I0651418

H. V. Stitzel

What Came of It

A Novel

H. V. Stitzel

What Came of It
A Novel

ISBN/EAN: 9783337001469

Printed in Europe, USA, Canada, Australia, Japan

Cover: Foto ©Andreas Hilbeck / pixelio.de

More available books at **www.hansebooks.com**

What Came Of

A Novel.

BY

MRS. H. V. STITZEL.

God is behind all things, but all things hide God.
— Victor Hugo.

Portland, Oregon :
PUBLISHING HOUSE OF GEO. H. HIMES.

1878.

TO THE READER.

WHEN the old Knights, from Amadis to Quixote, rode forth into the domain of adventure, they did not expect that their course would remain unchallenged; and so, in these halcyon days, when an author, in the shining mail of the types, invades the disputed realm of literature, he cannot be wholly unprepared for rude buffets and deadly thrusts. And yet the following pages appear under circumstances which may mitigate the asperity of that criticism which cannot, in the nature of things, be escaped. Not that MRS. STITZEL has passed under the friendly ægis of the maxim *de mortuis;* not that the book is the first effort of an unpracticed hand; not that ill-health, distracting household cares, and philanthropical labors are pleaded in extenuation of its faults—but that it does not fully represent the mental power and culture of the author. Shortly after the death of MRS. STITZEL, in January last, her unfinished manuscript, in the crude and imperfect condition of the first writing, was placed in the hands of Mr. SAM. L. SIMPSON, who has simply conducted the story to a natural conclusion, and prepared the whole for publication. The author herself, had her life been spared, had undoubtedly made a better book of it; but her husband and friends were unwilling that even the unripe fruits of her toil should perish utterly, and thus, under exceptional conditions, WHAT CAME OF IT is submitted to a generous and sympathizing public. It is, at least, the production of a good heart and a bright and active mind, and in whatever else it may fail, will cast no vicious stain upon the abounding river of human thought.

CONTENTS.

What Came of It.

CHAPTER I.

T some distance from the public road, and but a few miles from the metropolis of British America, there was, in the days through which this narrative extends, a little white cottage, over whose front porch a rose tree and a honeysuckle were striving for the victory of space, challenging admiration by the sweet perfumes they breathed through their dancing leaves, among which the sunbeams played at hide-and-seek with the cradled darlings of fond mother birds.

In a commodious chamber, with a southern aspect, of this retired though pleasant dwelling, reclining in an easy chair, was a venerable, white-haired woman, habited in a soft gray morning gown. Her lower limbs were paralyzed, and the hard lines of her aged face, as well as her general manner, testified to no ordinary degree of mental disturbance and bodily pain. Sometimes she would sit for hours abstractedly gazing out of the window, and again she would seemingly be possessed of the demon of unrest, muttering incoherently and moaning like one in agony. At such times

Echo, her grand daughter, was the only one that could sooth her perturbed spirit.

At the close of the day, Echo, seated on a low chair at the feet of her grandmother, Mrs. Clifford, was reading, in a sweetly modulated voice, from the family Bible. The perfect form of the girl was arrayed in a white dress of delicate texture, while falling over the pin which secured her ruff, was a cluster of purple pansies and creamy rose-buds.

Beneath her transparent complexion the full blue veins were distinctly traceable, while the masses of her rich brown hair, tinged with gold, fell luxuriantly about her shoulders, and constituted the flowing frame-work of a face transcendent in its loveliness. Her eyes were of a brilliant brown color, with those shifting lights and smouldering gleams of purple which give such eyes an ineffable splendor and power of fascination.

At the commencement of our story Echo was just gliding into the dreamy age of sixteen. She possessed considerable book-culture for one so young, but of society and its ways she knew comparatively nothing. She had lived a peculiarly secluded life in the little white cottage, with her grandmother and an aged nurse —the latter having died some three months previous to the beginning of this narrative. The only changes she could remember in the quiet monotony of her life, were the transitions of the seasons, the advent of a stranger to the country parsonage, the death of her venerable nurse and instructress, and the recent sickness of her beloved guardian. When a child she had often wondered if she was like other children who had mothers, for she had

never heard the name of her's mentioned, and she early
came to understand that the subject was a shrouded
mystery in the household. All she knew of her father
was from a painting of a roguish-looking boy hanging
in her grandmother's room, and smiling down upon her
with eyes marvelously like her own.

She had been taught obedience, and was forbidden to
speak of her parents, but, naturally enough, her thoughts
often invaded the *terra incognita*, and there built up
shadow-structures of the wildest character. It came to
be a region of enchanting dreams, where her ardent
imagination disported with the joyous freedom of
youth, her clouded parentage being at once the motive
and the shrine of her roaming fancies.

Mrs. Clifford belonged to a noble old family whose
reputation was without a blemish, and Echo's father
was the only Clifford whose crimes, or misfortunes, as
the world may be pleased to regard them, had cast a
stain upon the bright escutcheon of the race. Carefully
educated, with a pleasing face and elegant manners, she
loved and wedded a gallant young officer of the British
army, whom she accompanied to India. The courageous
and faithful services of her husband caused him to be
rapidly promoted, but having received a severe wound
he was transferred to England, whence, having apparently recovered, he was assigned a command at Quebec, Canada. Here the old wound broke out afresh,
however, and he soon after died from its effects, leaving
one child, a bright boy, to be the care and consolation
of his bereaved widow.

After the death of her husband, the general, M

Clifford took a lease of the cottage we have described, where she lived in the strictest retirement with the members of her own household, which, besides herself, consisted of her son, a single servant, and her son's instructress, a thoroughly educated but impoverished gentlewoman, a distant relative of the family.

Cleave was a handsome, passionate, wayward boy, who at times seemed to possess the attributes of an angel, and at others those of a devil. In the course of events he graduated at Yale with honor, and then went to the celebrated University of Heidelberg, Germany, to complete his studies. He resided three years in the University, during which time Mrs. Clifford received many loving letters from him in answer to her own, which invariably inclosed generous remittances and much good advice—both of which were prodigally wasted. Then came a strange rumor of his marriage, after which his correspondence was fitful and unsatisfactory, and at last ceased altogether.

One Christmas night, shortly after retiring, Mrs. Clifford was awakened by a startling sound. It resembled the wail of an infant, and seemed to proceed from the vicinity of the door, outside. Having called her servant, she opened the door with no little agitation, and, to her dismay, discovered a large basket upon the doorstep, which was soon ascertained to contain a girl baby, warmly wrapped in several shawls, to one of which was pinned a note in the hand-writing of her son. With dimmed eyes she read :

"DEAR MOTHER :
This child is mine. Take her to your heart in the

place of your wayward but loving son. My wife was false, and my hands are stained with the blood of her destroyer. Let the memory of the deed, of me, and of her that was once mine, fall into the abyss of oblivion; but for my sake, I implore you, receive the child and rear her as your own. We shall probably never meet on earth, but will, I hope, in the shadowless hereafter. Till then, farewell!   CLEAVE."

It was after reading this letter that Mrs. Clifford sank under the first paralytic stroke. Time had mitigated the poignancy of her grief somewhat by thrusting the bright face of the child between her and the shadow of her son's misfortune. She hoped, in her sequestered cottage life, to shield her darling Echo from all knowl-edge of the sins and follies of the world, and the dis-honor of her parents. She now, however, saw the fool-ishness of withdrawing herself from all social relations and public interests. She had outlived the companions of former years, and her life, but for the summer radi-ance that breathed about her beautiful protege, was as desolate as an arctic winter. At her death the pension which sufficed for their moderate way of living would cease entirely, and her beautiful charge would be left alone in the world without protection and support. In that event the tender nursing which had developed the innocence and purity of her darling's character, and the diligence with which she had been guarded from the knowledge and contamination of worldly evil, would illy fit her for the trials and temptations which she must inevitably meet in the untried ways of life.

About a fortnight from our first glimpse of the quiet life in the cottage, the Rev. John Hoberg, rector of the parish, called upon Mrs. Clifford, and, to his surprise, was cordially received by the old lady, who was greatly improved in mind. It transpiring during the interview that the rector, accompanied by his son and daughter, the latter a young lady of Echo's age, was contemplating a visit to Quebec on the following day, Mrs. Clifford proposed that Echo should accompany the party, which was readily acceded to, the clear-headed and somewhat belligerent clergyman thoroughly approving of Mrs. Clifford's newly formed design with regard to the practical education of her grandchild.

"Right? Of course you are right, my dear lady. The fruit of that forbidden tree comes to us all, but we can make it a tree of life. Ignorance is not bliss; it is death. There is no room on earth for the idler and the coward, and, I fear, no hope in Heaven!"

Mrs. Clifford winced a little at this sturdy way of putting the question, but she knew that he was right, and was only anxious to relieve her past error by allowing Echo to take her place among the struggling millions of mankind, and work out a destiny of her own. These conclusions cost her a heart-rending effort, but she was strong of purpose when the path of duty became plain, and no selfish yearning for love and companionship in her old age could now deter her from the course she had determined to pursue.

It was nine o'clock the next morning when Echo kissed her grandmother good-bye for the tenth time, and said: "Mrs. Hoberg is coming to stay with you while I am away, so you will not miss me so very much, will you, dear?"

"Does the earth miss the sun, or the plant its leaves and flowers, Echo?"

"Then why do you wish me to go, grandmother?"

"Because, child, I have kept you too much secluded, and it is time that you knew something of the world. But Mr. Hoberg is waiting; a happy journey and safe return, my darling!"

It was a transcendently lovely morning. The earth was flooded with the liquid gold of the sunlight, and the stainless dome of heaven was a dream of the purest violet. Song, fragrance, youth, hope, beauty, crowned the perfect day, and these, with the exhilaration of the ride, and cheerful company, and the nameless stir and enthusiasm of her undisciplined heart, made the occasion linger, long after, like a glittering arch, in Echo's memory.

Having arrived at Montreal and secured their state-rooms on the steamer for Quebec, there was yet time enough at their disposal for a ramble about the city. From one of the towers of the Catholic Cathedral, three of which rise to the height of two hundred and twenty feet, they had a magnificent view of the city and surrounding country. The superb island upon which the city stands was flooded with sunshine, and lovely beyond expression. The massive quay, the splendid streets, the shifting gleams of the white sails on the sparkling river, and the sombre splendor of the northern forests combined to fill up a picture of surpassing beauty.

Having visited the principal buildings, including Government House, the Church of England, and the Bank, the party repaired to the steamer, and, in due

course of time, arrived at their destination. On the
Friday following they visited the fortress, or Gibraltar
of America, as it is called, which is built upon an
enormous rock standing out boldly to the height of
three hundred and fifty feet above the river. They
spent a delightful week in Quebec. Before embarking
for home, they ascended one of the steeples of the city
for a farewell view. To the imaginative soul of Echo
the curtain of the past lifted as she gazed, and the Plains
of Abraham were re-peopled with the shades of heroes.
Upon the sky great clouds, luminous with a soft splendor, roll back in fantastic shapes and disclose the star-
sown blue of illimitable space. But hark! what breaks
the stillness of the lovely June night? What means
the moving mass of shadows on yonder green-gemmed,
silver-girded Island of Orleans? The shadows are upon
the water, now, and pass like slow, sailing clouds, to the
deeper shade of the moon-lit cliffs of Abraham. Now
shade after shade moves laboriously up the rocky steep.
The shadows are troops; it is a storming column!
Up, up, steadily up, they go with bated breath and
fiercely beating hearts! What are their thoughts? Do
they think of to-morrow, and yesterday, and the years
long gone? Surely their minds are not wholly occupied
by the arduous labor and the petty details of their terrible enterprise! No; thoughts of home and dear ones
and the sweets of life come to them in a thousand se-
ductive shapes; but they are climbing to glory, and they
persevere! And then an electric flash of the rapt
maiden's soul reveals the tragedy of the morrow. It
is yet gray dawn when the vision opens, and an army

is drawn up in battle array on the plains above! Now
the risen sun flashes on scarlet uniforms, golden epaulets,
and polished steel! The command to advance is given,
and the serene summer morning is suddenly clouded
and roaring with battle! The stormy pageant passes;
Montcalm is wounded unto death, and the heroic Wolfe
has fallen with the memorable words of triumph on his
lips!

Echo started and blushed as a hand touched her arm,
and a kind voice said: "What, dreaming again? I
really fear that you will yet vanish into a myth as beautiful and unattainable as your classic namesake." It
was the younger Mr. Hoberg who spoke.

"Lo, Narcissus speaks!" said his playful sister; "I
should like to see the nymph that would pine away for
any modern youth! But, brother mine, do you not
think the scene enchanting?"

"Exceedingly so." His gaze was lingering upon the
fair face of Echo, and not the glowing landscape.

"Do you not believe," said Echo, turning to the pastor, "that the loveliness of earth is but a shadow of the
infinite glory of Heaven?"

"Are you not happier for believing so, my child?" he
said.

"Yes, indeed."

"Papa," interrupted the daughter, "we will surely be
too late for the boat if we linger here."

"Even so, my daughter; it is time to go."

The return to Montreal was accomplished without
incident worthy of note. Their carriage awaited them
at the wharf; and after a pleasant ride of short duration,

Echo was bending over her grandmother with tender caresses—a radiant wreath of summer over the hoary serenity of winter.

In the morning Echo gathered a fresh bouquet of flowers for her grandmother, who seemed to be wrapped in tranquil slumber, and placed them where her gaze would rest upon them the first thing when she awoke.

But, alas! in the dead hours of the night the inevitable visitor had silently entered the cottage door and quenched the flickering lamp of that aged life. The wrinkled hands were folded upon her pulseless bosom, and there was nothing left but the way-worn frame—the devastation and mystery of death!

CHAPTER II.

WHEN the funeral rites were over, Echo was taken to the house of the warm-hearted pastor. Tenderly helping her out of the carriage, he whispered, "Fear not, my child, the Father of the orphan is yours now; it will be His good pleasure to attend you in every trial. Learn to lean upon His arm with child-like trust; He is mighty and full of mercy and loving-kindness. We accept you as a gracious charge from Him, and this house shall be your home." Then gently leading the stricken girl to an easy chair, he called cheerfully, " Come, mother, welcome our daughter home!"

Although Mr. Hoberg had a large and growing family of his own, his heart and his home, to use a homely comparison, were in one respect like a city omnibus—there was always room for one more. His wife, though a kind-hearted woman, inwardly sighed as she endeavored to greet the poor girl in a motherly way, and thought of the lean family larder. Upon intimating her prudent course to her husband, however, he replied with his favorite quotation—" Seek not ye what ye shall eat, or what ye shall drink, neither be ye of doubtful mind. But rather seek ye the kingdom of God, and all these things shall be added unto you."

About a fortnight before Christmas, as the family at

the parsonage were grouped one evening about a cheerful fire in the sitting-room, one of Mr. Hoberg's
younger sons, who had just returned from the city with
the mail, handed the father a package of periodicals and
letters.   One of the letters was from his son, Arthur,
at Quebec, and announced the intention of that young
gentleman of spending the holidays at home.   He was
recently graduated in medicine, and was anxious to locate
for practice in some town or village with miasmatic
accessories and a general disposition to derange its
digestion and break its bones.

The other letter was from Mrs. Ainsley, a wealthy
invalid lady, and an old friend of the pastor's, to whom
she wrote for assistance in procuring a suitable young
lady to live with her as a companion.   The young lady
in question was to be of good character, educated and
amiable.

Echo was all attention as these things were being announced, and then, looking towards Mr. Höberg with
kindling expectation in her eyes, inquired:

"Do you think that I have the qualifications required
by the lady?"

"Most assuredly you have," he replied, smiling.

"You will then be so kind as to recommend me at
once, will you not?"

"Is our daughter weary of her home so soon?"

"No, indeed; but I must be doing something for
myself."

"Well, dear, your happiness and prosperity are a precious charge to me.   The roses have been fading from
your cheeks of late, and perhaps a change and an ad-

ditional interest in the actualities of life will be best for
you. You cannot know how sincerely we shall regret
to lose your companionship, but, we shall not lose
you entirely, I am sure, and our prayers will attend you
always."

" Thank you, a thousand times, my dear friend; wherever I go my heart shall not stray from those who have
been so kind to me. When do you think of writing?'"

" Immediately, and if the answer prove favorable,
Arthur can accompany you to Mrs. Ainslie's."

The pastor's recommendation having been favorably
received, the necessary details as to salary, duties, and
the like, were readily agreed upon, and preparations
were made for Echo's departure.

It was three days before Christmas. The fire blaz-
ing upon the cleanly-swept hearth illuminated the
pleasant sitting room of the parsonage with a cheerful
glow. The family had accepted an invitation to dinner,
and Echo, at her own request, was left alone. The
snow had been falling in large, feathery flakes for some
time, weaving its beautiful ermine upon the bare limbs
of the trees, and covering the earth with a star-white
robe, embellished with crystal daisies. After her lonely
dinner, Echo seated herself at the piano and, running
her fingers softly over the keys, began humming an old
hymn tune, a great favorite of her grandmother. While
absorbed in music, she had not heard the arrival of a
horseman at the gate, or the manly step which had
halted upon the threshold of the apartment. She was
unconscious of the admiring gaze of a pair of dark
grey eyes, so steadily regarding her, and of the waves

of emotion passing over the intellectual face of the noble, dignified gentleman, who stood as if rooted to the spot, scarcely daring to breathe for fear of betraying his presence. As the sounds ceased, the gentleman suddenly became aware of the awkardness of his position, and, stepping slightly back, knocked upon the open door. Crossing the room, Echo stood face to face with Arthur. It was the first time they had met since her bereavement. Her face flushed hotly beneath his ardent gaze as he bowed over her hand, saying, in a thrilling voice, " Have you no words with which to welcome a homesick prodigal? "

" Your mother will be delighted to see you, Mr. Hoberg," she said with some confusion.

" Will you not be kind enough to call me Arthur? "

" Certainly, if you wish it."

" Is mother the only one who will be happier because of my return? "

" No. I presume that every individual member of the family will rejoice at your presence. Please be seated;" with a wave of the white hand and a gracious smile. " Your family will be agreeably surprised at your return, as they were not expecting you until to-morrow."

" No doubt; but all this reminds me of the French aphorism about language being invented for the purpose of concealing our thoughts; you have not answered my former question."

" I have forgotten what it was."

Rising from his chair, and seating himself at her side: " You were not wont to be so absent-minded. Are *you* not glad to see me?" He took her hand as he questioned her, and held it with a gentle pressure.

Her face flushed crimson as she endeavored to answer with indifference, " Of course."

There was a sound of bells, and a stamping of feet at the entrance. The door opened and then came expressions of surprise and pleasure at the presence of Arthur, and the evening was spent in agreeable conversation. The mother's eyes sparkled with pride and the father smiled approval as Arthur told of a difficult surgical operation which he had successfully performed—one which had spread his fame widely and marked him as a rising man. Every face expressed sympathy as he spoke of the loneliness and despair of the three weary months of waiting for the patients that never came. But now all this had changed. His signal success in a notable case had suddenly opened the door of fortune to him, and henceforth his way was broad and clear. Thus, after the manner of young men, Arthur grew eloquent about himself to the delight of his partial auditory, and the hours sped on fragrant wings. After reading of the Scriptures, and prayer by the good-souled pastor, they all joined in a vocal and instrumental praise concert, and the delightful evening was concluded.

Arthur dreamed of many delicious things that night, as became him, and then drifted off into a series of vague though startling adventures with a black cat, from whose machinations he was only relieved by the interposition of a maiden with nut-brown hair and magnetic eyes.

Not to steep an obvious fact in ethereal moonshine, it

may as well be said that the young people were in love
with each other. In due course of time, and in the
usual way, their mutual emotions were interpreted and
given a local habitation and a name.

They were engaged to be married.

And right here the reader is on slippery ground; for
if the course of true love runs smooth, the palatial plan
of this fiction will tumble into ruin and disclose a spectacle too ordinary to be attractive. We shall see.

The salary offered Echo was liberal, and she insisted
on fulfilling the engagement for a year. By that time,
Arthur would be fully established in his noble profession, and then the twin souls could flow together under
the arch of Hymen.

The thought of dwelling in the same city with her
beloved, mitigated the sorrow of the young lady at parting from the kind family at the parsonage.

Amid kisses, smiles and tears, Arthur helped his
fiancée into the sleigh and they were off. She kept her
handkerchief fluttering farewells in the air, and her eyes
filled with tears as she looked back and saw the family
group still lingering in the cold air for a last look—the
stately, reverend form of Mr. Hoberg the center of all.

"Do you remember our last summer's visit?" said
Arthur, as the mettled horses dashed along the snowy
track.

"How could I ever forget it?" she replied.

"I think that I never fully appreciated the beauties
of nature until then; it was on that day that I realized
for the first time how dear you were to me."

Their eyes met, and she dreamily murmured: "How sweet it is to be beloved!"

"My darling, earth contains no greater boon. Without the presence of love the human heart were an empty chamber of funeral echoes. It is the fragrance of life, the flower of virtue, and the fruit of hope!"

"Do you not think that excessive love is sinful? I have tried to exorcise the deep feeling which at times seems to absorb every other faculty of my being for fear of denying the dues of God alone." She said this softly, with tender pathos, as she nestled closely to his side.

"I hope that you will not succeed, dearest, for love is not to be restrained. It is the divine elixir which nourishes the soul to the fullest, freest, sweetest life—a glowing cup of joy in which doubt should cast no shadow and sin no stain."

"But you must admit," said Echo, thoughtfully, "that it causes much sorrow and suffering."

"Yes, dear, just as everything good and beautiful in nature may be wronged by our conception of it, perverted to ignoble uses and vitiated by impurity; and much more so all human faculties and sensations."

"Yes, it must be so, and I am thankful that it is. Since you assured me of your affection, vistas of happiness, golden, immeasurable, have opened up before me, and the very air is odorous with heavenly wings. Will it endure, do you think?"

"God grant it, my Echo; rest assured that I shall toil and pray for the perpetuation of our beautiful estate."

But the delightful journey was concluded all too soon,

and Echo, with the warm pressure of his hand at parting yet lingering in her veins, was ushered into the
magnificent mansion of Mrs. Ainsley, where, in a sump-
tuously furnished drawing-room, the lady was waiting
to receive her.   She was a small, faded woman, and in
the bloom of her youth had been a handsome blonde;
but in her manner there was an appearance of weakness and indecision.

A bright, amiable and attractive girl like Echo could
infuse new life into her stale existence, and they were
soon on the friendliest terms with each other.   There
was one pale cloud of trouble, however.   Mrs. Ainsley
had a son then traveling in Europe, upon whose susceptible heart she began to fear that her lovely companion would produce a dangerous impression.

CHAPTER III.

PARIS! the gay, volatile, magnificent, when calm, but dark and terrible when convulsed with rage, laboring with in-bred wrongs and thundering forth complaint! The beautiful city, as we look upon it, is marked by mighty changes. A new god, Equity, is enthroned upon the ruins of splendid monarchies, and a new phrase, " The inalienable rights of man," is in the mouths of Frenchmen. The people have refused to give that brow-sweat which, under the providence of God, is the price of bread and all earthly goods, for the barren splendor of hereditary royalty, and the glittering pageant has dissolved.

Standing in the Elysian Fields, in the midst of classic splendor, you are led to ask yourself, Where now are the graceful fancies, the fertile imaginations which shaped these lovely fountains and pillars of gilded bronze, these superb marble statues, and invested them with the glowing life of genius? There, too, stands the grand triumphal arch erected by Napoleon in commemoration of his Italian victories—a stately suggestion of the mockery of ambition, and of the foible side of the iron Emperor. What dizzy triumphs were those of Napoleon, and yet France, the monument of his glory, is the sounding sepulchre of his perished vanity! As the years sweep along, the multitudes thronging in the city he enriched with a thousand victories will forget him, and only along the sepulchral corridors of history will the great name resound. The breath of posthumous fame has a taint of the charnel, and its living voice is plebian with garlic and cabbage.

O Time! shapeless and absorbent shade! how the good, the brave, the beautiful, feed thy monster famine! Gone are the thinkers whose minds and hands enriched the Elysian Fields with works of art; but the solid structure of their massy thoughts remains to instruct and gladden us still.

As our feet tread the soil of the Place de la Concorde the red spectre of the guillotine, the shame and horror of France, darkens upon the mind. and there moves again the ghastly procession of doomed beauty, valor, wisdom and royalty. It was here that the mills of retribution ground out punishment to Robespierre, and the despoiler was in turn despoiled. Again, as the vision passes, the beautiful head of Charlotte Corday, bends beneath that historic blade, and again the indignant clouds flush crimson at the scene!

But the crime of Paris is not unique. The Reign of Terror goes back into the dim history of the past, and blackens the stream of tradition. The human race has fought its way to the dawn, and stands forth now but half redeemed, grim with battle-blood and scars. Alas! when shall the happy day arrive when intellect shall be crowned above the passions, and the jewel-clasp of mercy shall bind all hearts in universal love?

On the banks of the Seine and in sight of the *Champs Elysees*, or Elysian Fields, as it is more frequently called, which is only a continuation of the grand garden of the Tuilleries, there stood a magnificent old mansion which nature had done much and art still more to beautify and adorn. The taste and refinement displayed in furnishing and embellishing this spacious mansion within was altogether in keeping with the acute discernment and application of an elegant taste in the ornamentation of the exterior. A portly, pleasant-faced old lady standing at the casement said, in a mixture of French and bad English, "*Wont ma chere madame see ze beauty of ze sunset?*" The interrogatory was addressed to some one within, who nonchalantly approached the window and looked forth with a restless air which betokened a heavy heart or preoccupied mind. The individual was a lady of attractive presence, whose form, features and general expression suggested cultivation of mind and purity of character. The dark face, in its frame of silver hair, at once arrested marked attention. Her voice, when she addressed some careless remark to the lady mentioned, was observed to be low and musical, with a strange quality in its tone capable of thrilling effect. She was arrayed in deep mourning, only relieved by a ruff of rare old lace at the wrists and neck. There was a pathetic, hungry look in her deep dark eyes, haunting the beholder with their mournful splendor, like a melody of Beethoven.

Does the reader detect any resemblance between this lady and our young heroine? There should be; it is Lady Clifford, the mother of Echo. Gazing a moment on the fading pageant of day she returned to her seat with a heavy sigh. Her old nurse, Ninée, closed the window and drew the curtains, saying,

"*Mais ayons, patience, Madame.*"

Patience, Ninée, is the frozen rock to which we cling in the shipwreck of hope—the *dernier* resort of broken souls. And then there must be hope, or patience has a darker name—despair," she said wearily, as if in revery.

"*Je n'en doute pas*, my Lady."

"Ah, Ninée, you will never learn English, I fear."

"*C'est vrai.*"

"Only think, Ninée," said the lady, after a pause, " my little one is almost seventeen, that is, if she be living. If I could see her only once and know that she is pros-perous, a heavenly content would be mine.

"A thousand questions concerning her recur in my mind. Has he taught her to hate me, or does she think me dead? What have I done that the duties and priv-ileges of a mother should be taken from me and intrusted to a stranger," she continued. Though the criminal injustice of believing a wife unchaste without positive proof was detestable, the prodigious misdeed which sev-ered the tender relationship between mother and child is more inhuman and revolting.

She mused awhile and resumed, as was her custom, talking *at* instead of *to* her nurse:

"Maternity is the crowning dignity of womanhood; it has a secret, ennobling influence upon the character, and elevates the purposes of life. It broadens and deepens the subtle currents of the mind and fructifies the soul. The unselfish forbearance of a mother ap-proaches, at a tender distance, the immeasurable goodness

of Christ, the divine kindness that burst in crimson
flower on the cross! Oh, the blind jealousy of my
misjudging husband! The way to make me the false,
vile thing he thought me, was to deprive me of the innocent trusting eyes and clinging arms of my little one.
But, all these years, the thought of her has saved me.
The hope that we will ultimately be united has sus-
tained me in every trial."

"Ze 'ell is hot with zoul like Monsieur."

"You mistake, Ninée, the fire is quite out, or never
was."

"*Il faut qu'il soit rallumé*, for *Monsieur*."

"It is no satisfaction to me to think that his injustice
will be punished."

"*J'en ai bien de la joie.*"

"For shame, Ninée! your revengeful feelings are
altogether un-Christian, but it is growing late, we must
retire."

"*Je vous souhaite une bonne nuit, Madame.*"

"Thank you, Ninée."

Strange dreams, that night, hovered about her un-
easy pillow.

> "Faint, sweet sounds came floating down
> From wings of gold."

An indescribable calm enveloped her being. She
seemed to float in central space, surrounded by impenetrable vapor. Presently the woofy clouds rolled
away, and she saw an enormous tree, whose vast roots,
like precious veins of metal, spread over all the earth,
and whose branches towered and spread into the bound-

less regions of the infinite. Over all was a magnificent
drapery of foliage, white, black and red. While she
was yet gazing in surprise and wonder at the phe-
nomenon, a vibration of the fragrant air gently shook
the tender leaves from the branches. Some curled and
withered as they fell, while others were swept down
a broad avenue, where, drifted by chilling winds, they
fell into silver-fretted boxes. Then there sounded a
mournful symphony, like the wail of nature over her
dead children. Again other leaves were blown along
the avenue where sunshine and shadow wavered together, but the greater mass of leaves was piled in the
shade, where the ground was rough and sterile, and the
soft, smooth spots of green appeared more charming for
the contrast. Upon one leaf she saw that her own name
was written, and her whole interest was immediately
concentrated in watching its movements. A propitious
breeze wafted it gently along the sunny side of the
avenue. Anon the wind suddenly changed, and, catching the leaf up fiercely, hurled it along in the darkness.
While the invisible heart-strings of Nature wailed and
shrieked in sympathy, the heavy rain-drops smote it
sharply, and it was bruised and frayed on the cruel
rocks. At last the sorely wounded leaf sank upon a
rain-smitten bed at the end of the avenue, and was blown
no more. A beautiful and fragrant little leaf then fell
upon its bosom, soothing its pain, and then there came
a sweet memory of the parent tree, borne upon the
angelic murmur of its waving foliage, and the full
splendor of the sun flowed over its beauty.

Lady Clifford awoke with a start, and the golden

morning was aflame in the lace curtains of her boudoir. From a neighboring mansion came the sound of music, and she arose with a strange presentiment of happiness in her heart. In relating the strange dream to her old nurse, she said: "I shall always believe, Ninée, that the dream was prophetic, sufficiently interpreted to my own spirit. I am sure that my little daughter, grown womanly and beautiful, will yet be restored to me. But what shall I do in the meantime?"

"If Madame would seek happiness," said Ninée.

"Happiness! What is happiness, Ninée, but a false light along the path of duty—an ideal entity that mortals never grasp." With this philosophic expression, so entirely at variance with the prophetic movements of her own bosom, Lady Clifford relapsed into silence.

Just here it is well enough to develop something further concerning the hidden springs of this romance. The man whom Mr. Clifford had so brutally attacked was simply the victim of an unhappy circumstance. He was privately, or, more correctly speaking, clandestinely engaged to be married to a young lady friend of the Cliffords, and, imprudently, the Clifford residence, without the knowledge of the husband, had afforded a trysting place to the lovers. Love matters of this kind usually go wrong, somehow, and, in this instance, carried destruction to the bosom of a family. To forward this sinister result there was an Iago, appearing among men under the ordinary surname of Legrand. Pierre Legrand was a distant relative of Lady Clifford, and a discarded suitor for her hand. He was next in the line

2

of heirship to the immense fortune held by his cousin, and was therefore animated by the powerful motives of greed and revenge in attempting her destruction. After the flight of Mr. Clifford he had assumed the place of best friend and counsellor to the stricken lady, and swore that he would follow the husband over the whole earth, if need be, to recover the child.

He was gone a year on this business and returned to report that both father and child were dead. Then, insidiously, he set himself to work in the hope of ultimately winning the heart of the mother; but she, poor woman, mourned continually, and gave him no notice. As the years rolled on, her purse was perpetually the prey of his rapacity, but his passionate appeals for her sympathy and affection, made no impression on her stony heart. When she told him her dream and said: " My daughter is not dead," he affected to give her some encouragement, suggesting with a sigh, that he might have been deceived.   •

In pursuance of the ideas suggested by this conversation, Monsieur Pierre Legrand, amply supplied with money, was soon sailing over the ocean for America.

Six months of waiting passed, and then one day there came the following telegram from the New World:

" NEW YORK, April 6, 18——
LADY CLIFFORD:
Your hopes are verified. Will return immediately with mademoiselle. ,   PIERRE LEGRAND."

On reading this brief line—ah, upon such a slender thread hangs human happiness!—Lady Clifford was for a moment overcome with emotion, Thenceforth the rose of happiness blossomed in her delicate cheek, so that Ninée said one day—

"*Ma foi!* you look like one that has come from Heaven, Madame !"

"You are wrong, then, Ninée—I only see the gates of Heaven."

CHAPTER IV.

ROSSING the Atlantic in the same vessel with our wily friend Legrand, was a troop of ballet girls. Among these gay and worldly terpsichoreans, who were going out to conquer anew, in the interest of art, the mighty land of Columbus, was a handsome girl with blue eyes, delicately arched eyebrows, and long light hair. Her form, naturally fine, had been developed by the training of her profession, and there was upon her that glowing vesture of physical beauty which has again and again desolated the empires of this world by the quarrels it has provoked. Her heart was as dry as a pin-cushion, and no more the fountain of noble impulses than is that article of household economy. The world is bleak with the loveliness of such creatures, and little space need be accorded to a *resumé* of her coarse attractions.

It eminently became M. Legrand, both as a man and a Frenchman, to make overtures for an acquaintance with this young lady, a consummation which tolerable features, loud attire and a waxed mustache happily forwarded. Your elegant villain inevitably drifts towards feminine allurements of the kind displayed by the dashing Zarina, and the pair were soon on terms of the closest intimacy. They were well met. Perhaps they were to become necessary to each other in the mazes of the plot which the cunning brain of Legrand was busily weaving.

Sunset on the open sea is always a solemn and beautiful pageant. Looking on such a scene we realize the inspired splendor of Byron's ovation, and the sound of the great islander's harp fitly accompanies the marching world of waters.

> " Roll on, thou deep blue ocean, roll
> Ten thousand fleets sweep over thee in vain !"

The glory of the parting sun was marshalled on the sea, as Legrand and Zarina paced the deck of the good ship " Achilles."

" Very true, monsieur," said Zarina, gracefully clinging to Legrand's arm, " the emerald sea is all the more beautiful for a golden setting."

" Everything on earth is the more beautiful for a golden setting, mademoiselle," said the gentleman, with a meaning glance towards his companion. The glance was returned sympathetically, and then he resumed:

" There is a difference, mademoiselle; the sea has no care, but, we, *Ma foi!* must scheme and labor for the golden setting of our lives."

" Alas, it is true, monsieur!" And thus these worthy people enjoyed the scene.

But a fatality lurked in the beauty of the sunset. Strange, copper-hued clouds suddenly arose as the mighty orb dropped beneath the horizon. The bronzed mariners recognized the signs of danger, and the sails were close-reefed against the expected tempest. The vessel, with bared arms, head to wind, was soon rocking gently on the swell of the ocean, bravely awaiting the struggle. Then there were vivid flashes, and the sudden crash of angry thunder. A few flying rain-drops struck the deck like bullets of steel; there was a sudden flash of foam to windward—and the storm was on! A staunch ship struggling with a storm is a sublime sight, and the "Achilles" went into the battle with the prestige of a hundred victories.

When the storm was at its height, amid the roar of the waters, the shrieks of the timid and the prayers of the faithful, Zarina, clinging to a pillar of the great cabin, was pale but calm.

Legrand, white and terror-stricken, approached her, and she turned upon him with a sneer.

"Monsieur Legrand, thou flower of chivalry and soul of daring! how fares it with thee? *Mon Dieu!* the man is no longer a man—he is a rag! A woman does not love a rag, monsieur, and yet you ask my love! Come, it is too bad of you to abandon your beloved to the tender mercies of a post!"

"Have done, mademoiselle; it is not the storm I fear, but the prayers of yon gray-haired woman. *Pardieu!* a man has lived too long who has lived to be afraid of his grandmother!"

"Pardon, monsieur, but it seems that you are not a saint since you tremble at the spectacle of an old woman in prayer!"

"Ah, wicked mademoiselle, the saints are a long while dead!"

"Ha, ha, ha! the sword of my *preux chevalier* is

broken, yet he will not fly to the consolations of the
Church !"

The storm came on with redoubled fury, and the vessel seemed to be breaking up beneath their feet. The
last remaining fibre of courage in the bosom of Legrand
gave way under the additional shock, and he fell upon
his knees with a shriek of prayer—in which it could be
made out that he renounced all his impious schemes and
vowed the remainder of his life to religion.

Amid all this scene of terror, there rang out an appalling sound. The reckless dancer, with a flush of
fury on her cheek, was clinging like a serpent to the
painted post, and fairly screaming with demoniac laughter at the pitiable sight the man presented. It was
horrible !

"Hush, Zarina, we are lost !" moaned the man.

"Lost ! you fool ! Nay, not so. You will live to
retire to your nunnery, and I to quaff the cup of pleasure. Look ! the ship is righting now, and the fury of
the storm is spent !"

It was so. The vessel shook herself free, and soon
there was an appreciable falling of the tempest.

"Zarina, my peerless beauty," said Legrand, rising
awkwardly from his knees, "do you, then, have no fear
of death ?"

"Do I fear to fall asleep ? Really, monsieur, you
must know that I believe in the irrevocable fates, and
that the leading tenet of my creed is contained in the
command to our happy ancestors in the Garden : "Pluck,
and eat !"

"It was the praying of the old lady that unmanned

me. I remembered that my mother knelt thus and prayed for me at the time she died; and then when one, you know—ah, none of us are pure !"

"And my mother died, gnawing her arm for very hunger, and begging the deaf Heaven piteously for food. Bah, there is no God !" said Zarina, with sombre energy.

"You are right," said Legrand, becoming more assured, "there is no God, and the devil is a dream !"

"And fright a delusion," continued the reckless girl, with an intolerable sneer. "Beware, bold philosopher, we are yet on the open sea !"

But Legrand replied, with a visible effort to change the subject, "The sea is very rough yet, but the wind is in our favor, and we are driving along at a fearful rate. The captain thinks we shall reach New York the day after to-morrow. It is time that we sought repose from our fright in sleep."

"Our fright ! ha, ha ! Good-night, monsieur; soften your pillow with prayer !"

Thus, danger has its ludicrous side; and it is remarkable how soon the average man or woman will forget a deadly terror, and begin to flaunt their silly impertinences in the face of Deity. It requires all the mighty battle-fields of history to convince us that man is ever heroic.

Thenceforward the ship flew rapidly along, and in due time touched the busy piers of the great metropolis of the New World.

M. Legrand, fiercer than ever, when he found his feet on solid ground, procured a cab and conducted the fair Zarina to an elegant hotel, whither the remaining members of the ballet troupe soon followed, with the desire of being near their friend, whom they had begun to suspect of treason to the management.

These fears were well grounded, for Legrand had completely won Zarina over to his schemes, and the twain were made one, according to the rites of the Holy Church, in the course of the week. The bridal tour comprehended Quebec, Canada, as the terminal point; and upon reaching that city, Legrand left his wife in handsome quarters, and proceeded alone to Montreal. He had visited Clifford's mother on the occasion of his former visit to America, and had been shown the letter which the maddened son had written his mother when the child was left to her care. That was the last trace of the wanderer discovered up to this time. The whereabouts of the daughter, however, had never been made known to him, that portion of the letter having been studiously withheld.

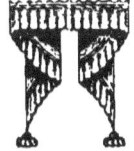

CHAPTER V

IN the rugged northland, on a winter's evening, the ruddy glow of a generous fire falling through an unveiled window upon the snowy scene without, is always a thing of beauty and a joy forever to the belated traveler, and so thought Monsieur Legrand, as, muffled in coat and furs, he alighted from his sleigh at the door of the parsonage occupied by our old friend, the Rev. Mr. Hoberg. The wanderer was always welcome in that genial home, and in the course of half an hour, the Frenchman, who could be amiable enough when he liked, was basking in the rose-light of the crackling hearth and ingratiating himself with the good pastor by his easy, yet deferent, manner and rippling flow of talk. From the domestic adytum of the establishment there was, occasionally, borne a faint odor of relishable viands, and the instincts of the gentlemanly traveler, sharpened by his bracing ride, informed him that there was about to be business in hand, which, however insignificant it may appear, when we survey life with particular reference to the Marathons and Pharsalias that dot its varied expanse, is not to be frustrated without endangering the mighty fabric of society.

The important matter of refreshment being concluded, M. Legrand, by a dexterous maneuver, brought the conversation round to the subject of the Cliffords, and was delighted to observe that the pastor became immediately interested, and entered upon the story with a zest and candor unclouded by suspicion.

" Did you have the good fortune to know the dear old lady, M. Legrand? "

" No," replied that gentleman, " I was not fortunate enough to know the excellent mother, but the son I have met in Europe."

" Indeed! Do you know whether he is living yet? "

" Assuredly, my dear sir, he is living; and I may as well be frank with you, who are the esteemed friend of the family, and say that my present visit to your magnificent country is concerned with his business."

" Well! well!" ejaculated the pastor, elevating his gold-mounted eye-glasses and gazing at Legrand in astonishment, "that is marvelous!"

" Marvelous, but true, your reverence, and I only hope you will assist me generously in clearing up the mystery of this affair and righting any wrongs that now exist and are not irreparable."

" Most willingly, my dear sir; the friendship I bore Mrs. Clifford extends to her descendants, and you may consider me at your service to the full extent of my ability to serve them in this important matter."

" Yours is the language of a Christian, sir, and allow me humbly to thank you. You speak of a casket that was left in your charge to be given to the daughter at her marriage; have you any objection to my seeing it? "

" None in the world. The casket is locked and sealed, and its contents, I believe, unknown to any living per-

son, and must so remain until it is given into the hands
of our darling Echo on her marriage day, according to
the will of the deceased. Excuse me, and I will bring
it from my study."

The minister soon returned, bearing in his hand an
ebony box, elegantly inlaid with pearl, which was, perhaps, four inches in width and depth, respectively, and
twice as many long, the aperture for the key being
covered by a blue seal artistically stamped.

There was a sinister light in the Frenchman's eyes as
he took the box and surveyed its workmanship with
curious attention.

"*Ma foi!*" he said at length, "it must contain the
fairy lamp of Aladdin!"

"Whatever it may be, it is secure in my hands, I
hope," said the pastor with a smile of pardonable pride.

"It is well said, your reverence; the casket is a sacred
trust, and as such, being faithfully observed, cannot but
bring peace and prosperity to your noble house."

"Do you know anything of the mother, Cleaveland's
wife?" said the pastor.

"Dead, long ago dead," alas ,for the uncertainty of
all our lives!" replied Legrand with a pious grimace.

"It is a sad, sad, story," and the pastor gazed ruefully
at the falling ashes on the hearth and bethought him of
the infinite sorrows of life.

In the further conversation that ensued before the
hour of retiring, a shrewd observer would have noted
the fact that M. Legrand was exceedingly vague with
reference to his particular mission in the Clifford inter-

est, but the pastor was, in the boundless charity of his
nature, unconscious of the discrepancy.

Elaborately polite and gaily voluble was M. Legrand
the next morning as he entered his sleigh with reitera-
ted farewells and showering compliments for the pastor
and his family. So high and airy was the conduct of
that gentleman, in fact, that one would naturally expect
to see his horse bound away for the moon when given
the rein, but instead of that he took the city road like
an animal of ordinary spirit, and was soon out of sight.

When, at the conclusion of his journey, M. Legrand
burst into the apartments where Zarina was patiently
awaiting his return, it was sufficiently apparent that no
funeral gloom came with him, and there was a joyous
ring in the interrogatory of his bride as she extended
her arms for an embrace.

" It is victory, my gem of women, and you do well to
reward me with a kiss."

" Victory? and, pray, what does victory mean?"

" It means that Monsieur Pierre Legrand, being as
handsome as he is fortunate, had the good taste to marry
an heiress. Ha! ha! I must really set up for a wit."

" Please use your wits in making yourself intelligible,
my dear; why do you call me an heiress?"

" For the reason, my love, that having been educated
for the accomplishment of difficult steps, *a la danseuse*,
you are now enabled to step into a great fortune. Ha!
ha! ha! better and better, as I live!" and the room re-
sounded again with the artless laughter of M. Legrand.

His wife looked at him in astonishment, but quietly
waited for him to proceed.

"Yes, my dear," he said at length, "a fortune of millions awaits you in France, and by these signs are we to conquer." He opened the mysterious casket, the seal of which had already been broken, and from its bed of velvet held up to her gaze a gold chain and locket of beautiful workmanship and of great value. Touching the spring of the locket it opened and disclosed the photograph of a lady unknown to Zarina. It was the photograph of Echo's mother, taken in her youth.

"It was careless of you, Zarina mine, extremely reprehensible in you to leave a precious heirloom like this drifting round the world."

"What interest is the handsome necklace to me?"

"Listen to me, Zarina; this necklace will identify you as the daughter of the rich lady whose photograph the locket contains. The daughter was lost; the heartbroken mother engages the services of a wise and handsome man by the name of Legrand and sends him to America in search of the missing one; Legrand returns with the daughter, identified by the charming ornament worn when she was taken away, and there is your romance, wife of my heart! and your golden millions."

"Ah, I see!" said Zarina, and she looked at her husband with something like respect for the deepness of his trickery and the artistic finish of the villainous plot he had disclosed.

"But you must pirouette through the boarding schools, Zarina; the daughter of the Cliffords must have culture and refinement."

"I am not unequal to what will be required of me, I think, Pierre. I have some skill in acting, and as for the rest, an intelligence naturally keen and polished in the obdurate mills of necessity, will doubtless serve me well."

"Ah, Pierre," continued Zarina, after a short pause, "you are as wicked as you are delightful."

"You are right, Zarina; Pierre Legrand and his native innocence parted company so long ago that their association can scarcely be remembered. A man must live in the world, even though he disgrace the memory of his mother. Alas! had she lived, and the world gone more smoothly with me, while I might have wandered with the waywardness of youth, yet, like the prodigal son, I should have returned long before this and become a pillar of reform."

"And then, were I the mother, in that event the fatted calf should live and the prodigal be led to the shambles. The prodigal son came home only because he had no other place to go, and I do not wonder that his good brothers grumbled at the distinction shown the vagabond."

"Yet, my beautiful logician, you seem willing to enjoy the fruits of my wickedness, if such a name can be applied to the triumphs of diplomacy, and should, therefore, pitch your moral song a little lower."

"Indeed I willingly share these prospects with you. The test of a life is success, and I am not one of those who will waste breath in laying up the treasures in Heaven."

"You will not fail me, then?"

"If I do, may the fiery demon of the Book receive me!" said the young woman with energy.

"Ha! ha! The evil one has the patience of immortality, my dear; he will wait for you."

"In the meantime we had better order some refreshments. The discovery of your wickedness has not destroyed my relish for the good things of the world."

Food and wine were soon before them, and Legrand, lifting his glass, brimming with Bordeaux, gaily cried—
"I drink to my successor."

"Your successor?"

"Aye, the Lucifer of the great Englishman's poem."

"Ah, it is well that you drink to him now, for a time will come when he will play the host for you, and they say he is frugal of his wine."

"Zarina, you nobly sustain your sex—the last word is yours."

"Nay, not so; for it has been intimated that the devil shall take the hindmost."

"Ha! ha! good, upon the faith of a gentleman!"

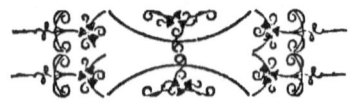

CHAPTER VI.

DMOND Ainsley was at home again, and his gentle mother was in a flutter of enjoyment. The weak-fibred lady was in this one thing thoroughly in earnest: she was devoted to her son. The young man had grown in a hot-bed of luxurious affection, and his character was the natural product of the gushing order of agriculture—too fragile in its cellular development for the winds that sometimes blow roughly on human harvests. To be candid with the subject, it may as well be admitted that Mr. Edmond Ainsley, of Ainsley Hill, was an ethereal snob. The fantastic legend, "*Vive la bagatelle!*" was indelibly graven on the fret-work, so to speak, of his facial angle. He was an authority in the mysteries of the toilet, and a glass of fashion to the circle in which he moved. He knew a little about horses and dogs, was a mild sportsman, and found books "a deuced bore." He not only got himself up well, with the aid of his tailor and a purse infinitely deeper than his intellect, but, to give some one we know his due, he was actually handsome. He was of medium stature, nicely proportioned, with a small, shapely head, crisp brown hair, low, white forehead, regular features, perfect teeth, and wore a drooping brown mustache. With these attractions Edmond had been fatal even among the Amazons, and it is not, therefore, a matter of wonder that among the plastic beauties of the period he was a perfect simoom of destruction.

At fashionable parties this king of hearts was a high card—indeed it was the opinion of many that the fussy little game, merely for amusement, you know, which we call "society," could not go on without him. Furthermore, it may be safely hinted that a large number of estimable young men in his set, outwardly decorous, and supposed to be of a religious turn of mind, would nevertheless have given freely of their substance in order to discover, by experiment, what kind of ornamental leather the hide of the said Edmond would make when properly prepared according to the processes of the tanner's art. But that is neither here nor there.

The instincts of a pure woman, when unimpaired by false associations, are nearly always correct. Therefore, even to the inexperienced heart of Echo, the elaborate effort of the redoubtable Edmond to subjugate her affections to his control were promptly discernible, and the studied graces of the beau-ideal were wasted on desert air. Sometimes these high-flyers are captivated by the irrepressible beauty of their mother's governess, but the motives of their assiduous attentions oftener lie in a coarser substratum than sincere regard.

Many women are so hopelessly weak! They are swept away in the lawless current of man's desire without a struggle, or, self-impelled, drift upon the rock-bound coasts of dishonor. Perhaps the fault is in the grain, perhaps is attributable to some fatal effect in our social varnish; at all events it *is,* and all the ways of life are strewn with wrecks that breathe miasma on the air. The soul of a strong woman is wrung with unutterable anguish at the recognition of these things, and she becomes austere, hateful, perhaps, in her contempt and loathing of feminine frailties.

A young woman's protecting ægis is the love of a true, strong man. The sentiment yclept the tender, is, in its virtuous growth and maturity, the crowning glory of our sex; perverted, the whole woman falls with the crash of its ruin. The social wrongs that sin against the strength of youth are indeed cursed, as Tennyson sings. Love may be stifled in the heart, but the soil in which it grew is blasted forever.

Well, what of it ? Only this, that the spectacle of a happy love-match is lovelier than the landscapes of Claude and the marbles of Greece. Thank God it is not altogether rare, but it is not common enough to be contemptible; and then climatic influences are so fruitful of blight !

Echo and Arthur loved each other wisely and well. Each, as to the other, was enveloped in the rose-hues of a romantic apotheosis, but it is not absolutely clear that this sublimating tendency of young hearts is much of an evil, after all. To a mere spectator a lover is simply a clumsy clod, subdued by a soft, tail-wagging puppyism, but the fault is in the prosaic, unleavened wretch who surveys the sufferer from telescopic distances. What food lovers flourish upon, what language they speak, and what golden arches bend above them always, it is no business of the uninitiated, unvolatilized pagan to inquire and know. The lover's world is not our world, and it is well that a purple mysticism glorifies them forever.

Arthur and Echo were everything to each other, and it follows that the young lady had neither eyes nor ears for gilt-edged Edmond Ainsley.

About three months after the return of Edmond Ainsley to the home of his mother, at the close of a lovely spring day, Echo was seated in an easy chair before the window; one soft white hand lay upon the book from which she had been reading, and the other, upon which the engagement-ring sparkled, toyed with the tassel of her chair. Her dainty feet tapped the rich carpet thoughtfully, as she sat, and the ruddy glow from the grate glorified her golden hair and pure complexion, the effect of the picture being grandly heightened by the crimson velvet linings of the deep-backed chair. The marvelous eyes were gazing through the window upon the western sky, suffused with the last glow of day. A few clouds, like golden brackets, framed the sapphire spaces of heaven, and the light that lingered upon the world was as soft and tender as the last kiss of a parting lover. Her thoughts had that touch of ineffable melancholy which belongs to such a scene—

> "Which resembles sorrow only
> As the mist resembles the rain."

The clear eyes mirrowed the matchless shadows that moved upon the fading horizon, and her soul was floating far in a glowing argosy of dreams, when suddenly a shade fell upon her face and a warm kiss electrified her lips.

"Arthur! How you frightened me!"

"The opportunity for a surprise was too tempting, love; I hope you are glad to see me?"

"Assuredly; but large bodies should not move through space without some attendant satellite as an *avant* courier."

"A dog, for instance?"

"Yes, or even a wide nimbus of musk, like one I could mention!"

"By the way, Echo, is Edmond Ainsley at home?"

"He arrived a fortnight ago, and," with a merry twinkle of the eye, "has doubtless inscribed upon his banner — all young gentlemen carry banners since Mr. Longfellow's 'Excelsior' came to fame — the Cæsarean boast, *veni, vidi, vici.*"

"Alas! am I then to grace his triumph?"

"Well, the court takes that question under advisement; and, in the meanwhile, you may consider yourself on your good behavior."

"Is this Ainsley, (*this* Ainsley!) entirely irresistible?"

"The Apollo Belvidere, appareled under the direction of the immortal Worth, could not be more so."

"Then I must really get a dog."

"Ah! and why?"

"To keep the young ladies from devouring this delightful creature; I shall interfere in the interest of humanity."

"Hedge him about with the odor of some of your

detestable drugs, Arthur — that were a safer and surer plan."

Now the reader will hardly believe such a thing possible, but it is nevertheless true, that the young lady had not once looked up during this dialogue until the gentleman burst into a roar of laughter at the conclusion of the last remark, and then she sprang up with a smothered shriek and a face of flame.

"Mr. Ainsley! villain ! how dare you insult me!"

The young man shrank for a moment before the towering indignation of the young governess, but partially recovered, and stammering out: "Forgive me, Echo — the sight of your wonderful beauty lured me irresistibly into difficulty. I love you, darling," and he moved forward as if to take her hand.

"Back! at your peril! There are those who will avenge this insolence!" and hot tears of rage and shame were coursing down the fair girl's cheek.

There was a pause of a moment, which was broken by Mrs. Ainsley who, wakening from her afternoon siesta, called —

"Echo, will you please ring for lights? Why, Edmond, you here?" for the young man, glad enough to escape the tempest he had aroused, had hastened to her side at the first movement and greeted her with a filial kiss.

"Where should I be, mother, but watching over the slumbers of those I love?"

The grateful, loving look which she gave him for this little speech expressed affection enough to fit put a paradise, with all the modern improvements. Mother-love is the saddest, sweetest thing in nature.

In all ages the existence of a Deity has been doubted; while Love, the attribute and essence of God, sits on an unshaken throne.

> Love rules the court, the camp, the grove
> For love is Heaven, and Heaven is love!

Echo ordered the lights as requested, and retired to her own chamber.. There, agonizing under the insult to which she had just been subjected, the desolation of orphanage came upon her as never before, and she threw herself upon the bed and wept bitterly.

"Why," the poor girl murmured, "am I to suffer this cruel wrong? It is thus that the poor and weak are ever trampled upon in this world. That young man cannot understand that he has done me an injury; his education tends to such outrages, and the light-headed wretch is scarcely to blame. In his eyes I am, simply a chattel—a part of the paraphernalia of his luxurious home and a legitimate victim for his pampered wickedness. The young lady who formerly acted as companion to his mother was ruined by him; she hid her shame ·in the dark-flowing river, and he — curled darling of his mother! — traveled in Europe for his health! How can I endure to remain here any longer ? If I disclose what has happened to Mrs. Ainsley she will dismiss me in disgrace, and what am I to do ? May the Lord help me in this heavy trial!"

When the paroxysm of her grief had subsided, Echo rose and bathed her swollen eyes and hot temples, for she was expecting a visit from her affianced that evening and wished to appear before him naturally.

That gentleman, *bona fide*, this time, was soon announced, and Echo, hastening down to the drawing-room, greeted her lover graciously.

"I believe that I have a surprise for you, Arthur," she said; "your sister Mary is to be married on Christmas day."

"That is news to me, surely, but young people are committing that kind of foolishness every day now," and he pressed her hand as though there were some sort of comfort in that condition of things. Then there was a delicious pause of a few seconds, the young lady not knowing how to controvert this dangerous position with reference to the prevailing idiosyncracies of young people.

"Come, dear," he said, "let us talk business. Do you know that I have been negotiating for the little cottage you fell in love with during our ramble the other day? I shall close the bargain, with your approval, to-morrow by paying one-third of the purchase money in hand, the remainder when we take possession."

"That dear little cottage! Oh, I am delighted! But you must let me furnish it. You know that I have a few hundred dollars from the sale of grandmother's effects, which, with the addition of what I have saved from my salary, will be sufficient to fit our home nicely. I shall make Mary a present on the great occasion, and will need something for my own modest *trousseau*, but there will be enough left for the furniture of the cottage."

" Verily, Echo, you would make a talented minister of finance," he rejoined, playfully, " but this sacrifice must not be made; it must be my pleasant privilege to furnish a home for you."

" Shall I contribute nothing, then?" she said sorrow-fully.

" Nothing, indeed! Why, Echo, you contribute ev-erything in contributing your delightful self. You are the priceless gem for which I, in my poverty, can only provide a paltry setting."

But the conversation is getting wild, and we will ring down the curtain and dismiss our characters to the happy realms of sleep.

It was midnight; dark, drear, silent as the tomb of elder chaos. The sky was heavily obscured in clouds, and a cold wind was blowing in fitful gusts. Suddenly the black, breathless pause of the night was broken by a hideous clamor. Fire! fire! fire! boom! boom! boom! Bells and voices were proclaiming the red ap-parition of an enraged element.

" Good God!" cried a man in the street — " it is the Ainsley mansion!"

A hundred men rushed up the broad flight of front steps and thundered at the knocker. There was a sud-den, inarticulate cry of alarm from the people in the street whose gaze was riveted on the stately dwelling. It was caused by the bursting of a black volume of smoke, mixed with bloody tongues of flame, from the roof.

The crowd was still hammering at the heavy walnut doors, and the confusion and alarm were becoming ter-

3

rible, when the mighty portals were flung back, and
Edmond Ainsley, half stifled with the smoke which
already filled the lower rooms, rushed out.

"A thousand dollars for the rescue of my mother and
the governess!" he shouted wildly.

A hundred resolute men sprang forward, but they
were beaten back by the hot smoke that rushed down
the great stairway.

Some of the upper windows shivered, with a terrific
crash, and the pent-up demon leaped forth in smoke
and flame.

In apartments remote from the uproar of the street,
Echo was suddenly roused by the bursting of the glass
in one of the windows, caused by a stone some one had
hurled from below, and leaped forth to see the clouds
ruddy with reflected flame. For an instant she was stupefied with fear, for the roar of the people below was
awful to hear. She came of a mettled race, however,
and soon recovered, when she hastily donned a wrapper
and opened the door leading into the hall. A stifling
smoke rushed in, and the door was closed. Then, seiz-
ing a blanket from the bed, and stooping low to take
advantage of the purer air near the floor, she rushed into
the hall. Thus shielded by the blanket, she was making for the stairway, when Edmond flew past her. At
the same instant she heard the voice of Mrs. Ainsley,
elevated to a shriek that chilled one's blood —

"Help! help! Arnold! Arnold! my son! Good God!
do not leave your mother in the flames!"

Echo turned, and with difficulty made her way back
to the apartment whence the fearful cry proceeded.

She found the poor woman on her knees in the middle
of the room, paralyzed with terror. She sank forward
insensible as the brave girl approached; and just then
a man, blackened and singed by the flames through
which he had passed, rushed into the room with a rope
in his hand. He paused an instant as if to recognize the
woman he had come to save, and then without a word,
passed a noose under the arms of the young lady and
lifted her tenderly and swiftly through the window —
and she was lowered to the ground amid cheers that
rent the air. Then followed the other lady, and lastly,
the man himself, his hair on fire, fell, rather than slid
down the rope, just as the flames leaped through in wild
pursuit.

When Arthur Hoberg recovered from the swoon into
which he had been precipitated by the concussion of his
fall, the Ainsley mansion was a heap of blackened ruins,
and every tongue was sounding the praise of the daring
young physician.

He was badly burned and bruised, but a sweet face
bent over him when he looked up to find himself in a
strange room. It was a face that he knew and loved.

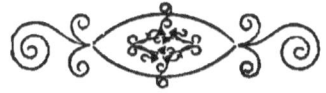

CHAPTER VII.

ROM the frightful experiences of the fire, Mrs. Ainsley received a nervous shock that completely prostrated her for a time, and when she had partially recovered, her physicians recommended easy travel and change of scene. The weak lady now leaned more than ever upon the companionship of Echo, as a shaded plant will lean towards the warm embrace of the sun. Mrs. Ainsley felt that the society of the governess was indispensable to her; in fact, she announced her intention of remaining in Quebec unless Echo should agree to accompany her in the contemplated round of travel. To one of the young lady's generous, sympathetic temperament, there was but one course. She would go.

There was the prospect of an early marriage and the inestimable pleasure of Arthur's society to be given up, but duty demanded the sacrifice, and she determined to make it.

California, the far-off golden land, whose very name is redolent of romance, was fixed upon as the terminal point of their loitering journey, and, accompanied by two faithful servants, they were soon on the way.

Edmond was to remain and supervise the re-building of the family mansion. This last was an important consideration to Echo,

The parting of the lovers was affecting in a high degree, and yet not utterly devoid of its humorous points. When a young man is seriously possessed of the tender passion, he is prepared to be miserable on all occasions. But if you really wish to give him up to the devouring torments of jealousy, let the object of his love go traveling without his protection! A situation of that kind fairly bristles with possibilities for the torture of the involved and irredeemable soul.

"Ah, Echo, you are going to leave me?"

"For a little time, Arthur, and I assure you that I shall count the moments until the painful days of absence are accomplished."

"Yet human nature is so fickle, dear, and I fear there is some truth in that homely old maxim, 'Out of sight, out of mind.'"

"Arthur! how can you say such cruel things?" and the sweet eyes filled with tears.

"I do not mean to pain you, darling, but you have had so little experience, and there are so many more charming men in the world than your poor knight, that I—"

"That you are a dear fidgety goosey!" said Echo, laughing through her tears delightfully, and dropping the warm shadow of a kiss on his bearded lips.

"You will write to me constantly, wont you, Echo?"

"It is the thought of writing to you and receiving long, loving letters in return, that sustains me in going, Arthur."

"You must not be too affable with strangers, my love;

there are so many smooth villains traveling that ladies are always in danger of insult."

"Oh, dear, Arthur! Mrs. Ainsley and I will be enveloped in such an odor of sal volatile and other medicaments that we will be effectually protected from the social overtures of strangers, I think. At any rate, "confidence" people will make nothing of us, I can tell you. Mrs. Ainsley's serving men are equal to any emergency of that kind."

"Of all men in the world, those Californians are the most impudent with women." O, miserable young man!

"A woman is panopolied in her purity, Arthur;—and feel that I shall be safe everywhere. With God's help, I know that I need not fear."

"I shall be very unhappy until you return."

"Oh, but you must not be unhappy, dearest; I shall continually pray for you, and the consciousness of my undying love should be with you always. Then you will have the cottage to look after, you know."

"That is true—if I may venture to anticipate the future to that extent."

Echo burst into tears at the continued gloom of his speech, and, so contradictory is the nature of a man in love, his manliness immediately returned, and from that time forth he bore his fate with heroic fortitude and charming grace.

Softly folding her in his arms, he said: "Forgive me, loved one! I have not doubted your sincerity for a moment; but we do not always understand our own hearts.

Let us be happy, then, sweetheart, and confident in our future."

She lifted her tear-softened glance to his face, and creeping closer to his side, replied : " You think me very foolish, no doubt, but as the dreaded time of sep- aration draws near, strange misgivings begin to shadow my spirit. My reason tells me that we shall soon be re-united, and that all will be well; but, somehow, there is a sense of gloom and impending evil that I cannot shake off."

" How foolish I have been, Echo—how criminally mean to be harping away on a wretched minor key about your journey. I might have foreseen that your gentle bosom would soon be disturbed by such idle fore- bodings."

A servant here announced that the carriage was in waiting, and the lovers, with one long, clinging, soul- ful kiss, terminated their interview with the whispered, inevitable " Good-by " that becomes so familiar to us in the sorrowful experiences of life.

Professional engagements detained Arthur in Que- bec, and this was therefore their parting. The overland journey has been so often described that we will not take more than a flying glimpse of the many wonders that bewilder and enchant the traveler in the mighty panorama of its mountains and plains.

There lay the brown, wide, interminable pampas of the buffalo and the Sioux, suggesting ten thousand wild tales of border life. Yonder, a dim wavy line of blue along the horizon, lay the gigantic mountain chains— the historic Rockies of the bold adventurous West.

Pulpit Rock, standing alone at the debouchure of Echo Canyon, is memorable from the fact that Brigham Young, the great leader of the Mormons, is said to have harangued the faithful from its summit for the first time in Utah.

" Almost anything is believed of Brigham," said Mrs. Ainsley; " he must be a great man."

" He has accomplished wonders, certainly," said Echo; " God allows error to ripen and fall, and I predict that the time is not far distant when the great religious society he has erected here in the desert will crumble into ruin."

" Let us not talk about ruins, my dear," said Mrs. Ainsley, fretfully; " I cannot forget that my own dear home is in ruins."

While the train was slowly creeping through Weber Canyon, an amusing incident occurred. An old lady, who was puffing painfully at the stem of a " cob " pipe, taking the unsightly object from her mouth for a moment, exclaimed :

" An' what might that are be?" pointing to the object of her curiosity.

" I believe that is called the 'Devil's Slide,'" answered a gentleman, kindly.

" The law sakes ! It must have ben wearin' on his trousers !"

There was a musical smile among the passengers, at this sally, at which the old lady took offense. Turning her brown, wrinkled visage slowly around the car, she disdainfully observed: "People are a gittin' mighty peart these days !" and resumed her wheezing cob. Perhaps she was a mother of heroes, but it would never-theless have been interesting to have had her opinion of the Medician Venus.

When the grand Sierras had been conquered, and the westward flying train swept down from the eternal win-ter of those granite solitudes to the summer of the Sac-ramento valley, our travelers were amazed at the won-drous change. On, on they sped, by waving fields and flowering orchards, under skies as soft and pure as those of Italy, and were soon at their journey's end.

CHAPTER VIII

T has been remarked, in tuneful verse, that hope vegetates eternally in the human breast. It was at least the impalpable but sufficient nourishment of our young heroine during the period of her separation from that daring Esculapian whose name, destined to be graven with a scalpel, on the heights of professional fame, she was fond of murmuring to the breezes and birds.

They were comfortably settled in the patrician city of Oakland, opposite the mistress of the Golden Gate. Before them lay the beautiful bay of San Francisco, studded with brown islands and stirring with commerce. Around them were the fruits and flowers of the semitropics, and upon all, glorifying all, the rich atmosphere of sunland.

How bleak and unlovely was their own northland when compared with this favored region! Yet Echo, notwithstanding her impressible, poetic nature, was more observant of the operations of the mails than of the vaunted excellencies of Californian life. It was natural enough; had she arrived at Elysium, her first inquiry would have been for a post-office.

"Do you know," said Mrs. Ainsley, reclining one evening in her easy chair, holding a letter she had just received, in her jeweled hand, "that my dear boy thinks of coming out to us immediately?"

"Yes," replied Echo, growing faint with apprehension at this unexpected piece of news and bending lower over the "Overland" she was reading, to hide her pallor; "I understood that business would detain him in Quebec for some time."

"Oh, he has arranged all that. The poor boy is homesick for 'Mamma,' no doubt, and I shall welcome him with a grateful heart."

"I presume so." It was all that she could say, her bosom was so shaken with vague alarms.

"My Edmond," Mrs. Ainsley closed her eyes with a soft ecstacy at the idea of proprietorship expressed in these words, "has a well-balanced mind and is jealous of the family dignity, but he is so strikingly handsome that *parvenu* belles are always fluttering about him, and I feel safest when he is with me. Don't you think he is 'like Paris fair,' as the poets say; though I cannot see why a city can be compared with a man, my dear?"

"Aye, 'and like Hector brave,'" rejoined the governess, her beautiful eyes sparkling with a merry reminiscence of the fire.

"You see it is this way," continued Mrs. Ainsley, who was evidently talking with an object, "Edmond must not make a misalliance; there is not only a possibility but a great probability of his coming to a title, by and by; and besides, our family has an aristocratic name to be regarded in the event of his marriage, which, I do

hope, may be happily consummated one of these days.
It is the source of constant anxiety to me."

"I can well believe that it is."

"Edmond has been so occupied with the improve-
ment of his mind and tastes that I think he has been
unconscious of matrimony so far; at least, I have never
heard him express the slightest interest in the matter."

"How would a Californian heiress suit you?" said
Echo.

"Oh dear; these Americans are dreadful people —
but as there is no such thing as caste here, I cannot say
that a rich, beautiful and accomplished American would
be entirely inadmissible."

"I suppose you will go into society here?"

"Oh, yes; if they support such a luxury in this bar-
barous country."

"It is said that Californian heiresses have a penchant
for pistols, and that they are accustomed to surround eli-
gible young Englishmen with revolvers and demand
their affections, a la Duval."

"Monstrous, Echo; how can you report such things?"

"Edmond is heroic, however," pursued the young
lady, michievously, "and will stand fire."

There was a point in this little innuendo which Mrs.
Ainsley did not see.

"Your friend, Hoberg, makes such a sorry figure beside my Crichton. Do you not think so?"

"They should not be mentioned in the same breath,
Mrs. Ainsley." Echo bit her lips as she pronounced
this two-sided opinion; but the other, absorbed in the

object of her vanity, did not realize the bitterness of the retort.

"I am glad you think so; rather, that you are frank enough to acknowledge the truth, my dear."

"It were useless for any one to endeavor to conceal so evident a disparity."

"Well, we must not be hard on young Hoberg; he is only a poor clergyman's son, and having to work for his living, it is necessary that he should be of coarser clay than Edmond."

There is a good deal of suppressed cat in the sweetest of female characters, and it is quite possible that Mrs. Ainsley's eyes were in imminent danger at this juncture.

"I verily believe that it was through the boorish awkwardness of this Hoberg in lowering me from that dreadful window that so much injury was done to my nervous system."

Echo nearly shrieked with indignation, but managed to say, with cold emphasis—"Perhaps. He should have left that delicate task to your son." Still the miserable mother could not see, and rejoined with indolent admir-ation.

"So he should. Edmond could have saved me so nicely."

"Ahem!"

The governess could not articulate a word. There was a murderous shadow on her lovely face.

"Still, it is a very good match for you," said Mrs. Ainsley, persistently extending the disagreeable theme; "and I shall take pleasure in making you a handsome wedding present. Hoberg is called a rising physician;

and if he shall make money enough, I suppose people will not care to remember that his grandfather was probably a hod-carrier."

"It is immaterial to me what they remember, so they do not forget that he was an honest man. Let us change the subject, please."

There was something in the girl's tone which impressed the dull wits, of even Mrs. Ainsley with a sense of warning, and the subject was dropped.

In due course of time Mr. Edmond Ainsley made his appearance upon the scene, and then Echo's lot was almost intolerable. One of her most tiresome duties was to furnish soothing music as an opiate for Mrs. Ainsley whenever that elaborate invalid desired to sleep. Of music itself the young lady was passionately fond, but it became utterly nauseous when thus administered as a medicine. And there was another more potent reason for disgust with it — Edmond Ainsley chose these occasions for paying her his intolerable attentions.

One evening, while thus engaged, she was suddenly conscious of his presence, although he had come up stealthily. Bending over her so that his hot breath actually scorched her cheek, he whispered —

"Dear Echo, have you determined to kill me with your cruel indifference?"

The white fingers swept the ivory keys evenly — not a muscle of the mobile face moved. There was no indication that the player was even conscious of his presence.

"Will you not hear me? I have been devoted to you from the first; in the blaze of your transcendent beauty

I wander like an enslaved satellite. Everything that I have and am I willingly lay at your feet. Is not such love worthy your acceptance?"

Still not a note was dropped, and not the quiver of an eyelash betrayed her excitement. Her unspeakable repugnance to the man rendered her impervious to his influence.

And yet the perfumed rake was unabashed—in truth, he seemed to take courage from her silence, and continued, while the touch of his hand on her shoulder chilled her blood:

"Do you consent—will you be mine? The prejudices of my mother can be circumvented by a secret marriage; and, the happy knot once tied, she will readily receive you as her daughter. Oh, dearest Echo, tell me that you accede — that you will bless me with your love!"

Still the tender melody flowed on through dreamy mazes, and the dozing invalid in the adjacent chamber harbored no suspicion of the little drama that was enacting so near her, else the rippling notes of the piano, had roused her like a thunder-crash.

"Speak, my darling; will you marry me?"

The young lady's touch became softer, and the music fell into a whispering echo as she spoke for the first time, her voice cold and cutting as the north wind—

"Have you done, sir?"

"I am waiting your answer, beloved."

"Then have it; had I not known you to be a miserable reptile before, the vile scheme you have hissed in my ear would have betrayed your slimy, sneaking na ture. I could sooner love the mangiest cur in the streets than such as you! We understand each other now; let this be the end.

The young man trembled with passion, and his face became purple as he hissed through his clenched teeth, "No, by the eternal, you flaunting beggar! you shall rue this!" and he hurriedly strode from the room.

As often as the opportunities of the mail served, Echo was made happy by the receipt of letters from Arthur, supplemented, occasionally, by less enthusiastic communications from his sister, Mary.

Then an alarming circumstance in connection with this correspondence appeared. Contrary to all precedent, in such cases, the letters of the young physician began to grow colder and more concise. A clue to the mystery was not wanting long. A troubled letter from Mary explained that Arthur had become insanely infatuated with a young lady, a niece of one Dr. Combes, who had just arrived from England. The sympathizing girl wrote that her father was stricken with grief at this turn of affairs, and it was their hope and prayer that the erring son and brother would yet regain his reason and fulfill his engagement with their darling Echo, than whom none better or more beautiful ever lived.

We will not attempt to analyze the suffering of the governess on the receipt of this intelligence. The blow had nearly unseated her mind; yet there was a straw of hope that there was some mistake, or, at least, exaggeration. Then came the climax, in a whining, pusillanimous letter from Arthur begging a release from his engagement.

Without a word of censure or complaint, she gave him what he asked, and then sat down to confront and contemplate the appalling misery of her situation. As a natural consequence, she fell dangerously ill, for it is thus that the body relieves the tortured mind.

Mrs. Ainsley acted as became her. She protested that there was a conspiracy to desert her in a strange land, and that Echo was not doing her duty by so munificent a patron in succumbing to a trifling ailment. "Bring me the smelling bottle, Edmond, you at least are here;" and the poor creature ended with a sob and a gush of hypochondriac tears.

There are, in San Francisco, a number of assignation houses, supported mainly by the extravagant licentiousness of stock-gamblers. Under pretence of having Echo removed to a Sister's hospital for treatment and experienced nursing, Edmond readily procured her admittance, by the liberal use of his money, into one of those gilded palaces of ruin referred to. It was no part of his programme that the young lady should die, so he procured her the services of a skillful but unscrupulous physician.

Then the fever fiercely ran its course, and life and death fought implacably for the possession of the smitten girl, babbling incontinently in her delirium of love and faith, inconstancy and despair.

CHAPTER IX.

NIGHT came on in the beautiful and vivacious world of Paris. Lady Clifford, in the solitude of her spacious living room, was pacing to and fro in feverish unrest. The machinations of Legrand had thus far succeeded. Zarina, in the character of the long lost daughter, had been received as became the occasion, and the heinous fraud bade fair to prosper. The restoration of the necklace was a master stroke of policy. Its identity with the necklace worn by the babe at the time of its abduction, could not for a moment be doubted, and the sight of the familiar ornament unlocked a flood of blessed memories in the mother's bosom. Painfully, again and again, would she pore over the features of the clever young actress, striving to recall traces of her child, but could not, and she would murmur wearily to herself : " My heart does not respond to the daughter that Heaven has restored to me, but I must be content; it was long, long ago, and the infant has become a woman." Ah! this grievous wasting of the wounded heart—that longing cry of her soul : "Will they come ! will they come !" in the thorny days of expectancy, only for this at last ! These hearts of ours, which are but living dust, and must crumble to dust again, are continually athirst for dews that never fall on earth. The woman was most unhappy, though Prov-

idence had seemingly answered her prayer. And how
had wealth attended her cultured taste in the adornment
of her home ! The carpet that covered the floor where
we beheld her chafing against an indefinable sorrow,
was of a gorgeous pattern, mingling the richest hues
of the rainbow in a very garden of silence ! Pictures
from the hands of the masters, garnished the walls with
vivid portraits and mellow landscapes. The mantel
was a *chef d'œuvre* of mediæval art, and costly statuary
was disposed in appropriate places. An ebony case,
heavily embossed with silver, contained the best books
in magnificent binding, for there was no room devoted
specially to a library, and the windows of heavy plate
glass were draped in damask and lace. And yet the
mistress of these luxurious appointments was complaining to God of sorrow!

While thus engaged, a visitor was announced — M.
Legrand.

"Show him in, Fantil," said Lady Clifford, I shall
receive him here."

" Ah, madame," said Legrand, entering, with a low
bow, " I hope that I find you happy !"

" I am beginning to believe, monsieur, that happiness
is not of earth."

"No! then my success in the restoration of your lovely
daughter has turned to ashes," and the graceful hypo-
crite tried to look as though his heart had fallen into
one of his polished boots.

" Nay, nay—I know that I am ungrateful; again receive my thanks for that inestimable service; but my

cup of joy is dashed with the bitterness of unreasonable doubts and fears."

"Human nature is a mystery, madame, and the motto of the Greeks, 'Know thyself!' implies a harder task than any of us can perform. With your permission, however, I have still another matter to submit concerning the highly romantic history of your daughter. I feared yesterday to try your nerves beyond endurance, and so kept back an important part of the evidence in the case. Will you see it now?"

"Ah, then, there is something more! You may produce it, if you please."

Legrand was examining a bundle of papers he had taken from an inner pocket of his coat: "Will you recognize the handwriting of monsieur, your husband?"

"Yes, I should know it anywhere," said the lady, with a slight gasp, feeling faint from the emotion his question had aroused.

He silently handed her a time-stained paper. Lady Clifford grasped it with a trembling hand, and, for a moment the written words danced before her eyes in a hopeless maze. Recovering, however, she made out to read it to the end, and then fell fainting to the floor.

It was the letter of Cleaveland Clifford to his mother; that brief and gloomy epistle in which the despairing man had announced the ruin of his home and had implored the maternal affection for his child.

"*Diable!*" chuckled Legrand, as he eyed the prostrate form, "an enemy becomes a philosopher when he can take his revenge like a gentleman."

"He rang furiously for the servants and told them to

hasten to their mistress with restoratives, as she had fallen in a swoon.

Under the treatment of her experienced nurse, Ninée, Lady Clifford was soon able to sit up, but she only called for M. Legrand, who had awaited her recovery in the next room, to thank and dismiss him:

"I have no longer the slightest reason, monsieur, to doubt the truth of your assertions. The letter is my husband's, and is of priceless value to me." She hesitated a moment and then said: "You may go, now, but come again to-morrow, and we will discuss the affair again."

"When I hope to see you much improved, madame, and till then allow me to give you good night!" and he was gone, with a satanic smirk on his keen features.

"Alas! my poor husband!" murmured Lady Clifford when left alone in her chamber, and all through the night she baptized her pillow with tears.

"*Mon Dieu! Mon Dieu!*" cried Ninée, rushing into the presence of her mistress one day soon after these events, bearing in her hand a broken bird's nest, " mademoiselle has destroyed the home of the heavenly bird!" and the dear creature sobbed wildly.

The lady's face flushed as she turned towards the despoiler and said, with sorrowful reproach, " Oh, my child; is it possible that you can take pleasure in the sorrow of another! Surely you must tell me that you did this accidentally!"

"Ha! ha! ha!" laughed the young lady in a voice silvery, yet cruel, " Is it possible that the antique nurse's heart is an egg that lies at the bottom of a bird's nest?

I could not resist the temptation to tease her, and then
the birds should have been better behaved than to build
their unsightly nests in the lilacs. On my life, mamma,
I think Ninée is out of her mind; it was only yesterday
that she saw a magpie fly across my path, when she
must fall down and pray!"

A slight frown of displeasure darkened the pure brow
of the mother.

"But, my dear, you certainly know, or have heard,
that it is an evil omen for the magpie to cross one's path
in flight. As for the swallow, whose humble nest was
on the wall, shaded by the lilacs, it is venerated by the
peasantry of France, and is called ' *La poule de Dieu*.'
These may be prejudices which will clear away before
the light of education, but while they remain, people of
good feeling must respect them."

"As you will, mamma," said Echo, for by this name
she was called now, I regret having been the occasion
of so much disturbance and will ask Ninée's pardon,
and hope to receive your kiss of pardon." The kiss
was given with all a mother's tenderness, and the ruf-
fled waters were quiet again.

As time went on, it occurred to the mother that her
daughter should be brought out in society, and to this
project M. Legrand joyfully acceded.

Mademoiselle Clifford therefore made her debut soon
at the house of one of the nobility, on the occasion of a
brilliant party. We have before referred to the personal attractions of the young lady, which, it may be
readily conceived, lost nothing by the accessories of
splendid apparel and artistic toilet. She was bold,

graceful, dashing, witty, wealthy, and, in fact, all that the dissipated, courtly society of Paris could require.

Among the host of admirers who immediately fell into the train of the young *debutante*, was La Croix, a rich and dissolute count of the Empire, who was soon more conspicuous than his competitors in the race for mademoiselle's favor, and boasted of his success at the fashionable clubs.

"*Ma foi!*" he would exclaim in the elegant lan- guage of the turf—"the girl is of good form and a proud stepper."

A dangerous intrigue between the two was soon in full flower, notwithstanding the surveillance of the thoughtful mother, vitalized in the almost constant com- panionship of Ninée.

So, one happy day, while the moments were dissolv- ing languidly in the gold-tinted air of June, Echo, en- veloped in a gossamer cloud of summer dress, was seen to enter a green-wreathed arbor in the garden and seat herself as if to read; but the newly cut volume of "Monte Cristo" was suffered to lie idly in her lap and the lady fell to musing. Very soon a sound was heard as if some one had vaulted lightly over the stone wall in the rear, and the flowering vines that secured the en- trance were gaily pushed aside by a handsome young man, dressed in the height of fashion, and perfumed be- yond the rivalry of the roses—

"Queen rose of the rose-bud garden of girls!"

quoted La Croix, in greeting, being proud of his famil- iarity with English literature and language.

"Good morning, count," replied the young lady, with a slight flush on her cheek, "You are a scholar, then, as well as a handsome knight."

"Nay, mademoiselle," said the young man gallantly, kissing the hand that she extended, "I am nothing but your slave."

"Be seated, then, and regale me with some of the gossip of your delightful, frivolous world."

"Rather let us talk of love in this atmosphere of roses," he exclaimed, seating himself at her side and printing an ardent kiss on her lips: "Do you know that I begin to suspect that you will get me into trouble, my dear?"

"Say, rather, that I shall destroy you with kindness."

"A death that an angel might desire," he said rapturously," claiming another kiss—"but the danger that I apprehend is from a harsher hand—that of M. Legrand."

"Ha! ha! M. Legrand is a kind of godfather of mine."

"I think he must be a lover of yours; he glares at me ferociously whenever I approach you in society, and one of these days I am sure that he will honor me with a cartel."

"There is little danger of that, dear count, and," with a blush, "you are secure in my favor—is not that enough?"

"Enough! it is the joy of Paradise in a single draught."

CHAPTER X.

"WHAT, monsieur; you here!" exclaimed Echo, otherwise Madame Legrand, as, on leaving the arbor, she almost ran into the arms of her husband.

"Nothing more probable, madame," said M. Legrand, with a dangerous sneer, his face white with suppressed rage; "let us return to your trysting bower—I have words for you which are quite as important as the idle flatteries of a libertine."

"*Pardieu!*" thought the false Echo, following her husband into the arbor, "there is trouble already, and it shall be a match of wits and hardihood." But the mocking smile faded from her lips, nevertheless, when, motioning for her to be seated, he stood calmly before her and began:

"I gave you credit for discretion, Zarina, if not for virtue. We are necessary to each other in the business we have undertaken, to say nothing of our legal union, and there must be no double masks—no treachery among traitors. I love you in my way, but when we have consummated our designs, you may go upon the town if you like; all that I require of you now is that your despicable gallantries shall not ruin the work we have begun. You cannot deceive me; I am the originator and director of this great scheme upon the fortune of

4

Lady Clifford, and I demand your implicit obedience till success shall be achieved. Have you an answer ?"

"Only this, monsieur," replied the subtle young woman, "that I am yours in everything, and that you have misconstrued the attentions which I have received from that insipid count. You know the freedom which we acquire upon the stage, and what I have done is simply the fault of my education. I swear that I love you and you alone, and that LaCroix is no more in my thoughts, and can be no more than a handsome poodle. Hereafter I shall be more guarded in my intercourse with men, so that I shall not receive such cruel reproaches;" and the guileless beauty actually had the cleverness to produce a tear or two.

What happened then has always happened since the world began. There was forgiveness and reconciliation, and the wife, *sub rosa*, was, a few minutes later, lying voluptuously in the arms of her husband, amid mutual murmurs of love !

"You will doubt me no more, then ?" she said, softly, disengaging her lips from a lingering kiss.

"No, my love, but I am impatient for the time when, with wealth at our command, we may feast upon the joys of wedlock without restraint."

"Well, monsieur, we have before talked of hastening that time; if there be obstacles, let us, as you have often said, remove them."

"You are right, my dear, we must move cautiously, but we must move. There are two great natural laws which will sanction our work—the universal law of self,

defense, and the command, not less obligatory and universal, to pursue our happiness."

The lady smiled her approval of his philosophy, and
he continued:

"I have been studying the nature of occult poisons
very much of late; it is a sublime science, and I flatter
myself that I have penetrated its arcana. Look here!"
and he took ·from his pocket and held before her a small
phial filled with a brilliant liquid. " This is one of the
most mysterious poisons that has ever been discovered,
and its preparation was, I believe, a secret of the Bor-
gias. Observe that it is colorless, odorless, and that its
taste can easily be disguised; that it is slow, insidious,
fatal, and that it leaves not, like a bungling assassin, the
footprints of its crime—and you, involved in the meshes
of a gigantic plot, must acknowledge and adore its
power."

" *Morbleu!*" said she, with a faint shiver; "it is like
the bottled genii of the Arabian story, and it strikes like
the unseen hand of God !"

" Yes, it is all that, love; two drops a day in food or
drink, will effect changes in the world and bring happiness to those who deserve it."

" Give it me," she murmured, and as a glance of deadly
meaning was exchanged, she took possession of the
phial.

" *Peste!* it is late !" he said, looking at his watch,
"and we must kiss and part;" and the delectable pair
parted with a caress that was worthy of better natures.

That night, in the secrecy of her chamber, the retired

danseuse held the potent phial to the light as she stood partially undressed, and admired its gem-like brilliancy.

"*Mon Dieu!*" she exclaimed, in soliloquy, "it glitters like the lightning! Ah, sweetheart—husband mine! you have put a powerful weapon into my hands, and you must look to yourself. Fool! does he think me blind, that I cannot see that he puts the burden of the guilt upon me, and, the deed accomplished, hopes to have me irrevocably in his power? The end is not yet, monsieur —a plot is as full of plots as an egg is full of meat!" With these virtuous thoughts to guard her pillow, the sleep of the young woman, when she retired a few moments later, was sweet and profound.

A few evenings subsequent to the events just narrated, Lady Clifford and the person known as her daughter, were returning from a successful dinner party, where the young woman, thanks to the maternal taste in dressing her, had attained the enviable distinction of being the cynosure of all eyes.

M. Legrand had a seat in the carriage, but he was apparently unhappy. There was a settled look of gloom and bitterness on his face, which, exert himself as he might, he was wholly unable to exorcise.

Echo was flushed with excitement and the glory of conquest. She had lost her head entirely in the giddy swirl of admiration she had created, and had flirted audaciously with a dozen men—La Croix among the number. For a long time she had been pouring forth a flood of comment upon the persons and characters of the guests, while her mother sat silently listening, or absorbed in her own thoughts.

"In the name of the inventor of speech, my dear mother, I implore you to answer some of my questions—express an opinion—or at least make a sign that you live, ·and can both think and hear !" she finally cried, exasper- ated by the indifference of her audience.

Legrand frowned heavily, and made as if he would have spoken, but thought better of it, and remained silent.

"I have been pained, my daughter," said Lady Clif- ford, "at your words, your thoughts, and your manner. I have hesitated to speak because my feelings were so deeply concerned for you."

"Ha, ha ! Mother, you are not a philosopher, like myself and the gay and versatile Monsieur Legrand ! Why, it is the acme of philosophy to think without feel- ing, and to speak without thinking. All serious thoughts are a useless abrasion of the tissue of the brain, and it is my opinion that the angels are immortal simply because they are happy, and,"—with a malicious glance at Le- grand—" I may confess to you that the knightly La Croix did me the honor to call me an angel many times this afternoon."

"For the love of Heaven, my daughter, restrain your idle tongue. Your conversation does no credit to your nature or your breeding, and you pain me beyond utter- ance. The love of admiration, when unreasonably in- dulged, is poison to a pure soul, and destroys every germ of good."

"Ah, mother, you do well to remind me of my breed- ing,"—Legrand eyed the speaker with á perceptible sneer—"therein lies the source of my foolish ways."

There was a mournful pathos in her voice that completely overcome Lady Clifford, who embraced her with misty eyes, and begged "the poor child" to forgive her.

Little more was said until the carriage arrived at its destination, and M. Legrand assisted the ladies to alight.

He clutched Zarina's hand with a painful grasp in assisting her to the ground, and whispered in her ear the one word—"Beware !"

CHAPTER XI.

PON the seventh day, stupor succeeded delirium. Arousing the patient with difficulty, the physician administered the medicine himself—remarking, philosophically, to the nurse: "It were better for her to die thus, while she lingers upon the threshold of sin, but the duty of a well-paid physician does not comprehend questions of such moral magnitude; and our frail, beautiful friend, here, will therefore recover, and go her way—alluring others, perhaps, by the false light of a fair face, to the ruin she has embraced. Hand me the blue bottle, and support her head a moment, please. There, that will do. It is a bitter draught, but not so deadly as the kisses that have betrayed her! Sick prisoners are often restored to health in order that they may be hung, but the rescue of this girl for a life of shame is still a ghastlier paradox. You know your duty, now, nurse. Good-day!" And the erudite *medico* passed down the handsome stairway, lightly humming a bar of the last opera.

On the evening of the second day from this, Echo gradually awoke from a slumber as profound and dreamless as that of the grave. Opening her eyes, she glanced around the dimly lighted room. All was strange. She tried to raise her hand, but it fell helplessly at her side.

With a dazzling sensation of recovering thought, she again closed her eyes, and her mind wandered back to the twilight border of fantasy. Presently, hearing the rustle of a woman's dress, she looked up, and saw a middle-aged lady, with a homely, yet kind face, bending over her.

"You have been very sick, dear," said the nurse, for such it was, in a soothing voice, as she tenderly smoothed the pillow. "You are better now, but must not exert yourself to .talk. Drink this, and compose yourself to sleep."

The poor girl obeyed without a word, and soon glided from the phantom land of fever into the soft embrace of a healing slumber.

The convalescence of the young lady was progressing favorably, when, one day, a note from Mrs. Ainsley was handed her. It contained words of sympathy and condolence, simply, which shaped themselves at the close into a whine of self-pity, and was accompanied by a tasteful bouquet of flowers, composed of a girdle of rose-geranium leaves around a pyramidal cluster of pansies, surmounted by a creamy tuberose.

The nurse observed, with surprise, that though at first the invalid pressed the flowers to her lips with a low cry of delight, she a moment later threw the fragrant offering from her with a moan of pain, as a purple flush swept into her white face, and her sensitive, pale lips curved with aversion.

"Take the flowers away," she said, "and please defend me from all other gifts from that source !" The

card attached to the bouquet bore the name of Edmond
Ainsley.

In narrating this incident to the medical attendant, the
nurse expressed the belief that her charge was the victim
of some cruel wrong.

" I never was more puzzled in my life with regard to
the character of a patient," said the man of nostrums; " I
am an excellent judge of human nature—it is incident to
our profession, and, were it not for the circumstances of
the case, I should say that this young woman is pure
as a lily."

And so he thought again as he stood at the bedside of
the woman he had saved from death. Very white, wan,
and plaintive was the face resting on the pillow. The
blue-veined lids drooped listlessly over the tender eyes,
and the long lashes swept the wasted cheeks. The
doctor looked kindly upon this picture of withered loveliness, and his heart was stirred with a noble sympathy.
He had a daughter of his own at home, a motherless darling like Echo, whom he loved devotedly, and thoughts
of her softened his voice magically when he bent over
the invalid and said :

" God and science have given us the victory, my dear;
the crisis is past, and you will get well. It must have
been a great mental and moral strain that brought you
so near the grave. I hope that you will give me your
confidence, and call upon me freely for any assistance
that I can render in removing the causes of your
malady."

" The time for the only service which you could have
done me has passed," responded Echo, sadly. " Oh,

doctor, you have done a cruel thing in prolonging my
life !"

"No, no, my child; those are idle words! I am not
a Christian in the true sense, and I am proud of the re-
sources of my profession; yet, believe me, dear, God
takes the lives that have accomplished their mission on
earth.   God wills it, therefore, and life is still a prize for
you, whatever misfortunes have gathered on your path.
You are young and very beautiful; take courage, then,
and we will assist you to tie the broken threads of love
and trust together again.   I find you in a strange place—
a place, the very shadow of which is deadlier than that
of the upas—but I take a vital interest in the life that I
have assisted back from the borders of shadow-land.
Come to my home, when you have recovered; I am a
widower, with an only daughter about your age, and
henceforth you shall have true and steadfast friends."

The doctor hesitated a moment, and a slight flush
mantled his brow, as he continued :

"I am wealthy and powerful in this community, and "—
the flush deepened on the broad brow—"I am lonely and
world-worn, will you share my name and home ?   I
know it is a sudden and startling proposition to you, but
judgment and feeling unitedly constrain me to be candid
with you.   Take time to think of this, if you wish it;
and, at all events, be assured that a home and a father's
protection beneath my roof are yours always."

The dreamy, dark eyes dilated with surprise, but not
a vestige of color dyed the marble whiteness of her brow,
as she calmly replied:

"Ah, doctor, your proposition, so far as it relates to a

holier bond than friendship, does more credit to your heart than your judgment. Even were things other than they are, I could not see you thus become the martyr of your pity. The title of wife should be crowned with the richest love of the heart, and my heart is dust and ashes now. When you are made to know all the calamities that have befallen me, you will understand me, and pity me more than ever. But do not, I beg you, withhold from me the fatherly affection you have said might still be mine—I need it sorely, sorely !" and she sighed most mournfully.

"I shall not annoy you with persistency, Miss Clifford, but you must yield me the high privilege of that paternal friendship which I feel for you. When you are well enough we will talk of the past and future, and in the meantime I caution you against all who are not proven and disinterested friends, and "—the doctor thought of declaring plainly the character of the gilded mansion in which she had unaccountably taken refuge, but concluded that she was safe for a time, and so concluded his sentence, "now, good-by, for to-day." He touched her hand affectionately, and withdrew.

Regularly, on alternate days, during this time, Edmond Ainsley brought to the house where Echo was lying short notes of inquiry and commiseration. Trusting much to the habitual reserve of the young lady, he hoped by these attentions to quiet her mind as to the safety of her situation.

The days dragged heavily. The doctor began to exhibit some anxiety about the slow progress of his si-lent, uncomplaining patient. A dull apathy rested upon her, and she lay mysteriously becalmed half way upon the voyage of recovery. The bright world had opened to her restored sight, only to wither and darken again in the memory of her awakened sorrow. The vision of life had returned again, but it was the garden of betrayal and despair, sunless and songless to her broken heart. The vestal flames of hope had been extinguished there, and the sighing, slow winds that waved the drooping flowers, were heavy with the burden of her soul's Gethsemane.

Physic, therefore, was no longer needed. The physician had paid his last visit, and gone to more stirring scenes on the wide battle-field of death. In the meantime Ainsley was in the full feather of anticipated victory, and standing before the glass forty times a day, complimented himself as one of the greatest generals of the age—a man that knew how to crush his enemies !

The nurse could not help admiring the appearance of her charge, one evening, as, reclining on a sofa drawn up by the window, she gazed out mournfully on the waters of the bay, the tender, solemn eyes harmonizing sweetly with the spiritual delicacy of the thin, transparent features. She was simply attired in a white cambric wrapper, relieved only at the throat and wrists with soft ruchings of tulle. A delicate white rose-bud nestled in the gold-tinted hair above one shell-like ear, the single ornament of her toilet.

Suddenly turning her mesmeric glance full upon the nurse, she said, in the low, thrilling tones the latter delighted to hear :

"I hope you will not think me ungrateful, kind friend,

for the unwearied attentions you have bestowed on a
ship-wrecked stranger. I shall pray the good Lord to
reward you bountifully."

"Do not mention it, child," said the other, with brisk
kindliness; "I did no more than my duty, and that, I
fear, but poorly. There is something on my heart, however, concerning you, and since you have spoken, I will
speak. I do not wish to intrude upon the privacy of
your inner thoughts, but my interest in you compels me
to ask if you have counted the cost of the step you have
taken—if your feet have taken deadly hold upon the life
you contemplate?"

Wholly innocent of any suspicion concerning the real
peril of her situation, and thinking the interrogatories of
the nurse referred to the rejection of the doctor's offer,
and the consequent acceptance of a lonely life of drudg-
ery, Echo replied—"Oh yes; had I not disobeyed the
command of God and turned idol worshipper, these calamities could not have befallen me. Alas! each of us,
like Æschylus, sings to some enthroned image of the
heart. 'Jupiter is the air; Jupiter is the earth; Jupiter
is the heaven; all is Jupiter.' But, alas, for the heart!
when its idols are fallen and its songs are dead!"

"I was young and pretty once, myself," said the nurse,
with a half smile at the singularity of the reminiscence,
"though not beautiful like you. I, too, have a heart-
history, as who, indeed, has not? Bereft of my parents
at an early age, I was left alone in the world, without
relatives or friends, and found the struggle for existence
severe. I was betrothed to a young missionary who
went out to India, whither I was to follow him at the

end of a year, but he fell a prey to the fever, and the star of my youth went down never to rise again. I am old and gray, now, but the grave of my perished love is still green in my heart. It is a sorrow that has kept my soul pure in the midst of temptations and bitter trials, and at last my life has been crowned with a heavenly calm, that is not despair, because it is fragrant with hope, and not joy, because it is mellowed with regret. The stricken heart should not become a waste—a *hortus siccus*, for fountains and flowers shall not be wanting to minds that lie open to the sunshine and showers of heaven. The memory of a pure sorrow will become a thing of beauty, a golden anchor to the storm-tossed soul."

"You are right, my kind friend; happiness is a young dream that will visit me no more. My prayer is for courage, patience, strength, purity, and that serenity of which you have so clearly spoken."

"To be good, we must do good, my dear. Pleasure vanishes in the grasp, because it is only the bloom-dust on the wings of a living, eternal good — the calm of a tried soul, which we may pursue, over thorny ways it may be, and surely gain. To be plain and practical, I see no consistency in your noble purposes and the life you have espoused."

"True," musingly, "my words and actions seem to conflict, but my aspirations are holy, and I shall prayer-fully seek the right way. My position in life is humble, but no shadow of dishonor shall fall upon it."

"Miss Clifford, I am astonished at you!" There was a flash of scorn in the fine old face.

"I do not understand you, nurse!" said Echo, quickly,

with a movement of alarm. "What can you mean?" and the invalid clasped her hands nervously, as she regarded the other with an appealing look.

The nurse bent over her work and seemed at a loss for a reply, when Echo continued, imploringly: "Oh, you must listen to my story and then you will not be cruel! You have told me of your love; it was a sweet reality, but mine was a phantom and a curse. You can remember a mother's kiss and a father's care — blessings I never knew. The love that I leaned upon, and oh, it was a golden chain from Heaven to me! broke, and I was cast down into the starless abysses of despair. Arthur Hoberg was the loveliest, noblest man on earth to me, and in my secret soul I worshipped him as though he were a god. Once he had rescued me from the flames of a consuming building, at the peril of his own life, and thus had another title to the life he had saved. I came to California as the companion of a rich lady of the city of Quebec, whose burning dwelling it was from which I had been gallantly rescued by Arthur. She has an only son, Edmond Ainsley, who has persecuted me with his base attentions. He is a soulless dandy, a vicious libertine, whose very presence is contamination, and I repulsed him with unutterable disdain.

"Ah, nurse! I can almost hear the soft sighing of the wind around my little white cottage home in Canada; the lullaby of the birds at evening, the humming of the bees at noon-day, and the soft lowing of beautiful old Floss as she came through the meadows at sunset. Still can I see the smooth, green lawn, with its flower-beds and gravel walks, the cleanly porch, shaded with clambering vines, where dear old grandmother used to sit with her Bible in the fragrant days of summer. Oh, that I could feel those kind hands on my weary brow to-night, and know that in all the world there was at least one warm, pulsing heart that was wholly mine!"

There was a pause, and the nurse broke in agitatedly, "Child! child! you perplex me beyond measure. Your story bears every evidence of truth; and, yet, how came you in a house of ill-fame, represented as a fashionable young man's mistress?"

Echo was almost stupefied with wonder—"House of ill-fame! a mistress! Good God!"—starting forward with an agonized expression of face—"is this the horrible phantom of a feverish dream? Has God really forgotten me, and allowed the fiends of hell possession of my soul! It cannot be! it cannot be!"

The nurse started up and laid her tender hand upon the arm of the excited girl—"Compose yourself, dear, you are safe now, and the wretched designs of your enemies shall come to naught. But tell me—how came you here?"

"Why, it was effected while I was unconscious. When the news of Arthur's unfaithfulness reached me, the blow was more than I could bear, and I sank into the desperate fever through which you have attended me. The notes that you have brought me were from Mrs. Ainsley, saying that she had caused my removal to a Sisters' hospital, and this I supposed to be the character of the place, though I have sometimes wondered that none of the good nuns have appeared in my sick room. But why are you here?"

"I am a nurse by profession, dear, and go wherever duty calls me. I trust that I have done much good in such places by sowing the seeds of reform."

Echo turned resolutely towards her bureau — "Come, then, let us get ready, and leave this poisoned air!"

CHAPTER XII.

AT eight o'clock the following morning, while the inmates of the house were still wrapped in slumber, Echo, closely veiled, and leaning upon the arm of the faithful nurse, entered the coach which had been ordered the night before, and was driven rapidly away. Before night the two—for the nurse had now established a gentle protectorate over the young lady—were comfortably settled, in quarters of their own in a distant part of the city, far from the bustle and roar of Kearney and Montgomery streets.

During the following month, mainly through the untiring effort of Christian Newbury, the nurse, Echo secured a large class for instruction in music, and the grim battle for bread was fairly launched.

One day, when returning from the home of a pupil in the neighborhood of Telegraph Hill, the attention of the music teacher was drawn to the piteous cries of a little girl, not more than four years of age, whom a group of street *gamins*, "hoodlums," as they are now known to odious fame in the Bay City, were industriously tormenting. As the teacher reached this scene of cruelty, one of the grimy young devils kicked the feet of the child from under her, and she fell heavily to the pavement, fracturing her arm. The gallows buds then fled, with a

scattering yell of triumph that had an Apache ring
in it.

"My arm, my arm, my arm !" screamed the child, as
she scrambled to her feet, and clung to Echo's dress.

"Poor little thing," said the latter, pityingly stroking
the child's disheveled hair; "Where do you live ? Tell
me, and I will take you home."

"Don't you know ?" said the child, looking at Echo
through her tears, which she was trying to dry with her
sleeve. "We's ben livin' in the alley, but we's goin' to
live in the sky now, where there's a garden, and flowers
and birds and sunshine allus, and where the good Lord
has made us a house full of jewels, and close and goodies
and everything. Mamma's gone there now, and I'm to
go, too, as soon as the pretty angels come for me, and
you are so pretty and kind I know you're one, and you're
goin' to take me now, aint you ? And you won't let the
hoodums hurt me any more, will you ?"

"Yes, poor child," said Echo, deeply affected, "dry
your tears, and we shall see what can be done." Then
the young lady looked around in much bewilderment,
as if she would question the very street for some information concerning the child. As if in answer to this
inquiring glance, a girl of about twelve years of age here
stepped forward and observed :

"The young one's name is Wistlt, Miss, and her
mother died yesterday. I guess she hasn't got no home
nor folks now."

Echo's heart filled at this sententious tale of woe, and,
gazing at the little wanderer with misty eyes, she murmured :

"Poor little waif, uncouth, unloved, desolate! We walk in the fields and crush the tender flowers at every step; lo! the relentless destinies tread us down with their iron feet in the same way! What will become of this tiny nursling of the street, if I do not give it a home and protection? Surely I have been divinely appointed to this humane office; and perhaps in saving and nourishing this periled life, I may restore much that has been lost from my own. Come, my child, you must go with me, and perhaps we shall find mamma and the beautiful garden of the sky."

The grimy little hand was laid confidingly in her own, and they went on together.

"Can't you tell me your name, dear?" said Echo, coaxingly, after they had walked a little way.

"I'm only Wistit, ma'am!"

"But what did your mother call you?"

"Mamma called me darling, but everybody else called me Wistit," replied the child, moaning with the pain of her arm.

At this moment a well-dressed gentleman overtook them, and greeting Echo respectfully, said:

"Pardon me, madam, but I noticed the accident from a window, and observing that the little girl was hurt, and that you were seemingly a stranger to her, I have ventured to offer my assistance."

Echo responded to his salutation, and was thinking of what she should say, when the gentleman stooped beside the child, and said, gently:

"Let me examine your arm, little one; may be I can help you."

He rose in a moment, and said :

"The poor thing's arm is fractured, and she must have immediate assistance. I should advise you to give her in charge of a policeman, whose duty it will be to convey her to the city hospital for treatment."

He was a man of about thirty-five, of commanding stature and shapely proportion, with a dark face, cleanly shaven with the exception of a flowing black mustache, and full, brilliant eyes. As he concluded his remarks he touched his hat, with a white, shapely hand, and handed Echo a card, on which, in clear script, was the name— Cleaveland Farrish.

Before Echo could answer, the child broke in :

"No, no, no ! I'm afraid of the p'liceman, and I won't go to the hospil ! You will take me to mamma, and she will make me well !"

Mr. Farrish pondered a moment, and made another suggestion :

"Perhaps, then, it will be better for me to call a coach and accompany you to the office of some physician. When the arm shall have been dressed, I will cheerfully assist you in arranging for the future of the homeless child, if you will kindly allow me that privilege. It is too great a burden to fall on you alone."

Echo hesitated a moment, and replied :

"Very well; I wish only to do what is best."

There is a Latin phrase which counsels us, very indefinitely, to resist beginnings. The purport of the warning evidently affects evil beginnings only, and yet, in that circumscribed sense, it leaves an individual in hopeless entanglement. Causes, both good and evil, as regards results, are woven together in an undistinguishable maze, and all that is left for the wayfarer is to be candid, courageous, yet cautious, too, and as wise as he may, in taking up the threads of destiny, and leave the rest to the merciful care of Heaven.

To Echo, inexperienced as she was, there seemed to be no impropriety in thus associating herself with an unknown gentleman in a passing work of charity, with which matter, indeed, her mind was wholly engrossed. The course of our lives, or rather of the possibilities of our lives, is marked by an infinite number of lines, which, lying in contact at the beginning, seem to be parallel, but really diverge widely as they extend, and lead to contrasted results.

Then, as if to explain her intentions, Echo said :

" I had concluded to take the forlorn little estray to my home."

Mr. Farrish cast at her a quick, inquiring glance, and suggested a doubt, with just the shadow of a fleeting smile on his dark face :

" Are you sure it will be best ? Perhaps your people will object to the spontaneous philanthrophy of your act ?"

Echo thought that Mr. Farrish was rather spontaneously thrusting himself into other people's business; but she replied, with mild gravity :

" My parents are dead. I have only to serve my own taste, convenience and sense of duty."

" Ah, then, that relieves you of all embarrassment."

And the gentlemanly Mr. Farrish seemed to approve her independent state. Then, in pursuance of the stran-

ger's counsel, the office of a physician was visited, and
the fractured arm skillfully set and bandaged.

Mr. Farrish accompanied Echo to the door of her residence in the carriage he had called, and there gracefully,
and wisely, took his leave.

"In the name of the seven wonders, what have you
here ?" exclaimed nurse Newbury, as she opened the
door and gazed upon the ill-assorted pair with consternation.

"A young lady in distress, sister," answered Echo,
cheerfully, "whom the laws of humanity and chivalry
constrain us to protect."

"Well, well ! A dog, two cats, and a street waif, all
in a month ! Bless me, Echo, I hope you have reached
the climax now ?"

Meanwhile the child, glancing from one to the other,
clung pathetically to the dress of her deliverer, and
trembled with apprehension. Seating herself, and taking
the child tenderly upon her lap, Echo then recounted the
history of the case.

"The gentleman was right," said the other, when she
had heard all; "the child should have been sent to the
hospital immediately. You do not seriously intend keeping her, my dear ?"

"I do, if you consent, sister," said Echo, gravely.

"Why, child, you have enough to do in caring for
yourself, and so have I. There are organized charities
which look after such cases more effectively than we
can."

"Organized charities ! Oh, sister, do you not know
those institutions are the last resort of the wretched ?

Charity, the 'twice blessed,' is there measured out by the inch, and loses its flavor in the grudging dole! Something has interested me strangely in my little "Wistit," as she quaintly calls herself, and I must care for her personally, even at a great sacrifice of time, comfort and convenience."

"Let us take her, then," said the nurse, softened by the earnestness of her friend; "God will provide, and we shall make out somehow."

Echo hastened to sanction this understanding with a kiss, and the little girl was brought between them and received the kiss of formal adoption.

It transpired during the following days that Mr. Farrish had taken more than ordinary interest in the street Arab, now cleansed of alley stains, prettily clothed, and nourished in the bosom of a warm affection, from the fact that he called several times with propitiatory gifts of bon-bons for the child and genial courtesy for nurse Newbury, Echo, on these occasions, not being visible.

One Thursday evening, at prayer-meeting, great was the astonishment of the nurse and Echo, when their pastor, at the conclusion of the services, advanced with this same Mr. Farrish and introduced him to our friends as an old and valued friend! All suspicion of fraud thus set at rest, Mr. Farrish, being an intelligent and attractive man, was thenceforth an acceptable visitor at the residence of Echo and Aunt Newbury, as the latter now came to be called, and the mills of destiny ground slowly on.

CHAPTER XIII.

THE brow of M. Legrand began to wear a sinister gloom. He daily became more and more bitter and morose, and was an enigma to his friends. Chagrin poisoned his meditations, and jealousy was gnawing at his heart. He saw Zarina pursuing a systematic course of flirtation with the debonair count, and he knew she was already false in sentiment, and in a fair way of becoming criminal in deed. Vain, giddy women of Zarina's order, are susceptible of the deepest corruption. The empty pride of fair features and splendid dress, and of the venomous babble of flattering tongues, is an eternal Sphinx that haunts the highways of society with those remorseless riddles of chastity and honor which tinted lips cannot answer. The wrecks of female loveliness and truth are gay with ribbons, diamonds and rouge!

The physicians of M. Legrand advised country air and remission of labor; but the jaundiced plotter sniffed danger in the atmosphere and would not desert the field. He resolved to restrain Zarina with a strong hand, and force her inexorably into the accomplishment of his designs. He had come to admire the woman extremely, as well as fear her, so well had his villainous teaching prospered in the fruitful soil of a vicious nature, and he felt the necessity of bracing himself for the impending

struggle with unusual effort.   He was a good swords-
man and a dead shot with the pistol, not lacking in natural courage, but, an affair with the count, might lead to
disastrous discoveries and ruin all.

On the other hand, Zarina was really infatuated with
La Croix, and her brain was whirling with the intoxica-
tion of pleasure.   She was desperate, demoniac with the
awakened fury of her passions and capable of the wildest excesses.   A man is ordinarily governed by reason,
but a woman is moved by intuitions.   Corrupt the causes
of action, therefore, in women by vitiating the source of
her intuitions, and she will head for the lakes of sulphur
with blinding velocity.

While things were in this condition, Lady Clifford
gave a magnificent dinner party.   The guests were nu-
merous and fashionable, and the enjoyment supreme.
Zarina, whose real name will be used when she is spoken
of, and the assumed when she is addressed, was queenly,
in a delicate, shimmering green silk and over-dress of
costly lace, embellished with grand golden lilies, whose
diamond petals gleamed and glowed with starry splendor as she moved in the dance.   She had advanced rapidly in the graces of high life, and was considered *au
fait* in amorous intrigue by a host of perfumed gallants.

During the evening she managed to have a moment's
tete a tete with La Croix on the balcony.   These two,
being "birds of a feather," inspired each other magneti-
cally, and the brief interview in the odorous moonlight
was rich with sensuous kisses and endearing words.

"Ah, my prince," said Zarina, returning his embraces
with unabashed warmth, "stolen [waters are sweet, but

the moral philosophers have called them deadly. Do you know, my dear, that your passionate glances and amorous behavior have aroused mamma's suspicions this evening, and that M. Legrand devours you with the eyes of a tiger?"

"The full cup foams over, love; but what of that? I swear by the crimson blood of my heart and the nectar of your glowing lips that you shall be my wife. I shall seek an immediate opportunity of proposing the matter to your mother."

"No! no! count, that will never do!" exclaimed Zarina with vehemence. "I implore you to believe that the course you have indicated would snuff out our young and happy love like a wax taper. Be patient yet a little longer, and the time will come, and that ere many months have passed, when the desire of your heart, and mine, shall be fulfilled. It is my opinion that great changes are about to occur, and that M. Legrand, the arch-enemy of our happiness, contemplates a long voyage."

"Your speech is dark with enigmas, sweet-heart, but your lips blossom with a confession dear to my soul, and I shall be content to wait. But, *parbleu!* we must not grow too serious and tragic, or, tamely common-place. It is better to be the butterfly of a brief, bright summer than the toiling, unhappy bee of a dozen seasons."

To which Zarina, shaking her jeweled hand at him warningly, replied: "Butterflies we will be, then, count; anp we must have a care that we do not singe our wings. But we must not tarry here too long. *Au revoir!*"

In retracing her steps to the drawing-room, Zarina

paused a moment by the fountain in the conservatory to arrange her hair. While engaged in this graceful task, M. Legrand stepped out suddenly from the shadow of a mighty cactus in crimson flower, and grasped her arm with cruel force. The man was utterly hideous with jealous rage, and his eyes flashed daggers —

"At it again, hussey! By the grave of my mother! you shall repent this one day! I have raised you to a giddy height, vile *danseuse*, but the descent is greater and the rocks below have fangs like lions! Tell me, viper that I have nursed! do you think to baffle and ruin your benefactor, and yet walk this horrible precipice in safety?"

"Ha! ha!" she laughed, with a scornful curve of her fine lip and a murderous flash of her eye, "you appear to great advantage, to-night, monsieur — never better that I remember, except, may be, the figure you made during the storm at sea. There is a royal magnificence in your carriage that overpowers me. You must be inspired by wine as dry and old as the mummies of Egypt. Come, name the brand of your god-like tipple that I may instantly shout its fame!"

"Hear me, harlot!" he hissed with awful fury, "you have made me desperate and this masquerade shall end. This very night I shall expose you to madame, and then you may pirouette down stairs, the laughing stock of all you have deceived, and exchange these diamonds for the tawdry spangles that better become your flimsy and false character."

She felt that she had gone too far, and hastened to repair her error,

"It is you," she said, "who are threatening us both with destruction. You spring upon me like a wild beast, and shriek curses at me like a madman. I declare that I am true to you, and that you alone hold possession of my heart. Your jealousy would be simply absurd were it not so criminally savage. I walked a moment on the balcony with that monkey of a count, exchanging the airiest nothings of small talk, and, lo! what a scene my lord and master makes of it! Ah, husband dear, let us have faith in each other, and cease these wretched wranglings!"

Her voice was mellow with increasing tenderness, and the title of "husband" she had so softly spoken, crushed the uxorious villain into helpless pulp at once.

"Then, my dear," he said, twining his arm about her waist, "why do you annoy me and hazard our happiness by your idle flirtations? You must know how the world regards the appearance of evil you seem to court, and that it is never too charitable in its constructions. You must not expect me to stand by submissively and see my wife metaphorically, if not physically, in the arms of a libertine. But I shall trust you again, and sincerely hope that you will be more considerate of my feelings than heretofore."

She promised to be his slave in everything, and they were reconciled, as before, with a sickly plentitude of lip-service.

The dancing soon ceased, and the weary guests departed. The Clifford mansion was soon in darkness, with the exception of a single curtained light in an upper window. For a moment an outside observer might have seen a shadow on that curtained window—that of a contemplative female in partial undress, with her arm extended towards the light. Zarina was counting the blood-red drops remaining in the quaint little phial.

"There is enough for two," she said, "and my tigerish monsieur shall be generously served!"

CHAPTER XIV.

WHILE all these things were happening to Echo, Arthur, toiling away assiduously at his profession in the northern city, was wholly in the dark as to the conspiracy by which he had been despoiled of his treasure.

Our griefs and joys, and not our years, mark the flow of life on the sensitive dial of the soul. A great change had come over Arthur Hoberg, but it was more felt and seen by his friends, than understood.

A cankering grief in a man is ordinarily attributed to business cares; the same in a woman, to some physical derangement. A face may, or may not, reflect the disturbance of the heart. Then, we pay so little attention to these things. We never seem to know, or cease to remember, that every life has its own crosses—every soul its special burdens. As we weep by the graves of loved ones, friends group about us and sustain us with their sympathy; but to the secret sepulchres of the heart, we steal in silence and alone. Optimism is an amiable mood of mind when entertained in a hazy, impersonal way, but is nauseous enough, sometimes, when individually applied. The broad humor of Artemas Ward's readiness to sacrifice all his wife's relatives in the war, has the flavor of a pungent truth. That Job's friends bore his eruptive afflictions with neighborly equanimity, there can be no doubt. There is really little vicarious suffering in the world, notwithstanding the divine example. We cannot become thoroughly *en rapport* with the sufferings of others. It is a blessing that it is so, else our hearts would break with one mighty throb of sympathetic pain, and there would be an end.

"What in the world can possess you, Arthur?" impatiently queried Mary Hoberg of her brother, during one of his home visits. "In place of our former cheerful and chatty brother, there appears a grave and dignified stranger, wrapped in the solitude of his own thoughts. Are you passing through the slow and solemn stages of some horrible petrefaction?"

"If the boy of yesterday was more attractive than the man of to-day, sister, I am not to blame. Eternal youth does not tangle itself in our heart-strings or our hair. Then you should know that my mind is engrossed with professional cares," he said, with a grave smile.

"That plea of business absorption hardly deceives me, Arthur; but I think I have the clew to your secret pining." And pursing her lips with ludicrous affectation, she sang:

"It is, oh for the touch of a vanished hand,
And the sound of a voice that's away!"

"Asking Mr. Tennyson's pardon for improving upon his verse, I think that warble includes a complete diagnosis of your case, brother. But come," she continued, more seriously, "look up and be a man, Arthur. You simply made a mistake in supposing that swine had a relish for pearls, and all you have to do is to gather up your gems and find better patrons. Pshaw, man alive, the old adage about the inexhaustible number of fish in the sea, should be a wholesome panacea for the ills your mind is heir to !"

A woman can never understand why a man should break his heart for one of her sex, and Mary, having delivered her opinion, went on dusting the furniture as though she had crushed her brother with mighty bowlders of philosophy.

"For Heaven's sake, Mary," said Arthur, with some indignation, "have a care ! The person to whom you have alluded so slightingly, is the purest and loveliest of her sex. I worship her still, though hopelessly, and cannot bear to hear her traduced with such an idle tongue."

Mary raised her eyebrows with deprecatory surprise at this outburst, but said nothing. After a pause, he resumed, in a cold tone :

"But, please to remember that this subject is very disagreeable to me, and not refer to it again."

Then, noting the pained look in his sister's face, he was recalled to his better self, and took her hand, tenderly, as he said :

"Have not the least anxiety about me, sister, I pray you. Some would require probing, others simply to be let alone."

Placing her disengaged hand upon his shoulder, and looking him kindly in the eyes, she said, placidly :

"Hereafter I shall endeavor to comply with your request."

The family, with the exception of Arthur and Mary, had gone to church. In place of the usual stir and hum

of voices, a solemn stillness reigned in the vacant rooms.
Brother and sister, sitting side by side in the gloom of
the evening, wandered apart in their silent reveries. It
was that witching hour which gilds the royal castles of
the imagination with supernal beauty. The summer
moon, rising in full-orbed radiance, poured its silver
splendor through the room, and the atmosphere was
voluptuous with the scent of roses.

Mary's hands were clasped upon her lap, and she had a
rapt and far-away look, while the expression of her face
and the repose of her rounded figure, invited the thought
that she was spiritually conversing with some invisible
presence from the Fifth Heaven of the Midrash, the
felicitous queendom of " Gan Eden," where the daughter
of Pharaoh wields the scepter over the fairest and purest
of her angelic sex.

Of what was Mary thinking? She was thinking—
whisper it softly, reader, mine !—which one of her several dresses she should wear to the pic-nic that was to
be held in the parsonage grove on the morrow, and the
style of toilet that would best become her on that important occasion.

Arthur, absorbed in his own thoughts, was soon obli-
vious to the presence of another, and murmured his so-
liloquies aloud :

" Ah," he sighed, " what a delicious agony is love ! I
offer homage at another shrine ? Never ! As the orders
of flowers are printed on their leaves, so the glorious
lineaments of her beauty are limned upon the sacred tab-
lets of my heart. O, the violet perfume of her breath !
the heavenly bloom of her cheeks and lips ! her hair sun-

dyed, to ensnare the love of men! and her eyes, luminous as the purple stars of the highest heaven! And
what a dream of bliss was ours! We were alone upon
the broad, blushing sea of illimitable tenderness—the
liquid eternity of souls divinely dissolved and flowing
together. But, and by Heaven, there is madness in the
thought!—she may at this moment be reclining in the
embraces of another!".

"No," he resumed, after a moment of silent torture,
"I shall yet believe her to be true and pure. Why, we
should have been married before this, and had raised such
an altar of blessed domesticity as had propitiated the
favor of Heaven!"

And while Arthur wanders abroad in delightful fancies of the home that might have been, let us stand apart
and consider the tender subject he has suggested.

The tendencies of this age are against the sanctity of
the marriage relation. The theory of the law which
treats the hymeneal bond as a civil contract merely, has
been literally adopted by the masses, with disastrous consequences. It is in reality a spiritual, as well as physical
union, and should be a sacrament of the church, more
than a contract, between tiresome parties of the first and
second part, of which the courts have exclusive cog-
nizance. Marriage is the fulcrum of moral progress, the
fountain of social happiness and domestic joy.

The young man or woman, who, in mentally ro-
mancing along the misted future, sees no domestic shrine
shining its welcome for the aspiring soul, is hopeless of
earth and heaven. Courtship is the golden way that
leads to this shrine, and the delirious rhapsodies of love

the roses that arch over its lustrous portal, so that we must be patient with the ravings of Arthur.

"Good gracious, brother, we must both be moon-struck!" said Mary, starting up suddenly, when Arthur had made a pause in what she mentally termed his delectable rant. "Come to the piano, and lend your assistance as accessory before the fact, while I render the 'Moonlight Sonata.'"

He followed her languidly into the drawing-room, and soon the immortal melody of Beethoven was flowing into the silvery dream of the pale planet like a living soul.

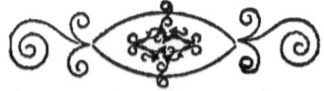

CHAPTER XV.

"ECHO seems to be still infatuated with her strange little protege," remarked Aunt Newbury to Mr. Farrish, one day, "and," she continued with a smile, "I never see her with the child upon her lap that I am not reminded of a little girl with her first rag baby."

"Ah," responded he, "I shall never forget how, once upon a time, while wandering about in a volcanic region, I was greatly refreshed by the beauty of a little flower which grew upon the side of an extinct crater. The simplicity and loveliness of the lone little virgin in the midst of that awful desolation where the giant forces of nature had torn and hurled the earth in a carnival of madness, impressed me delightfully. If a tiny floweret, one touch of grace and tenderness, in that sepulchre of dead horrors, could thus instruct and please a languid traveler, it is not strange that the young lady should find nourishment and pleasure in the contemplation of the human gem she has rescued from the volcanic ruin of a wicked and wasted home."

Somehow, by these remarks, the contrast of human lots was suggested to Aunt Newbury, and she was moved to ask — "Do you really believe, Mr. Farrish, that all men are born free and equal, as the Declaration has it?"

"No, indeed!" was the somewhat emphatic reply. "The idea is absurd in any other than the mere political sense in which Jefferson used it; and, even then, there are limitations and exceptions. Can one, for instance, conceived by ignorant and vicious parents, brought forth in squalor, and misled in shame and crime, have any sort of equality with one whose veins flow with pure blood, over whose cradle arches the rainbow of love, whose youth blossoms in the sunshine of plenty, and is strengthened and adorned by lavish culture — one, in fact, who enters life through golden gates and is forever girdled by the saving memories and influences of a fortunate Christian home? The parable of the sower is timely in this connection. There is, in human growth, stony and blighted soil which can produce nothing good. Blood that is clotted with hereditary impurities bears in it the seeds of death. It is the natural result of original sin; the angry ripples of Adam's fall widen and widen across the restless sea of human life."

"Yes, but I cannot agree with you unreservedly. Circumstances are powerful, but not despotic, in moulding our destinies. Many of the kings of intellectual achievement sprang from the low and sunless vales of life. The roll of the world's great men glitters with such instances. It was to all men, and no special caste, that Longfellow sang —

> 'Lives of great men all remind us
> We can make our lives sublime.'

I am afraid that your doctrine, fully accepted, is edged with a cruel fatalism."

"You seem to forget, madam," he rejoined in a bantering tone, "that the biographers of men who have risen from poverty and obscurity invariably remark that 'he was born of poor but respectable parents.' There's the rub. Honest poverty impedes, and vicious poverty destroys. Plant a germ and cover it with a paving stone, and you will find its growth distorted or destroyed. The street *gamin* ripens, but it is oftener for the gallows than the senate."

"It is a deep question, and difficulties involve it on all sides, I grant," said Aunt Newbury; "but the school of experience has taught me to believe in the equality of childhood. The character of a child is clay in the potter's hand and takes shape according to the will and skill of the moulder."

"But there is a difference of material, madam. You cannot make a porcelain vase from a lump of ordinary mud. I would not go to a tailor with a number of yards of shoddy cassimere and expect therefrom a broadcloth suit. Like produces like everywhere and always."

"Do you sink back then, my dear sir, on the velvet cushion of your natural caste theory and have no word of sympathy and encouragement for those struggling in darkness under the pressure of evil fates?"

"I simply recognize facts as they exist. Encouragement and sympathy to those born with a blight I would give freely; but I should expect my sympathy, in most cases, to be despised and my encouragement thrown away. You can build a pretty good ship with faulty timber, but it were infinitely preferable for the material to be without a flaw."

Aunt Newbury did not respond immediately, and he resumed —

" I acknowledge, too, that there are men who conquer circumstances. There are two great classes of men — the positive and negative — force and inertia. Positive men achieve the world's great victories and commit its wildest crimes. Negative men simply stagnate and breed malaria. The former may conquer circumstances, the latter are enslaved and destroyed."

At this juncture, little Wistit, who had been sitting quietly in a chair by the window, sprang to her feet with a scream and ran into the hall-way.

" What has excited the child?" asked Mr. Farrish, as he turned a surprised look towards Aunt Newbury.

" She has probably caught a glimpe of Echo. The little thing is extravagantly fond of her protector, and it does her credit."

Holding Echo's hand, and frisking at her side with extravagant delight, Wistit exclaimed, pointing towards the house — " You doesn't know who's in there?"

" No, darling; but you must tell me — " Who is it?"
" Guess!"

Echo named over several of the neighbors, but Wistit shook her head negatively.

" Guess more."

" Who can it be?" said Echo, musing, with mock gravity. " Come, Wistit, you must tell me."

" It is Mr. Bon-bons," exclaimed Wistit in triumph.

" Hush, dear," interposed Echo, unable to restrain her mirth at the suggestive appellation; " Mr. Farrish might object to that name, sweet as it is."

Flushed with her walk, her eyes luminous with a deep splendor, Echo was dangerously beautiful as she entered the room and greeted the visitor pleasantly.

The gentleman felt his heart dilate painfully in the glow of her surpassing loveliness, and returned her easy salutation with a perceptible trace of confusion.

" Your sister," he remarked to Aunt Newbury, when the other had passed from the room, seems to have rapidly recovered her health."

The sisterly relation, be it understood, was a mild fraud in which Mr. Farrish had been allowed to entangle himself.

"Yes," replied Aunt Newbury, "I do not remember to have seen her looking better. Tedious work seems to have done her good instead of harm. In fact, few of us realize the benefit we derive from the steady, but not strained use of brain and muscle. Echo, however, I fear is too ardent a devotee at the shrine of duty."

"I obtained two more pupils to-day, sister," said the young lady in question, returning from the removal of her outer wraps. "These make ten additions since Wistit came to us — thirty-five in all. If business keeps increasing at this rate we shall be able to support our third estate handsomely" — and she smiled indulgently upon Wistit.

"Ah, hopefulness is a glorious attribute of youth!" exclaimed Aunt Newbury.

"And most glorious when altogether unselfish," interposed the gentleman, with an admiring look at a portrait of President Lincoln which was suspended from the wall above the mantel.

"Life is too short and our capacities too limited for the accomplishment of much good," said Echo with a sigh. "I wish that I were able to found and endow a school where children of both sexes, *gamins* in the social scale, could be cleaned, clothed, fed and educated practically for future usefulness."

"The splendid philanthropy of such a scheme would be its only reward, I think," said Mr. Farrish. "The traditional needle that was lost in a haystack may have been, or will yet be, recovered, but in the soiled chaff of the streets you will not find many grains of valuable humanity for all your winnowing. If I desired to leave the imprint of my benevolence on human coin, I should not select the baser metals for an experiment."

"I differ with you entirely," said Echo. "Humanity is *sui generis*, and not to be compared with material things. Following the divine example we should all, each in his degree, strive to elevate and redeem the race. That we occupy higher ground and have a stronger foothold constitutes a sufficient reason for our extending all the assistance in our power to those who struggle in the darkness and *debris* of the ascent of life. The advent of Christ not only proved the necessity of redemption — it was the golden text of brotherly love, mutual aid, and eternal charity. The Christian who, intent upon his individual salvation, appears with confidence at the throne of judgment, will, like Cain, of old, be met with the startling interrogatory — 'Where is thy brother?'"

"Grandly true, and as eloquent as true," replied he; "and yet the human heart longs for human appreciation. If the government were, however, to found, liberally

endow, and sustain such a school, compelling the attendance of uncared-for children, the lower classes would
regard it as an odious tyranny."

"May be; but it would seem that a government which
is founded on the theory that all men are created free
and equal, might esteem it a duty to keep them so. It
will have to do so, finally, for self-protection."

"Well, Miss Newbury, I confess that you have taken
the very Redan of my position, and, if you will allow
me, will retreat with the honors of war."

Echo laughingly bade him retain his reversed sword;
and the overthrown Russ sauntered away towards North
Beach, ostensibly to look at the parrots and monkeys,
but really to dream dreams.

Echo taught Wistit to make original prayers, instead
of repeating a stereotyped formula, and, as they kneeled
together by the bedside that night, said — "Now, Wistit,
ask the good Lord for what you want."

The little hands were clasped, and this unique petition
ascended to the Throne:

"I pray the Lord my soul to take — and bring Mr.
Bon-bons, too — and I pray the Lord to make mamma
Newbury a new back, and good, pretty Echo, every-
thing she wants. Amen!"

For the information of the reader it may be remarked
that Aunt Newbury, poor woman! often complained of
a demoralized and painful spine.

CHAPTER XVI.

N O sooner do the skies which stoop over our individual worlds begin to frown, than time lags heavily and the spirit droops. With hues borrowed from the gloom of the present, our thoughts duskily tincture the future, and all things, material and mental, loom in sombre perspective. All the world outside may be bright, but if a shadow rest on the horizon of our own little cosmos, the sun no where shines, and darkness covers all. Human atoms cannot recognize the true insignificance of their microscopic areas in the immensity of creation, else a sublime stoicism would reign in the hearts of men, and the pigmy millions of earth would move placidly in the mighty progress of destiny. There must be lights and shadows in the eternal panorama of life, and the soul should not repine because its horoscope is gloomed by the *umbrae* of the planets that wait upon its terrestrial advent.

To Pierre Legrand, who sat watching the mournful drip and drizzle of the rain, the present and the future were obscured in funeral clouds. "How greedily does the insatiate earth drink the rain!" he murmured, as he tossed his half-consumed cigar through the window. "*Parbleu!* it might be satisfied with its pluvial Heidsick, and not be forever extending its mouldy arms to embrace its prodigal sons!"

When death, however lightly, touches the chords of
life, the sorrowful minor tone is at once recognizable,
with a thrill of secret dread, and the pallid hues of the
pale horseman are imparted to all our thoughts. These
are the times when, like the ever tender and musical Hood,
we smell the mould above the rose.

Lady Clifford having gone out upon an errand of
mercy to a poor pensioner, Legrand was temporarily the
autocrat of the family mansion. Wandering discon-
solately into the drawing-room, he sat down by the piano
and began listlessly turning over some pieces of new
music. There was a strange shadow of fear, suspicion
and anxiety in his sunken eyes, and a ghastly pallor overspread his face. "*Mon dieu!*" he murmured, "how
gay these authors of music are! *Peste!* laughter and
music seem to have died out of this life of mine!"

While these unhappy meditations were occupying the
mind of the schemer, Zarina, bright with the glow of
her animal beauty and the adventitious aid of fine attire,
came rustling into the room, and, folding her arms softly
about his neck, gave him a gracious salute.

A faint tingle of pleasure was communicated to his
veins by this airy trifle, but his solemnity was not dis-
pelled, and he said, reproachfully:

"We cannot live on kisses, Zarina; the little phial
lasts too long, and madame seems actually to be improving in health!"

"I am not in fault, monsieur," replied Zarina, in a low
tone; "Nineé haunts me like a spectre, and I find little
opportunity to administer the drops as you directed without the peril of discovery. The old woman is Argus-

eyed, and never seems to relax her watchfulness. Sometimes I fear that she suspects me, but surely that cannot
be after all the precautions I have taken. Then
madame, as you know, is under the care of a physician,
and it is just possible that she may have blundered upon
a panacea for the ill that threatens her."

"Time drags horribly," replied he, in a complaining
tone, "and I am wearing out in the struggle. *Peste!*
the poison seems to be settling in my heart, instead
of hers!"

"Believe me, monsieur, we cannot be baffled long.
Like desperate commanders, we have destroyed the
bridges behind us, and must win or die. I pledge you
that the apparent health which seems just now to mantle
in the cheeks of madame, shall prove to be the hectic
flush of approaching death!"

"And yet, my dear Zarina, the slow and heavy wheels
of time are grinding me to death upon the rocks of this
torturing suspense. The quick stroke of a Corsican
stiletto is the way to remove obstacles, after all. I am
courageous enough for sudden deeds, but this slow,
snake-like coiling about one's victim is maddening. The
deadly aroma of crape is continually in my nostrils, and
my very soul is shaken with strange alarms." Legrand
passed his hand across his clammy brow, and was awfully
in earnest.

"Fie, fie, monsieur, your digestion is out of order!
You remind me of a spider, which gathers poison from
the same flowers which have loaded the bee with honey.
Where is the Latin maxim you used to quote to me?—

Dum vivimus, vivamus! Have you lost the inspiration of that joyful motto ?"

"The only thing Roman that can do me any good now, is a priest. Sometimes I have been almost driven to try the exorcism of a confession."

"Heavens, monsieur!" exclaimed Zarina, really frightened at the dire possibility of such madness. "Your womanish hypochondria may ruin us yet! Come, there is another life than ours at stake now. Shall I tell you a secret ?"

He looked at her passively, and she stooped and whispered something in his ear.

"In the name of the holy saints!" he cried, starting up in agitated surprise. "I had not thought of that, Zarina," he continued, in a lower tone, while a strange, softening light broke over his sinister face; "we must be true to each other now. By heaven! it is something to live for and to suffer for, and it will propitiate the terrible fates!"

It is thus that the instinct of paternity ennobles the wickedest of men.

"Then let us swear," she said, impressively, lifting a small gold crucifix which was suspended upon a beautiful chain that encircled her neck; "let us swear by the sacred cross of Christ and the living pledge of our union, that we will have no confessions, no relentings, no cowardly shambling and shuffling in the path that leads us inevitably to prosperity, and that we will steadfastly abide by the decision we have made, come what may!"

"I swear," he said, solemnly, and kissed the potent emblem,

"And I swear," she said, kissing the cross in her turn.

Then disengaging the chain from her own neck, she clasped it around his, saying :

"Wear it as a memento—a talisman powerful against all devils, blue or black !"

"And you will discard the Count ?" he said, with a slight lowering of the brow.

"He is not mine, in any sense, to discard," she answered, simply; "but I promise that even his silly attentions, since they give you pain, shall be put to flight."

"Now swear again, Zarina," he said, playfully, extending his arms; "swear that you love me."

"Joyfully, pierre," she answered, meeting his embrace; "and seal my oath with kisses."

To have maintained the unities of truth and dramatic propriety, Judas should have been a woman. The cold, calm, lustrous, serpentine coils of female treachery, pale the puny efforts of man, in that direction, to immeasurable insignificance.

While patiently submitting to the prolonged manipulations of the maid, who was dressing her hair, Zarina revolved the incidents of the recent interview in her mind, smiling placidly at the recollection of her absolute victory in a crisis of great danger.

There was Pierre, a strong man—a wicked, scheming man—and an acute lawyer, besides, completely prostrated and pressed to earth, figuratively, by a single flourish of her rosy little thumb ! She was completely fascinated with the thought of her power over him, and resolved to play with the poor man's life mockingly, as a cat plays with the mouse she will presently consume. Nature and education had combined to make the ex-*danseuse* a fascinating fiend. Vain, selfish, completely imbued with the ideas of a coarse materialism, and inflamed with lawless passions, she was as cunning and false as hell itself.

As for Legrand, he soon sought the privacy of his own apartment, and, leaning abstractedly against the antique mantel, gazed down at the glowing grate. He was not in good spirits, even yet. Perhaps the red coals reminded him of the lurid Gehenna which must sometimes vex the reveries of wicked men. Perhaps the dissolving embers suggested a solemn phrase : " Dust to dust, and ashes to ashes !"

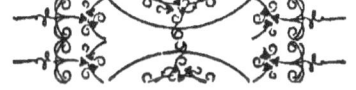

CHAPTER XVII

ONSIEUR Legrand could scarcely conceal his satisfaction, the following morning, on entering the breakfast room, when he observed upon the face of Lady Clifford the unmistakable signs of some serious bodily ailment; but he, nevertheless, in a voice of silken placidity, inquired after her health.

"With many thanks for your solicitude, monsieur," the lady answered, "I am sorry to say that my exertions of yesterday are followed by considerable indisposition. The most relishable viands will hardly tempt me this morning, but it is only a temporary lassitude, I trust, and will doubtless disappear in the course of the day. I am glad to see that you are looking brighter than usual of late."

"My mercurial temperment, madame, borrows its tone from the loveliness of the morning, but will now be overclouded again from sympathy with your unhappy depression."

"Dear me, mamma," said Zarina, seating herself at the table with an indolent yawn; "What can be the matter with the noble house of Clifford this morning? Here am I regretting that I deserted my pillow, and, a more serious affair, I notice that you are very pale and apparently out of spirits. As for monsieur here — good

morning, M. Legrand! he is never out of spirits, until
the bottle is empty. And then you have the advantage
of most men, and nearly all women, monsieur," regarding that individual peculiarly, "in possessing that quiet
. conscience which is said to be friendly to refreshing
slumber and the artless *rouge* of eternal youth."

"You are delightfully facetious, mademoiselle," he
answered. "Such excellent humor, however forced,
must inevitably restore the gay elasticity of your spirits
and sympathetically animate the entire household with
its more than Cliquot sparkle."

"And yet you would doubtless prefer the 'widow'
herself, eh, monsieur?" said the young lady, carving a
broiled breast of pheasant with surgical skill.

"Not at all, mademoiselle Echo; this is one of those
unusual cases in which the shadow is sweeter than the
substance."

"Spoken like a courtier, monsieur, who is always
ready to do homage to the reigning sovereign. Were I
absent, and the veritable Cliquot before you—ah, well,
it may be true that familiarity breeds contempt, but it
must still be said that absence is the mother of treason
and forgetfulness."

"It is the beginning of a superior day," said Lady
Clifford, who had taken no interest in this crisp dialogue,
"and I must invite you to accompany me upon a matter
of business, to-day, Echo. My attention was yesterday
called to a destitute family, consisting of a mother and
three small children, all sick, which must have immediate assistance. You will take my place in these matters
after a while, dear, and it is well for you to begin to un-

derstand them. Personal contact is an admirable stimulant to charitable feelings."

"I am ready to be sacrificed, mamma, on the grimy altar of poor people's miseries," said Zarina, with a shrug of her exquisite shoulders. "Call the garbage cart and let us hasten to the scene of slaughter."

"Echo! daughter!" exclaimed the mother, reproachfully. "Your light way of treating such subjects may be attributed to absolute cruelty of disposition. You cannot feel so, I'm sure."

"Your pardon, mamma. I hardly knew what I was saying. The fact is, I was engrossed with the peculiarity of M. Legrand's cravat, which has slipped around under his left ear, like an English hanging noose."

Legrand turned pale and cast at her a dangerous look as he rejoined — "It is really suggestive, mademoiselle. Perhaps I had better anticipate the dire event by attending the confessional."

This shot went home. A strange quiver passed over Zarina's face and she confessed his victory by dropping the subject. "Shall we walk or ride?" she queried, turning to her mother. "I should prefer the former, for the reason that it is a fine morning in which to air my new walking suit. I got it home only yesterday, and it is a marvel of millinery."

"We will walk, then," said the mother; "but I should advise you to dress more in accordance with your mission, my daughter. The contrast between our mission and your attire might suggest odious comparisons."

"If agreeable, I will do myself the honor to accompany you for a few blocks," said M. Legrand when their proposed route had been suggested, "as I have a little business with Cruzan, the jeweler."

"We shall be pleased with your company," said the elder lady.

In passing down the stairs there was an opportunity for a little by-play on the part of M. Legrand and his clandestine spouse. "I hope that you rested well last night?" he said, in a soft whisper, as he looked down admiringly into the fair face—fairer still for the slight paleness that overspread it.

"Well enough, my dear," she answered—adding significantly—"Remember me to the jeweler, Cruzan."

"Royally, my queen."

"Have I kept you waiting, mamma mine," said Zarina, as they assembled in the hall.

"Not long," was Lady Clifford's reply as she observed, without comment, the deprecated walking suit flaunting to the public gaze.

At a corner of the street, not far from home, the ladies and their escort met La Croix face to face. Legrand scowlingly acknowledged the nobleman's elaborate bow and pleasant "good morning." Lady Clifford returned his salute with easy courtesy, but mademoiselle was apparently studying the pearl handle of her parasol, as she gave the graceful knight no notice—a circumstance which that gentleman recognized with an angry flush.

"Why, Echo, is it possible that you did not see the count?" inquired Lady Clifford, surprised at her daughter's rudeness.

"The count! where? Upon my soul!" with a glance backward at the count's retreating form. "The magnifi-

cent La Croix must be practicing as a stage-ghost or as
sassin that he is able to glide by so stealthily."

Lady Clifford regarded her with a look of mingled
surprise and reproach, but said nothing. As for Legrand,
he could have knelt and kissed the dainty kids that enveloped her feet. Mademoiselle had achieved, inten-
tionally, an adroit *coup*.

Proceeding two or three blocks further, after M. Le
grand had gone his separate way, the ladies mounted a
flight of stairs leading to the upper stories of a mournful tenement-house. At the second landing, they turned
aside into a narrow hall, along which they proceeded towards the back portion of the building until they reached
the threshold of a dark room, where Lady Clifford hesitated a moment as if uncertain of its identity with the
one she sought. Entering, however, and gradually becoming accustomed to the dim light, they discovered in
one corner a pallet on which lay a woman, gray, dirty,
disheveled — a ghastly hag, whose form was shaken at
brief intervals with a sepulchral cough. A flannel che-
mise, and a tattered and grimy coverlet, were all that obscured her bony wretchedness. Her skin was sallow,
wrinkled, and as dry as parchment. Her sunken eyes,
overhung by shaggy brows, shot savage gleams in the
lair-like obscurity of the apartment. Her teeth, the
few that were left, were yellow and carnivorously
pointed. Upon her distorted lips sat a horrible snarl.
It was sin grown old, miserable and forsaken — that
hideous mistress whom, it is said, we at first dread,

> " But, seen too oft, familiar with her face,
> We first endure, then pity, then embrace !"

Yet, this can only be averred of vice in youth; vice grown old is monstrous with antidotal ugliness.

Lady Clifford could not repress a shudder at this leprous spectacle, and was about to turn away with silent disgust, but hesitated an instant, then turned and addressed the woman on the pallet thus: "Pardon me, we were looking for the apartment of a destitute woman who bears the name of Laselle; but," as a new idea suggested itself, "we are simply striving to assist our suffering fellow-creatures. Can we be of any service to you?"

"Hah," exclaimed the old woman in a hoarse, rattling voice, "it is the voice of an angel! Look at me, madame, look! a thousand curses upon the fiends of age, and want, and disease! Do I seem like one that has need of help? But perhaps you are only come with your soft voice and fine attire to show me how wretchedly unjust is the God to whom the lying spires of *La belle Paris* are pointing us the way! No matter. Do you not see that I am dying here like a whimpering old rat in the stinking vaults of a sewer? See! I have no dress. It has gone for food. There is not in this noisome dungeon of a room the sustenance that the vilest fly could live upon for a day. Come, I am old, neglected, dying — but I can curse like a Christian. Will you have pity and give me fire, and food, and drink?"

"Yes," said Lady Clifford, endeavoring by a strong effort to conceal her unutterable loathing of this human hyena; "I shall send you all these, and, in the meanwhile, shall leave you money for immediate wants. Echo, you are treasurer to-day," added she, turning to

the latter, who stood in the doorway with a look of scorn
and repulsion on her fair face.

As the young lady advanced, disengaging the clasp of
her *porte-monnaie*, the woman rose to a half-sitting posture, and, brushing back her bristling, gray hair with
skinny hand, regarded her with a glance of keen, horrible scrutiny.   There are those, particularly among the
lower orders, to whom the power of vision remains unimpaired to the extremest old age.   One of these was
the crouching horror of the pallet.   Suddenly, as if some
strange interest had arisen in her thoughts, she crooked
her neck forward and, shading her eyes with her corpse-
like hand, pored upon the features of Zarina with baleful
earnestness.

" Ha! ha! ough! ough! ough!" laughed and coughed
the nauseous wretch, sinking back upon her pallet.   "A
thousand curses upon that funeral cough! and a million
curses upon age, and want, and disease! but this is a
masquerade that it is worth living to see!   I am not to
be deceived, though I am dying in a dungeon like a rat.
It is Zarina, the *danseuse*, dispensing charity in the guise
of a lady!   Ough! ough! ough!   What? do you not
recognize me, Mother Mommet?" she howled, striking
her forehead savagely with her hand.

Zarina almost sank to the floor at this alarming outburst; but the instinct of self-preservation bore her up,
and, though pale and trembling, she turned to Lady
Clifford: " What, in the name of Heaven! does the old
woman mean?   Have we invaded the lair of a wild
beast? or a lunatic?   Come, mamma, we must hasten
from here, or I shall faint with horror!   Come!"—and

flinging several pieces of silver towards the pallet, she hurried through the door with a white, scared face.

"Do not be so frightened, my child. I do not think the good woman is dangerous. Weakened by suffering and in the semi-darkness of the garret, she has, no doubt, mistaken you for some one else," replied her ladyship soothingly, as Zarina tremblingly drew her along the hall. As she seemed so much alarmed, however, Lady Clifford thought it best to comply with her request to return home.

In the street, near their residence, they were intercepted by La Croix, who seemed to be desirous of consulting her ladyship about the best disposition of some surplus funds which he wished to appropriate to the cause of suffering humanity.

Of course, innocent Lady Clifford saw no impropriety in the polite count picking up, between thumb and forefinger, the dainty bit of costly lace, designated as a handkerchief, which careless Zarina, after winding nine times around her little finger, let fall.

The artful count, *au fait* in all the languages of love and intrigue, interpreted the handkerchief performance to mean —"Meet me at nine o'clock this evening in the arbor." The count, with a profound bow, left them at the door.

Lady Clifford went immediately to her own private room.

Zarina, without removing her wraps, entered the drawing-room, whither she had been preceded by Legrand. Upon her entrance he arose and met her. Noticing the coldness of her hand, he keenly scanned her face, at the same time asking eagerly: "What is it? you seem to be excited?"

"O, monsieur!" was the startling reply, "we are ruined. I was met and recognized by the only one whom I ever feared."

Leading her to a chair, and seating her, Monsieur Legrand said, reassuringly: "It may not be as bad as you think. Compose yourself, love, and tell me all of the particulars."

"After leaving you at Cruzan's, we proceeded quite a distance beyond the *Boulevard des Italiens* to a part of the city I have never before visited. Lady Clifford has the street and number, however, in her memorandum. Arriving at an old tenement house, we ascended a rickety flight of stairs to the second landing, where we turned into a hall-way as dark and damp as a cellar. From the hall, we entered a gloomy and desolate room, reeking with filth and disease, where, in a corner, upon a loathsome pallet, was a frightful old woman. As this creature received us somewhat after the fashion of a hungry wild beast, Lady Clifford was, for a moment, horrified and speechless. Recovering herself, however, she explained our mistake, and ended by offering to send her all the usual necessaries. As I stepped forward to hand the woman some money, at the request of her ladyship, I was terrified to meet the mother of one who was supposed to have committed suicide on my account. Her son, an only child, on whom she doted, formerly belonged to the same company as myself; in truth I flirted with him. He, foolish boy, took everything in earnest and became so jealous that I had to cast him adrift, and he, as I said before, destroyed himself. Would that his mother could do as well — it would certainly be a blessed deliverance for me."

For full five minutes Legrand waited, and then, rather impatiently, with a decided frown of displeasure on his pale face, and a keen glance of the deep-set eyes, said:

" Proceed."

The thought of a former lover was excessively annoying to him.

" Well," resumed Zarina, shivering, " as I handed her the money, she cried out in a voice so bitter that if all the bitter inflections which I have ever heard in my life were concentrated in one word it would have been sweet in comparison. Ah! I have it — 'It is she! Zarina, the ballet dancer, dispensing charity in the guise of a lady. What, you don't recognize me?' calling herself by name. 'Shall I refresh your memory? Mademoiselle, the ballet girl, has become a clever actress.' After saying which she fell backward with a horrid contraction of the face, and a sinking of the long, flat finger nails into the bloodless flesh, accompanied with a frigthful laugh which all the dark corners of the room seemed to re-echo. Of course Lady Clifford thinks her to be insane from suffering, at present; yet, she is almost sure to return, thereby giving the woman an opportunity which she will be *sure* to improve. My only hope is based on her propensity to acquire a 'bit of land' as she formerly called it. Should her greed prove stronger than her desire of revenge, she can be bought off."

Monsieur Legrand, thoughtfully stroking his beard, observed: " Nothing was said to give the woman a cue

as to your present name or place of residence, as you remember?"

Zarina, after a pause, replied, "No, I think not; I
am quite sure, in fact, that Lady Clifford addressed me
as 'my child' only."

Legrand, who had been slowly pacing backward and
forward before her chair, stopped short, and said rather
quietly, as one engaged in serious reflection, "That was
all the better for you. Though the woman might receive hush money, yet you would never feel safe, and
her present conviction would be verified by the offer;
while, on the contrary, if something startling should occur to the woman herself, that would drive her thoughts
in another direction, no doubt but that she would, in the
course of time, regard the whole affair as a sick fancy.
I hope, however, that this will teach you the folly of co-
quetting," added Legrand rather irrelevantly.

Zarina, who had been steadily gazing out of the window with troubled eyes and rigid face, flushed, but
said nothing. Presently she arose and turned to Legrand with an imploring look and out-stretched hands,
like a naughty child seeking sympathy from an offended
mother.

Monsieur Legrand responded by taking her little cold
hands between his large feverish ones and rubbing them
briskly for a moment, then, folding them caressingly
across her breast, while, looking fondly upon her, he said
in a softer tone: "My love, you will obtain possession
of her ladyship's diary containing the street and number
of the house which you visited this morning, placing the
same in the pocket of my light overcoat hanging in the

hall; after which you will drink a cup of strong tea to compose your nerves and retire to rest. You did well in coming to me immediately, as I shall not allow Mother-what's-her-name to give you further annoyance."

Echo's eyes lighted — "You have a plan, then, monsieur," she asked, eagerly.

"Most assuredly," he made answer, smilingly, patting her soft cheek. "It is only another obstacle to be removed."

Twining her arms about his neck, she bent his head, and while leaning her cheek against his, whispered in her soft, cooing voice — "You will succeed, then, you are so subtile. Do you know that I am loving you a little more every day, you rogue?"

Then, with a sudden start, and mock earnestness, "But, I had almost forgotten. Where is the testimonial from M. Cruzan?"

"You will find it in your dressing-case; but, remember that it is *sub rosa*, and not to be worn until a public marriage crowns our victory."

CHAPTER XVIII

ZARINA paused at the door of Lady Clifford's dressing-room, and, with lifted finger and bent head, appeared to listen. Hearing no sound from the interior, she gathered her skirts in one hand, so as to keep them from rustling, turned the knob, and noiselessly entered. The apartment was empty. Swiftly crossing the floor, she found what she sought on the top of the bureau, and stealthily retired.

Proceeding to her own apartment, she flew to the toilet, where lay the gift of M. Legrand. Upon opening the case, the effulgence of a full set of diamonds flashed upon her, and she could hardly repress a scream of delight.

"O, glittering beauties !" she cried, triumphantly, holding the diamonds towards the light, to note their streaming splendor. "It is, indeed, a royal gift."

Then, arraying herself in the jewels, she stood before the glass with half-closed, admiring eyes, and soliloquized, after the manner of women :

"If the giver were not so plebian and jealous, he would make a goodish husband, after all. With a little pampering, he would become one of the most uxorious of mankind—a condition, however, which would become a formidable bore to a wife not *en rapport* with his

weakness. These diamonds must have cost a small
fortune. A few such gifts would utterly wreck Legrand's exchequer, since he is living now mainly on
great expectations. Heigh ho ! if he were only younger,
handsomer, and had a title, a woman might go farther
and fare worse, as they say, in search of a husband; but
he is plain Monsieur Legrand, and can never be younger
or handsomer than he is. What do you say, queen of
the ballet and marvel of intrigue ?" simpering at her reflection in the glass; "shall it be ' countess' or ' madame ?'
The title, of course—I read it in every feature of your
piquant and lovely face ! The fates have decreed ! La
Croix will win, but not so much as he thinks; yet he
cannot complain. This is a world of second-hand goods;
every man's wife has been some other man's sweet-
heart !"

Having aired these chaste sentiments in the solitude of
her chamber, Zarina unclasped the jewels, put them
away under lock, and hastened down stairs with the
purloined diary, which was placed in the pocket of the
drab overcoat, according to directions.

In the course of half an hour, M. Legrand emerged
from the gilded gates of the mansion, and walked
leisurely down the street. Penetrating the business quarter of the city, he came to No. 42 *Rue de* ———, which
was a bazaar for the sale of ladies' furnishing goods, and
sported, in gilt letters, over its arched entrance, the name
of Madame Fleurot, that lady being herself in attendance upon some fashionable customers when M. Legrand entered.

Mme. Fleurot was a bright, active woman, of middle

age, proficient and popular in her calling. She greeted
Legrand in a manner which betokened mutual acquaintance, and, when her customers had gone, showed
him into a cosy little side room.

"Be seated, monsieur," she said, cheerfully, motioning
the lawyer to an easy chair. "I declare, it is an age
since you honored me with a visit!"

"Not so very long, madame. Your health and business are both good, I presume?"

"About as usual," answered the lady, with grave
courtesy. "Do you know, monsieur," she immediately
added, "that I despair of ever being able to pay that
mortgage?"

"Indeed!" said Legrand, with polite surprise. "Then
I am here opportunely, since my present business with
madame is for the purpose of making her a proposition
which will enable her to accomplish that very thing.
Madame surely remembers how her own son, innocent
though he was, came so nearly being convicted through
circumstantial evidence? Well, to be explicit, I have a
somewhat similar case on hand, though in this instance I
should be blind, as well as dull, were I not convinced
that false evidence will be given through pure malig-
nity. This, you, madame, have it in your power to prevent, while benefiting yourself," he craftily pursued,
impressively pausing to note the effect of this somewhat
dubious communication on Madame Fleurot.

Madame, all attention, answered, with a demure dropping of her eyelids:

"Had I no other motive, the debt of gratitude which

I owe to you would be amply sufficient to interest me in this affair."

"Thanks," said Legrand, gratified at the favorable opening of his subject; "not only for myself, but also for the poor sick mother whose only child is in danger."

"The part which I wish you to act in the affair is this," resumed he, after a pause, assuming an air of special confidence : "Take this money. After filling a basket with provisions, you will place the remainder in your purse. Taking some one along to carry your basket, you are to proceed immediately to the place whose direction I shall give you. It would be better, perhaps, for you to enter several rooms, leaving something in each, before entering the fifth room to the right of the second landing. Within this room you will find an old woman, in a complete state of destitution. There you are to leave the entire contents of the basket, and also contrive to drop your purse, unseen by the one by whom you are accompanied, though plainly perceptible to the woman herself. At the foot of the stairs you must first become aware of your loss. Upon your inquiring, she will be apt to deny all knowledge of it. Then you must have her arrested. The purse will be found in her possession, which will be proof positive, and she will be sent to prison for a short time, and thereby prevented, through your instrumentality, from grievously wronging an innocent person, while at the same time you will cancel a mortgage which would otherwise deprive you of a home."

"In case the woman should deliver up the purse," hazarded Madame Fleurot; "what then, monsieur?"

"Why, an altered case would most assuredly require a change of tactics. I do not anticipate such an event, however—that is, if you are not very fierce in your demand for its restoration. Of course, it would not be the best policy to speak of sending for an officer in the presence of the accused," he added, leaning his head on his hand, and slowly dropping his heavy eyelids over his keen, searching eyes. "Please remember that what is done must be done quickly," continued he, arising from his seat, hat in hand. "I shall expect to hear of the success of our plan by three o'clock this afternoon."

"Of our success, or failure, monsieur, whichever it chance to be."

"You will not fail if you bear in mind that to succeed is to cancel the mortgage," said Legrand, bowing.

"I will try to fulfill your wishes in a creditable manner, monsieur," promised the woman, with a blush of shame, though with a tone of resolution.

With this assurance the man and the woman separated, Madame Fleurot hastening to entangle one of her own sex in the meshes of the law, while Legrand lighted a fresh cigar, and sauntered up the street, with a satisfied air.

*   *   *   *   *   *   *

Punctually to agreement, Lady Clifford sent the promised help to the sick woman. The room was vacant— the woman gone!

Upon relating the incident to Legrand, her ladyship
asked :

"Do you not think the whole occurrence rather unusual, monsieur ?"

"Not at all," was the ready reply. "The woman was,
no doubt, delirious from fever, and has, in all probability,
been taken to some hospital. I am sure that such occurrences are happening every day."

"Yes, I presume so," answered Lady Clifford, with a
gentle sigh. "Do you know, monsieur, that the only
bearable thought which I could ever derive from this
great abysm of suffering, is, that were there no misery,
there would also be no happiness ? Strange," added
she, after a slight pause, "that life should be so constituted that pleasure and pain are made to travel on the
same roadways, and that the same poor heart should own
the dominion of each !"

"Exactly, madame. I myself have long been fully
persuaded that pain and joy are not only useful, but also
absolutely necessary to sympathy and knowledge, else
actions proceeding from the true conditions of life could
not be understood. Surely one state of sensation implies, augments, and necessitates the other. Who, for
instance, would commit the absurdity of expatiating upon
the tenderness of affection or the agony of a separation
to one whom they knew to be totally devoid of feeling;
for though the words to convey the ideas would not be
wanting, the experimental knowledge, which always,
with reference to these things, implies feeling, would be
wholly wanting. Plato was a fool to philosophize about
abstract good; it is an idea which can exist only in the

mind of the Creator. And," continued Legrand, complacently surveying himself in a mirror opposite, "it is this relative practical nature of good and evil that makes it impossible for persons who have health, youth, affluence, etc., to be humane and sympathetic. Their good fortune gives them supreme independence."

"Supreme independence is an attribute of God alone," answered Lady Clifford, with grave sweetness, as she stood at the window securely fastening a small cluster of purple pansies beneath the pin on her bosom, while her tender eyes wandered meditatively around the smooth, green lawn without, where a dream of sunlight lingered lovingly. "Perfect happiness! supreme independence!" she softly repeated. "Why, monsieur, there are blighted grains in every field, however fair the seeming. Even the calm, bright beauty of yon sky is borrowed from the atmosphere, while the awful sublimity of the lofty mountains is heightened by the accretion of the tiny snow-flakes. The mighty rivers owe their majesty to the little streamlets. The forests, celebrated in song and story; the luxuriant vegetation, both useful and ornamental; the flowers, bright souvenirs of Eden—all these are indebted to the richness of the soil, the warmth of the climate, and the proper condensation of vapor. Thus we find that nothing stands alone. Nothing is wholly independent, for everything is useful, everything is necessary. Those who despise first causes are like a giant oak who would close his million pores against the sap that gives him life, and shake the dew from his dancing leaves. While suffering brings its revelation of happiness, it is only through the antagonism of the two that we obtain a clear conception of either. In contemplating the utter helplessness of mankind, from their advent to their exit, one is led to ask : 'Who is free ? Who is independent ?' It is the darkness which covers one class of society, which forms such a cogent contrast to the light embathing the other. A demand always evolves a supply. No human being was ever independent in knowledge, or infallible in judgment. True, while chasing phantoms, stumbling over errors, and groping in darkness, intellectual meteors have gleamed here and there through our mental atmosphere, all the more prized because transitory; but it would be well for the egotist to remember, perhaps, that a real flame of knowledge is never allowed to be wholly extinguished, and that a broken lamp is always replaced when most needed. Though mankind, taken in masses, are mighty, and may even be called irresistible, yet their impotency, when separated, is pitiable, and would be truly ludicrous were it not so sad. In fact all thought, all knowledge, all reason, all language, all life, must have had a beginning; therefore, the whole is but the effect of a great first cause—orderly, intelligent, omnipotent, eternal."

"Ah me, mamma mine, as my poor brain refuses to digest philosophic fare, please do change the subject," exclaimed Zarina, who had entered the room unperceived by either Lady Clifford or Legrand.

"I, myself," said Legrand, unheeding the interruption, "could properly accept the doctrine of optimity were it not for those, to me, terrible interceptions of vital forces. No argument drawn from great expectations of future

happiness can convince me that this constant and ruth-
less destruction of human life is, was, or ever will be,
for the best."

"In the name of sanity, monsieur," said Zarina, with
affected wonder, "is it possible that you understand
yourself? *Ma foi!* you must have bad company when
alone, if this jargon be a sample of your thoughts! But,
look here, my good people, it is past nine o'clock, and
quite time that this little 'Diet of Worms,' gloomy repast! should have an end."

This sally closed the conversation, the "good-nights"
were given, and soon slumber reigned over that strange
household.

CHAPTER XIX.

UMAN nature presents strange contrasts. In some persons affliction produces a great commotion. In these, the very fierceness of grief exhausts its power, and the disturbing elements are cast forth as the thunder-cloud discharges its heaviness in lightning and rain. At the time of bereavement, they descend to the lowest vales of suffering and the midnight of despair, rending the air with their cries, and clinging to the dead ashes of their loved; but they emerge again with elastic vitality, and drink the sunshine with joyous ardor.

There are others, again, whose true hearts shiver like a mirror and are never restored, "but brokenly live on." With these, sexual love is devotional in its strength and absorbing in its power. Disappointment cannot be outlived. No dreamy lotion, no fiery elixir can soothe their grief to sleep or stir their hearts with hope. A persistent minor note mars the music of life, and the unbidden spectre sits with them at every feast.

Of this latter class ʼwas Echo; and her daily prayer was, not to be delivered from the gloom of her sorrow, but for strength to bear it. The sweet, mournful words of Longfellow were often on her mind:

"The air is full of farewells to the dying,
And mournings for the dead;

The heart of Rachel, for her children crying,
Will not be comforted!

"Let us be patient! These severe afflictions
Not from the ground arise.
But oftentimes celestial benedictions
Assume this dark disguise."

But, to pursue our diagnosis of the tender passion a
little further, it may be observed that there is an ideal
love, which invests its object with impossible attractions.
It is as regularly an incident of youth as teething is of
childhood, and quite as painful. It is the fragrance of
life's blossom - time, soon gone, but deliciously remembered.

Then there is a love which is justly included under
Blackstone's definition of "things corporal." It is simply
animal phosphorus, and not to be analytically discussed.

The highest and best love is intellectual and spiritual.
It is the substance of the peach when the rude hand of
experience has brushed away its treacherous bloom. It
survives the wreck of youth and beauty, and strengthens
with the lapse of time. It is the leaven of divinity in
human souls — our connecting link with the eternal harmonies of heaven. This love is the crown and glory of
every mortal life — the deathless germ that remains from
the lapse of Eden. Shall we not seek it with bleeding
feet through all the world? Who knows but, like
prayer, it may be our watchword at the gates of death?
Such a love was that of Echo for Arthur, and it still
survived all changes and disasters.

There is no heroism in this world as beautiful and
rare as self-denial, rising to the sublimity of self-sac-

rifice, through disinterested kindness to others. The de-
livery of Abraham from the sacrificial agony, has few
parallels in history. Ordinarily, the cruel play grinds on
to its tragic close, and the recompense of truth and faith
is among the treasures of heaven.

Echo, not destroyed by the blight of her love, or the
bleak loneliness and threatened struggles of her life, had
quietly taken little Wistit into her affections, assuming
the care of the draggled castaway as the heavy, yet
precious, burden of her days.

It is the crowning sin and shame of this Christian age
that the greatest enemy with which an unprotected hard-
working, independent girl has to contend, is calumny.
The leprous tongue of the slanderer is prone to seek
these unshielded heroines of toil, and the venomous drip
of its saliva has blackened many a fair name — blasted
the hope of many an aspiring soul. Thus far obscurity
had protected Echo from the "slings and arrows" of de-
traction, but there was danger at hand.

An amateur concert, for some charitable purpose, was
to be held in the church which Echo attended, the musical portion of the entertainment to be followed by a
basket supper. At the urgent solicitation of the mana-
gers the young music teacher consented to preside at the
piano, and to further assist the occasion by reciting that
beautiful poem — "The Miracle of the Roses."

Is there a fatality in occasions? Assuredly. The
fates often hand us the gossamer threads of our own destinies, in very derision of our vanity and blindness.

Echo, in order to escape the pursuit of her enemies,
had adopted the name of Newbury, and it was, of course,

7ⁱ

understood that she and the nurse, Aunt Newbury, were sisters. Mr. Farrish's mistake had first suggested the idea and the harmless fiction had been permanently adopted.

The entertainment, which was largely advertised in the city papers, chanced to fix the attention of Edmond Ainsley, whose eye, while carelessly running over the programme, was arrested by the name of Newbury. "Newbury! Newbury!" he repeated, thoughtfully, while drumming with his fingers on the table by which he was seated. Suddenly bringing his hand down upon his knee with force, he mentally ejaculated, "*Eureka*, by Jove! the name of that infernal old nurse at the seraglio on Stockton street! And she did succeed in Newburying my little bird, that is, as far as I was concerned, pretty effectually; but its gift of song has at last betrayed its place of retirement."

"To-morrow night at half-past seven o'clock," he added, referring again to the advertisement. "Rest assured I shall be there, *ma chere!*"

The evening was a propitious one; the church was full to repletion. Each and every participator performed his or her part creditably. Echo presided at the piano with the graceful dignity of a professional. When it came her turn to recite, however, Edmond Ainsley, who was seated in the second pew to the right of the middle aisle, half rose as she bowed to the audience and threw a bouquet of her favorite pansies, which fell at her feet, thereby attracting her attention. At the sight of him she started, faltered, and seemed about to run off the stage, but Mr. Farrish and some friends just at this critical moment came to the rescue by starting a storm of applause, during which she had time to collect her scattered senses, and then proceeded with a power and pathos which softened and electrified the whole assembly in an unusual degree.

"An elocutionist of rare ability and culture," remarked an old man, with gold-rimmed spectacles, as Echo, leaning on the arm of Farrish, passed him on her way to the supper table. "Too lovely for anything," lisped a sweet sixteen, to an envious elderly girl who was superior in nothing but years. "A splendid 'make-up' which came near being a 'break-up,'" said a gay belle to her attendant who seemed to her to be more favorably impressed with the young reader than was pleasing. "A perfect stunner, 'pon my soul!" This last was a *petit-maître*, who was seemingly trying to make up for the deficiency of his figure by the length of his finely curved and twisted mustache. "Yes, she understands acting to perfection, acting which has lost the merit of novelty to me, however," answered Ainsley, purposely loud enough to be heard by the Misses Richard. "How they came to receive her in respectable society is an Americanism of which I am unable to account," he added, shrugging his shoulders.

"Oh, for the matter of that," said the *petit maître*, nonchalantly, "these sirens seemingly understand that the charm of novelty is very cogent with us gentlemen, therefore they flourish for a brief hour. By-the-way, you must have met that little package of sweetness before, else you possess extraordinary intuition or exceptional confidence in your own acuteness of discernment."

"Perhaps we had better postpone our present discussion, and not force the blush of modesty to mount the fair cheeks of those who may chance to overhear our remarks," said Ainsley, filled with malicious amusement, as he glanced in the direction of the two listeners, rightly judging that he had said all that was necessary to blast the reputation of a young and handsome girl in Echo's situation. "All the knowledge which I have of the person under discussion, I am sorry to say," added he, hypocritically, "was a short but sweet *amour*, begining and ending, much the same as all youthful intrigues."

"Really! Come Ainsley, acknowledge that you are filled with remorse, not for the *amour*, but for the loss of so fair an inamorata. I swear, by the nine gods of Greece! that I will not rest content until you give me an introduction to her."

When the concert and its appendant feast were over, Aunt Newbury and Echo, accompanied by their friend, Mr. Farrish, no sooner entered their carriage than Ainsley, and his twirled and twisted companion, called a passing cab and followed them.

"'When found, make a note of it,'" said Ainsley, carefully observing the street and number of the house entered by the ladies, and making a memorandum of it in his pocket book, "and thus do honor to the manes of the illustrious Captain Cuttle," returning the book to his pocket, and begging of his *vis a vis* the inestimable favor of a "light."

CHAPTER XX.

THE week following the entertainment, Echo lost five of her best paying pupils. The grains of scandal dropped by Ainsley, had fallen in fertile soil. That ancient mustard-seed, spoken of in Holy Writ, which grew and flourished and branched out enormously, was never more productive.

The warmth of society's affection varies like the seasons; consequently, the 'summerlings' of to-day may be the icicles of to-morrow. Intuition is a pretty good barometer, and the Misses Newbury felt a sudden change in the weather of friendship. Without any apparent cause, its mercurial nineties dropped down to zero.

One dull, rainy evening, about nine o'clock, Echo, who was returning from the apothecary's, where she had gone to have a prescription filled for Aunt Newbury, left the street-car at the depot nearest her residence, Wistit being her only attendant. After walking two of the four blocks which still separated her from her home, she recoiled with a scream as a hand grasped the umbrella which she was carrying, and another, its mate, fell upon her shoulder, while a sharp, falsette voice smote her ear :

"An umbrella is entirely too cumbersome for such a pretty hand as this to carry !"

Echo's first impulse was to run, but as that was an impossible thing to do, incumbered as she was with a sleepy child, she recovered her presence of mind somewhat, and said, with dignity :

. "You are evidently mistaken, sir ! I hope you will have the kindness to release me at once."

"Very true, my girl—spoken like a queen !" said the fellow, with a tipsy leer.

"Please, sir," appealed Echo, to a passing gentleman, "will you not have the kindness to protect me from insult ?"

"Ha, ha !" laughed the ruffian. "Innocence abroad ! Come, Polly, no foolishness with a man you know!" And he attempted to put his arm about her waist.

At this instant the gentleman appealed to turned and took in the situation at a glance. He said not a word, but the shapely arm in broadcloth mail suddenly shot out, and the wretch lay writhing in the dust.

Echo gave a little cry of delight, as she recognized in her muscular deliverer, Mr. Farrish, who bowed to her with grave courtesy, offering his arm.

"Allow me the pleasure of seeing you home, Miss Newbury," he said. "The back streets of San Francisco are never safe for unprotected ladies after dark."

"I thank you most gratefully for your opportune interference," she said, accepting his escort. "I did not recognize you at first, and supposed that I was appealing to the natural chivalry of some gentlemanly stranger. We were detained longer at the drug store than we expected. Dear me, do you think he is dead ?" she added, looking back, tremulously, at the prostrate black-guard.

"Not dead, but sleeping!" he answered, with a laugh, as he followed her fearful glance. "In fact, we might erect some such epitaph as this to his memory:

'Struck by lightning,' is the inscription on the pavement where
    he lies,
Dead he is not, but prostrated, for the bummer never dies!"

"Really," said Echo, mirthfully, "you are like one of those horrible modern inventions which do so many things at once. You knock a man down and then plaster him with funeral poetry with a double-back-action ease that is astonishing. It's a shame to use Longfellow's pretty lines about Albrecht Durer, in that connection, however."

"Oh, as for that, he will recover from the blow soon enough, but the poetry will almost assassinate him, no doubt."

"But how can I ever thank you, and the Providence which directed your steps that way?" said Echo.

"By never mentioning my part of it, Miss Echo, and promising me to be more careful hereafter in your travels," he answered, kindly. "Ah, here we are!"

Farrish, by invitation, ascended the steps with Echo and Wistit, for he was always welcome at the Newbury home.

Echo, having seen the gentleman seated, excused herself for a moment, and retired to administer the medicines brought for "sister" Newbury. She soon returned, saying:

"Sister is sleeping well, and I trust she will be much improved by to-morrow."

"That is hopeful," said Mr. Farrish, gently. "But I notice that you are looking very pale." Then, with a sudden impulse, "Ah, my dear, I wish you were my very own, to love, protect, and cherish always!"

"Yes," she answered, unconscious of intentional cruelty; "if fate had been more kind, I might have been your daughter."

"My daughter!" he repeated, dropping his hand in consternation.

"Why, my dear friend," said she, smiling involuntarily at his manner, "is the thought so very startling, then?"

"Startling? No;—it were better so, perhaps, but I was thinking of a tenderer bond. Do you think that it can never, never be?" And he advanced and laid his hand gently upon hers.

The face of Echo flushed crimson at this appeal, and, softly disengaging her hand from his clasp, she answered, with down-cast eyes :-

"No; no! It cannot be! I have loved, and I know the agony of blighted affection. I like you very much, sir, but God help you, if you love me truly!"

"But you might learn to love me, dear. The heart loves because it is its nature to love, and it is not fatally blighted by any of the disappointments of life."

"It is not so with me, sir. There are plants that blossom but once in a century, and hearts that love but once. Love is involuntary. Were it otherwise, a mere matter of option, I should take pleasure in returning your affection, because "—

"Because what?" he asked, as she hesitated, with a smile.

"Because I respect you, and believe you to be sincere."

"Thank you, for that concession, at least," he said. "I will not prose about my attachment, and enter into a philosophical analysis of the capacities of human hearts, but I hope that you are mistaken as to the dead blight of your affections. So warm and true a heart must necessarily love. I confess, however, that I would have all the advantage in an exchange of hearts."

"Your last expression is flattering, but none the less sophistical."

"Why, may I ask?"

"It is easily established, sir. You have money, friends, position, and manly independence, while I have nothing but the hard earnings of brain and hands. Even my friends—and every one has friends—may be numbered one, two, three," checking them off on her rosy fingertips. "Then, recently, a chilling cloud has come over my prospects. The social atmosphere, so lately warm and fragrant, has fallen to a wintry temperature; my acquaintances have suddenly grown cold—and for what reason, I cannot divine. There must be an enemy at work, somewhere. I am confident that my character has been secretly assailed, and I feel prostrated and helpless. The consciousness of innocence may sustain me in the struggle, but it cannot compensate me for the loss of that good name beside which the great Shakspeare has said that shining lucre is but 'trash.'"

"Pardon me, Miss Echo; but in reference to the first

part of your answer, I will say that money, position, friends, and all that, are the merest trash in comparison with the love and wifely companionship of yourself. As to the trouble in your social experiences, I have simply to say that the fact indicates your need of the best friend and protector you can have on earth—a strong, true-hearted, loving husband." Mr. Farrish' face was crimson when he concluded these remarks, and his breath rather short.

"Upon such a protector," she answered, with tender pathos, "I could only call in the high and holy name of love. As to the inestimable value of my companionship, you should be more reasonable."

"In affairs of the heart, one needs a more subtle and unselfish guide than reason."

"There I agree with you—that is, if reason, which is said to be the chief attribute of man, causes him to be so inconstant."

"As for that, Miss Echo, women usually worship certain ideal characteristics, mostly mere abstractions and impossibilities, which they attribute to the men of their choice, while men, more reasonable, certainly in this, bow before the force of beauty, which, while it lasts, is a reality, and, departing, ordinarily leaves its devotee too far gone for a relapse—to say nothing of moral and intellectual excellencies that remain—with a power of enchantment borrowed from the faded bloom."

"I am not so certain about that. The common experience of men, is, that beauty is a false light on a treacherous shore. But all this is neither here nor there. I want to be candid and considerate with you concerning the delicate subject you have introduced. I want you to see my heart as it is. As your wife, I should undoubtedly occupy an honorable and easeful position, but the contract would be wholly wanting in the necessary consideration from me. Such contracts melt into contentions, and are concluded by divorces. Should I so bestrew the quiet of your future with sour fruits of discord, you would soon learn to hate me. The most barren poverty or direful misfortune in the power of circumstance to inflict, shall never force me into a contract in which I should lose my own self-respect. Had it pleased God to have granted me such a father or brother as yourself, I should have indeed been blessed. As a friend, you shall ever have the first place in my affections. Though I respect and honor you greatly, yet the thought of marriage is too extremely repulsive to be entertained for a moment; and though the truth sometimes seems unpalatable and harsh, yet, believe me, dear sir, it had best be spoken. You must try and understand me, and not wholly withdraw your sympathy in withdrawing your suit for a worthless hand. From my earliest remembrance there has been a blank in my life which parents alone could fill—a sort of innate longing for a mother's peculiar love and a father's tender care. Strive as we may, there are times when nature cries out mightily against such deprivement. The cold philosophy of not grieving for the inevitable, may be abstractly correct, but it is surely not practically useful to the human heart."

As the truth-freighted voice ceased, the long, fringed, drooping lids were slowly lifted from Leathean eyes,

within whose magnetic depths the gazer found oblivion.
To Farrish, Echo never looked more bewitchingly beautiful than as she sat there with her elbow resting on the
arm of her chair, and her head bowed on her shapely
hand.   Between this fair young girl of eighteen and
this man of forty-five, there existed a strong attachment.
On her part there was a reverential regard, more felt
than understood, while on his part there was a worship-
ful compassion for her tender years and hard lot.

A few minutes passed in which Farrish arose, then
suddenly sank back in his chair, as if overcome with
emotion.   While involuntarily running his white fingers
through a mass of dark hair, he broke the silence by
saying, respectfully :

"You have been frank, Miss Echo; I will be no less
so.   Conscience forbids my taking advantage of your in-
experience. Such friendship, as you seem to desire, existing between a man of the world, such as I am, and a beautiful young girl in your situation, would be more detri-
mental than beneficial. This world is full of evil-thinkers,
as well as evil-doers; such are utterly incapable of com-
prehending true friendship. In my estimation the man,
who, for the pleasure of a woman's company, would
compromise her good name, is a selfish villain, unworthy
of her notice. I sought you at first, as a man of the
world, bent upon his own pleasure, would naturally seek
a lovely young girl. Your innocent frankness at first
bewildered, then disarmed me, while your unprotected
condition appealed to my better nature. You see before
you a man whose faith in the purity of woman had been
violently shattered, one who, in fact, regarded her as a

boy usually regards a painted toy. In you I found a living demonstration of feminine goodness, as inward purity steals out like some subtle ether and envelops the actions of every-day life. The necessity of our separation seems almost unbearable, and though the breaking up of our present friendly intercourse would be a loss to me irretrievable, yet, should it continue, your reputation would suffer—and it must be."

While encountering the earnest, sympathetic gaze of her companion, two great tears rolled slowly down the soft, flushed cheeks of Echo, and fell upon her lap unheeded, as she somewhat pathetically expostulated :

"Must it, then, indeed be broken up ? Why, sir, your cheery company has been to me what that delicate flower growing in its rocky crevice is said to have been to Mungo Park as he wearily lay down in the desert to die. Is there to be no more of those friendly walks and drives, those familiar talks in which thought called forth thought, and the storehouse of your mind gave ·forth its goodly treasures ? Is it right that I should be deprived of a friendship so tenderly compassionate, so divinely good, so helpful to my ignorance ? Are those quiet evening hours which were so refreshing, after days of toil, to have no existence but in memory ? Are not the needs of the heart as great as those of the body and the mind, and human sympathy as precious to the weary, struggling soul, as water to the traveler in the desert ? I, then, bow to the dire necessity of a separation, brought about by a society of evil-thinkers, who frown down upon me sorely on account of circumstances over which I have no control, and who not

only ostracise me from their one circle, but also invade
the associations of my home.   Charity ! charity ! where
is thy dwelling place ?   The only treasure poverty
affords is friendship.   Robbed of that, nothing remains
but the hard fact of a barren existence, and a little self-
respect, perhaps, which goads one on to observe life's
most common proprieties, however hateful."

"My dear, impulsive child," said Farrish, arising and
taking her hand tenderly, "the conventionalities of society are inexorable, and must be observed.   Ah, my
dear, you had better reconsider your first decision, and
give me the right to shield and cherish you."

Oh, why did Echo's heart beat so wildly ?   Her feeling for this man was not to be compared to that being,
instinctive passion, which she had experienced for Hoberg; and yet this parting fell as heavily upon her throbbing heart as did the sound of the first clods which fell
on her grandmother's coffin.

"No, no, no !" said Echo, in tones vibrating with emotion, as she also rose.   "Do not tempt me, for I have an
inward monitor which constrains me from entering into
a marriage contract with one while loving another, and
that other still living.   I do not wish to dictate to others;
but as for myself, I must be 'firm in the right as God
gives me to see the right' in the present, regardless of
future consequences."

"Oh, fairest, and best, and sweetest of woman kind !"
cried Farrish, in a voice of impassioned tenderness, "I
honor your motive, while deprecating your sacrifices,
and should future events cause you to change your present decision, you can always hear from me by dropping

me a line through my solicitor. The lateness of the hour forces me into saying good-night and good-bye in two successive breaths."

As Farrish clasped Echo's extended hand, their eyes met; his were full of earnest entreaty. But her's, though tear-suffused, shone with a steadfast purpose. Farrish suddenly bent his head and gravely touched Echo's forehead with his lips, then rather reluctantly resigned her hand and was gone in another moment, after pausing at the door and regarding her with a look which is not often given except to the dead, and then only when the coffin lid is about to close upon them forever.

" Dear God !" was the impassioned cry which involuntarily burst from Echo's lips, "give me wisdom to know, and strength to do, the right."

CHAPTER XXI

ECHO, wrapped in thought, stood perfectly still fully ten minutes after Farrish's footsteps had died away in the distance. She thought, with dismay, of the displeasure of Miss Newbury, who seemed to favor Farrish's suit, and the loss of his cheerful company weighed no less heavily upon her over-charged spirit. Thoughts of the insult which she had received that evening brought a flush of indignation to her face, while the loss of her pupils and the increasing coldness of the members of the Church to which the nurse, her fictitious sister, belonged, and that of the choir also, where she, herself, was in the habit of singing, chilled her with no small apprehension.

As the little time-piece on the mantle chimed out the hour of eleven, Echo entered the room from which proceeded a slight noise, and found the nurse awake and feeling better.

"You are surely sick, yourself, child," was her first salutation to Echo, "that is, if looks are to be trusted," she gravely added.

"Pray, do not give yourself unnecessary alarm, dear sister," replied Echo, while straightening the covering of the bed, smiling pleasantly.

"Some one rang the door-bell about half an hour after the departure of yourself and Wistit. I am not sure

who it was, of course, as I was unable to attend, but pre-
sumed it to be Mr. Farrish."

"That lady whom you wished me to see, personally,
kept us waiting more than hour. We were then forced
to return without the money. We were also detained
at the apothecary's a short time. In consequence of the
lateness of the hour I experienced no small difficulty in
keeping Wistit sufficiently awake to move. In all probability you were wrong in your presumption in regard
to Farrish, as he met and escorted us home without
mentioning the fact of having called before this evening,"
said Echo, in explanation.

"I think that he is almost on the point of making you
a proposal of marriage, Echo, dear, and I would advise
you to accept," hazarded the nurse. "To be frank, he
intimated as much to me some weeks ago, but I advised
him to wait."

"It is time that you were taking your medicine, sister,"
said Echo, with irrelevant tenderness.

"Pray have no hesitancy in ringing the bell in case
you need anything," she added, as she kissed the nurse
good-night. After reading a chapter from the Bible — a
nightly free-will offering to the Father — Echo entered
the adjoining room, leaving the door of communication
open. Then lying down, she gathered the sleeping
child, Wistit, to her aching heart, and strange as it may
seem, appeared to be comforted thereby.

In the silence and darkness of the night one is often
startled with spontaneous thoughts which come and
go like dreams. That night the returning stream of
memory sent forth before Echo's mental vision a reflec-

tion, as it were, from that picture of her unknown father which had been taken in his boyhood. As this reflection .vanished, that of Farrish's face took its place, and she was startled at the resemblance existing between the smooth-faced, beautiful boy and that of the man, bearded and handsome. Ah! were one but wise enough to heed these inspired thoughts which, like the wind, are felt but not seen, whose action all behold, but whose source is unknown!

As thought goes keenly searching through that mysterious repository where past events lie covered, how often does it shudderingly turn away from that cemetery by whose monuments acts are perpetuated which their doer would fain obliterate. Are not those silent chronicles to be the book of God's remembrance? and every immortal stone reared in that awful graveyard ol memory a witness which shall condemn or exculpate its builder at the Judgment? If, as has been asserted, the mind does not relax from its functions when the body is in a state of rest, why may not this indwelling god — this discerner of good and evil — live on independent of its corporeal body? Surely, the all-wise God and subtile serpent are both reported in the third chapter of Genesis to have declared that a knowledge of good and evil made man god-like. Moreover, does not the case also specified in Holy Writ, where man is called to render an account of imparted talents at the day of reckoning hint of the mind's progression in a life beyond?

At seven o'clock, the following morning, Echo awoke. She arose and dressed with care, for she was regularly neat in matters pertaining to her toilet.

As plants are easily distinguished by their leaves, so are women by their outward adornings. The richest apparel, if carelessly donned, would not be as adequate to the purpose of attracting and impressing the thoughtful as less presumptuous garments, properly adjusted. The beauty of one's dress consists more in its suitableness to the style of the wearer than its fineness of texture or brilliancy of color, and a woman who carefully studies herself and surroundings is never ill-dressed, however small her income.

"Well, how are you feeling this morning?" pleasantly asked Echo, who, upon entering the adjoining room, found the nurse awake and sitting up in bed.

"Almost well. The pain has vanished in the nighttime like the famed palace of Aladdin," replied the nurse, who had been suffering from a severe spell of inflammatory rheumatism, "so I shall arise and go to the breakfast table with alacrity."

Not till the breakfast had been prepared and eaten, Wistit washed and dressed, and the house tidied, and everything in order, did Echo see fit to reveal last evening's occurrences to the nurse.

After they were cosily seated, Echo busily engaged on a hood which she was knitting in biroche stitch for Wistit, while the nurse, seated in an easy-chair, was no less busy on a pair of slippers that she was embroidering for one of her lady patrons, did Echo broach the subject which lay uppermost in her mind just then, by saying, "I was grossly insulted on my return last night."

"By whom?" queried the nurse, indignantly.

Echo's cheeks reddened slightly, "By a man, of course."

"Say a brute, rather! But relate the affair just as it occurred."

Echo began: "After leaving the car and proceeding a short distance, I was startled by a hand grasping my umbrella and another being laid upon my shoulder, while a voice half whispered something about the weight of the umbrella being too heavy for my hand. I was too badly frightened to catch the exact words. It was raining heavily. The street was dark and almost deserted, the wind soughed dismally, and, if I was afraid before, how much more so then? As soon as possible I replied, telling him that he should never address a lady without being sure of her identity. Receiving an insulting reply, I appealed to a passing gentleman for protection. Judge of my relief on recognizing the voice of our friend Farrish as he replied to some more of the man's remarks by knocking him down, and I do not know as he was able to get up again," she added, raising her soft eyes to the nurse's, in troubled doubt.

"It is to be hoped not," answered the latter, spitefully. "A brute acknowledges no law but that of force."

"And yet one should pity them after they are conquered. Suffering, by no matter whom or what, ever calls for commiseration," continued Echo, carefully picking up the stitches all along the back of the hood upon which she was engaged.

"Humbug!" exclaimed the nurse rather fiercely, stabbing the needle in and out the cloth she was working. "For all suffering there is a cause. Two-thirds of all the miseries of this world could be avoided by the exercise of reason, coupled with a little self-command. In my humble opinion, involuntary sufferers should have the fullest commiseration, as it is only by pain and toil that the majority of mankind can be taught wisdom. Think, for instance," she jocularly resumed, "of a lazy, sluggish set of Adams and Eves fooling around the garden of Eden with nothing to do but kill time — no motive whatever to exercise that God-given faculty, the mind! Why, even the mute creation would have been their superiors, and alas, for the day of elevated manhood, they had been without the trick of mixing mint-juleps as they lounged around vacantly, and with no money to bet on the merits of the various animals straggling by! Moreover, awful to contemplate, there had been no corner saloons before which men could congregate and chew their cigar-stubs while they canvassed the beauties and frailties of passing ladies.

The idea of women having no children to care for, no trowsers to mend, or carpets to protect from sun and stains! Finally, most weighty consideration of all, there had been no sailing down the church aisle of a Sunday, full-rigged, colors flying, unmindful, perhaps, of the buzzing and neck-stretching on either side the restless stream.

Imagine, if you can, the angels rushing around waiting on those great, indolent, overgrown hulks of babies, who, if not furnished a substitute for breathing, would have ceased to live through pure inertness. I remember an anecdote illustrative of the subject: An Indiana farmer, going one day into the harvest-field, saw five of his hands lying supinely under a shade-tree, though noon had long since passed. With a merry twinkle in his eye he approached the group saying, as he took a greenback from his pocket, 'Here are ten dollars for the laziest man in this crowd.' While four of the men sprang to their feet, each claiming his right to the money, the fifth lay perfectly still, without so much as moving a muscle. 'I think that this fellow has given us the most convincing demonstration,' said the farmer, extending the bill towards the man. 'Won't you put it in my pocket?' drawled out that worthy, rolling on his side.'"

Echo, much amused, laughed heartily, for the drollery of the nurse's manner and argument were not to be withstood.

"If one-half of the wasted pity and charity were discriminately dispensed among those who are really worthy creatures of circumstances, the world would be gainer thereby," the nurse more gravely continued — "The man or woman who has most thoroughly learned the lesson that under all ordinary events, self-help is the most reliable efficacious and sustaining of all helps, is almost sure to make his or her mark in the world."

Silence fell between them, which was broken by the kind inquiry of the nurse:

"Are you well, Echo?"

The heavily-fringed lids opened wide, then drooped suddenly over the luminous dark eyes as she answered somewhat abruptly —

"Certainly, but why do you ask?"

" On account of your increased paleness and seeming abstraction."

" Oh, is that all ?"

" All, unless you wish to disclose more," said the other reproachfully.

Echo smiled but answered not.

" You must remember, continued the nurse, " that mutual confidence is conducive to friendship. Just as you please, however."

" Echo blushed painfully, while the delicate scarlet lips tremulously articulated —" Mr. Farrish made a proposal of marriage last night."

" You accepted, of course ? "

" No."

The nurse, looking at Echo in utter bewilderment, slowly ejaculated, " Is — it — possible ? "

" It is my friend."

" The ground of your objection, please ? "

Echo, drooping her eyelids demurely, answered softly, " The strongest in the world — want of proper affection."

" You amaze me ! "

" Why so, pray ? "

" You surely loved that man ? "

" As a very dear friend, only, in the same way that I love you, dear nurse."

" He is rich, handsome, wise and loving; what more can you desire ? " said the nurse, much disturbed.

Echo's face expressed varying emotions, while the fitful color, in its ebb and flow, was charming as she raised her resplendently lovely eyes to those of her companion, and replied with solemn pathos:

"What equivalent have I to give for the possessions which you have named? A body devoid of a heart; a will forced into wedlock; a mind teeming with inbred thoughts of another! Is this marriage? Bah! methinks that the very ink would pale and fade from the 'license' when touched by the acid of truth. Is wedlock but a summer cloud that it needs no sustaining truth? Know you not that a bond, light as a gossamer web in seeming, can be made as heavy and rough for the sensitive soul as a criminal's clanking chain—to be broken by violence only? Oh, these broken contracts! these heartaches! whence come they? From want of understanding, surely. Love bridles the passions and gently guides the feelings of the truly married into verdure-clad fields of pleasantness."

A sweet light stole into the softened face of the nurse, as she answered:

"I was in fault, darling, and you must forgive me. A marriage of convenience is simply legalized prostitution."

Echo left her seat, and, approaching the nurse, kissed her with reassured affection, saying, "You, Wistit, and I will be sufficient unto each other. We will practice the strictest economy, and, in a short time we will have money enough to purchase a few acres of land somewhere on the bay, and we will have a little Arcadia of our own, raising fruits, vegetables and the like for the city market. It would be a dear, reposeful, happy life, and I am very weary of San Francisco. Really, nurse, the thought is an inspired one. 'We will be rich and contented, if not 'happily married,' as the novelists say. Come, dear, is it not a scheme among ten thousand?"

"It is a pleasing picture, Echo, and I am inclined to think that your Arcadia is attainable."

"And will there be flowers, and butterflies, and cherries, and swings, and things?" said Wistit, in tumultuous excitement, her eyes dilated, as she approached the knees of Echo.

"Yes, pet, all these — a garden of beauty and of love," and the young girl's hand stroked the hair of the "mith' erless bairn" with angelic softness.

CHAPTER XXII.

SOME twenty minutes after entering her own apartments, and dismissing her maid for the night, Zarina securely fastened her door, and softly stealing down the stairs, let herself out into the garden. Raising her skirts in her hand, and peering cautiously over and around the shrubbery in whose shadow she was keeping, she made her way with the greatest possible speed to the most secluded and uncultivated spot in the enclosure.

The light of the moon was obstructed at intervals by floating clouds. The arbor was made dim and cool by the density of its green surroundings even when the sun shone its brighest. To-night it was particularly dark, gloomy and chilly.

"Five minutes past nine," murmured La Croix, while consulting his watch by the light of a match. "Glad that my divinity is usually punctual. Deucedly dumpish trysting place this!" with a yawn.

After an interval of about ten minutes, the count removed the cigar from his mouth, and bent his head to listen.

"It is the rustle of her garments!" exclaimed he. "No, 'twas but the wind among the trees," he reluctantly corrected, after a moment of earnest expectancy.

"What in the name of Venus keeps her?" he rather

impatiently ejaculated. "She was not wont to have me waiting. I presume, however," he added, arising and walking backward and forward through the rather narrow frescade which led to the arbor, "that the pulse of time, seemingly, beats more sluggishly here than elsewhere."

The branches of the trees on either side of the walk interlaced, forming a leafy barrier through which the chill air crept regardless of its murmurings.

Just as his patience became thoroughly exhausted, the keen eyes of the count discerned what seemed to be a shade within a shade, or as it were a little black cloud scudding across the face of its lighter neighbor.

As the cry of a bird smote the air, the count hesitated no longer, but sprang forward and in another moment clasped the swiftly moving shadow in his arms.

"Have I kept you waiting?"

"An age!" kissing her.

"How long?"

"An hour in reality, an eternity in seeming," whispered the count, leading Zarina into the arbor, and seating her in a large rustic chair and placing himself beside her.

"This place is dark and chill as a dungeon," said she, shivering.

"It was," said the count, gathering her more closely to himself, "until warmed and lighted by your presence."

"Is that really so, prince of my heart?" inquired she, laying her cheek caressingly against his.

"Can you doubt it, life of my soul?" said the count, replying to one question by asking another.

"Demonstrations are conclusive," said she, smilingly,

and patting him on the cheek with her soft, white hand.
" Do you know, count," she resumed after a slight pause,
" that I have a peculiar request to make of you ?"

" Your lips are more potent than Mordecai's golden
scepter ; so draw near and touch, and *thy* request, no
matter what it be, is granted already," said he gaily.

" A bargain," kissing him. " I shall demand the ful-
fillment of your promise, remember ! You are probably
aware that Monsieur Legrand holds a small fortune in
his own right."

" So it is reported, but what has that to do with queen
Echo's request ?"

" Much, as you shall see. You have also noticed his
failing health ?"

" Yes," with the utmost indifference.

" Well, his physician privately informed mamma yesterday that he was liable to drop off at any moment."

" A sorry drop for him, but no concern of ours, however."

" You will change your mind, no doubt, when I inform you that he has made a will in my favor."

" Ah!" interrupted the count, immediately showing
signs of interest.

" Though an estate, when held at the will of another,
is the flimsiest of legal estates, yet, I do not think this
one at all liable to slip from my hands if a certain frailty
of his character is not provoked."

" Which is jealousy," hazarded the count.

" Right," asserted she, " and should you cease your attentions to myself suddenly, it would, I fear, cause com-
ments; therefore, I request that you leave the city for

about three months. By that time Monsieur Legrand
will have entered 'The Valley of Blessing,' thrice blessed
to us, surely, and the road will be clear."

The count's answer was a prolonged whistle.

"Not for a fortune, count?" reminded Echo, coaxingly.

" Three months—banished—from Paris—from you—
an eternity rather. Paris — you — *mon Dieu!* what
more of life? what more of heaven?"

"Oh, be reasonable!" exclaimed Zarina. "In staying,
you not only foolishly venture the loss of monsieur's small
fortune, but, in all probability, my own heritage; as Legrand will use his influence with mamma to have the
greater part of his large estate willed to charitable institutions if I persist in my present absurd infatuation, as
he calls it. Your friends seem to have but one opinion,
and that is, that you will marry for money only.
Mamma has repeatedly asserted that she will never consent for me to wed a fortune-hunter — so, for my part, I
think the chances of monsieur's success to be good, especially if her ladyship should put into practice her pet
idea of humanizing the masses and make an example of
herself by unlocking her vaults, maintaining that money
should be in circulation among the many, not hoarded
by the few."

"The devil take him!" involuntarily muttered the
count between his teeth.

" As for the matter of that, dear count, his satanic
majesty, perhaps, needs a breathing spell, as it certainly
requires a prodigious amount of activity, to say nothing
of strategy, to keep from being out-maneuvered, and

therefore, superseded, by some aspiring mundane wrestler."

"Really, I must not stay a moment longer," she added, rising. "As I retired under the plea of headache, her ladyship may chance to enter my room before bedtime. So what say you to my proposition?"

"On one condition, only, will I accede."

"Well! time flies. What is it?"

"It is," said the count, offering her his arm and escorting her outside the arbor, "that we be married in this arbor, clandestinely, to-morrow night."

"*Mon Dieu!*" exclaimed she, stopping short in her walk with surprise, then murmured:

"The long coveted title is offered me at last. Would that I could accept it! Why not? Bah! that would be bigamy, and bigamy is a crime punished by imprisonment. 'Nothing venture, nothing gain,' however; besides, after giving Legrand the *coup de grace*, the first marriage will be a thing of the past. What matters it whether it be a few days before or afterwards. In fact, the sin lies not in the doing, but in the discovery. The count but forestalls some one of those dignified, seemingly-pious gentlemen whose eel-like propensity enables them to slip right around the point of discovery, but who, nevertheless, manage at the husband's grave, between showers of grief and sundry handkerchief turnings, to give the sudden stroke which secures the coming wife, perhaps; and moreover, though widowhood is certainly the most subtilely sweet of all 'hoods,' yet, its enticements could have no charms for me, as my marriage is a secret and must forever so remain. Condensed in those two men are the materials which shall suffuse my future with the gold and purple tincture wherein human eyes behold fair, envious visions of great glory. Faugh! first a secret marriage; second, the defrauding of an innocent girl out of her birth-right, and a mother, thereby, of a child! Shall I, after all this, weaken at bigamy? and — ah me!" with a shudder, "my lips shall not coin the horrid act into words, for it is surely better that the mind should not take into account the work of the hands on this occasion. Monstrous crimes! indeed, but as necessary, alas! to my success as the ugly feet of the pea-fowl are to the brilliant plumage which flaunts above them."

"Have you plunged beneath waters of oblivion, or glanced at the petrifying Medusa? that you stand gazing into vacancy, apparently unconscious that a fellow-mortal awaits eagerly for an answer," asked the puzzled, but petulant count, with capricious irritation, breaking in on the mental conflict between conscience and desire somewhat raging in Zarina's prolific brain.

"I — I — was thinking, only thinking," rather irrelevantly answered Zarina, slowly resuming her walk.

The count, scowling blackly, interrupted her with slight acerbity, "No doubt but that my proposal struck Mademoiselle Clifford dumb with surprise. Surely, past events did not lead her to expect such presumption from one whom she has always treated with the utmost reserve (?). The idea of a man of my rank and title being duped — refused — pshaw!"

"I was thinking of the impossibility of meeting you at the time appointed," said Zarina, turning around abruptly and facing him with one of her peculiar glances and a return of her old manner, adding, in tones of icy crispness, "Rank and title, forsooth! an elephant minus a trunk, a dry river-bed whose supply of water has been cut off! Truly, past events should have taught us the absurdity of exhibiting surprise at such a wise proposal from such a source!"

"Why covet for yourself that which you affect to despise when possessed by others?" he said.

"Pray, what stronger reason can be given than that hateful fact, 'by others?'" she replied.

"Forgive my roughness, *mignon*," murmured the count, changing his tactics. "You both enchant and madden me, and," suddenly clasping her to his bosom and covering her face with kisses, "you shall not return to the house till you grant my request."

"Hush!" cautioned Zarina, laying her hand peremptorily over his mouth, "you may be overheard. We are now in close proximity to that part of the house occupied by the servants."

The count, transferring the plump, white hand from his mouth to his palm, where it rested with a soft, caressing touch, asked again, "You consent, then?"

"Foolish man! what would be the necessity? If Monsieur Legrand should hear you, all would be lost. But mamma is expecting company to dinner to-morrow, so, of course, you see it would be impracticable."

"The day after, then," rejoined the count. "To-morrow is Tuesday, the next is Wednesday, so, on the evening of that day, I insist that you shall meet your adorer and a priest in the arbor, at ten o'clock, precisely. If you dare to fail me—but you will not!"

"Suppose that I should, what then?" asked Zarina, with a shrug of her finely moulded shoulders.

"Why, then, I shall have my revenge by disclosing everything to Legrand," whispered the count, threateningly.

"I will not relieve his anxiety till the appointed time," thought Zarina, inwardly chuckling, "or mayhap he may think me too easily won." Then suddenly throwing her arms around his neck and passionately kissing him, she broke from his grasp and swiftly disappeared around a projection of the mansion.

Upon re-entering the house and regaining her apartments in safety, Zarina hastily doffed her clothes and sprang into bed. She had scarcely done so when Lady Clifford entered the room and found her, apparently, in profound slumber.

CHAPTER XXIII.

IN the Talmud there is a phrase to which all men, in all countries, of whatsoever sects and beliefs, seem to have given their unanimous assent and approbation, and to have studied for self-protection, as it seems to be on the outer edge of their memories, and always accessible in time of need. The phrase in question is this : " Descend a step in choosing a wife; mount a step in choosing a friend."

If, as has often been alleged, a man should be judged by the character of his associates, it seems that the before-mentioned phrase should read thus : " Mount a step in choosing a friend, and as many as possible in choosing a wife," especially as man and wife are merged into one, and every man insists on being that one. The average man needs many elevating accessories in order to be recognized as a success.

Matrimony admits of no "backward steps," to translate a Latin quotation, though, in truth, we have frequently known those who, in the vulgar parlance of a live language, have "*stepped down and out*." Perhaps 'twould be better for all enraptured candidates to pause before mounting that acclivity of final bliss, and forever decide whose individuality shall be swallowed up in the matrimonial crater. According to the theory of modern philosophers, the strongest should prevail; but that is a question not always decided by the accident of sex.

These observations are induced by the contemplation of the matrimonial alliance of M. Legrand and Zarina. Their accuracy may be tested hereafter—by results.

On the afternoon of the next day, directly after luncheon, Madame Fleurot was honored by another call from Legrand. When he had purchased some rare old laces, he was again shown into madame's little back parlor, where, when seated, he resumed the theme of the former occasion, by saying :

"I congratulate you heartily, madame; you succeeded beyond my expectation."

"You attended the trial this morning ?"

"No; but I received your note of yesterday evening."

"The money was not only found upon the person of the accused, but she also fought and scratched the officer who arrested her. Such talk ! such names ! why, it fairly makes one's hair stand on end to think of it, monsieur," said madame, indulging in a grimace, while smoothing down her hair with both hands. "The penalty was heavier than I thought, however."

"Very likely," said Legrand. "I presume his honor, the judge, thought that the ferocity of the beast needed severe discipline."

"Be that as it may, she surely received the sentence with stolid indifference. I, for one, was wholly unprepared for such a stupid calm after the storm of yesterday."

"A propensity of savage natures, when under the retributive lash," answered Legrand, producing a paper from the pocket of his coat and handing it to her. "This will cancel my obligation, I presume."

"Obligation, indeed! I owed you a debt of gratitude, which it was my sacred duty to have remembered," exclaimed the woman, taking the mortgage, however, and carefully locking it in an escritoire at hand.

Legrand smiled at madame's subtleness in metamorphosing corrupt motives into gratitude. When the hoop breaks the cask falls, to use a familiar phrase, and it too frequently happens that bribes are the golden hoops, and convictions the cask. It was so, at least, in this instance.

While many seek, few profit by Scriptural advice. Madame Fleurot was an exception. "Be ye therefore wise as serpents, and harmless as doves," was a motto which she endeavored to practice; and though a great student, she had been able to master the first part of this phrase only, and in so doing was always too busy to grapple the remainder.

With a few common-place remarks, Legrand took his leave, as well pleased with the termination of the affair as herself.

Returning home thoroughly exhausted, he retired to the elegant suite of apartments set apart for his occupancy.

After an hour's rest, feeling somewhat refreshed, he arose and glanced out of the window. Seeing Zarina alone in the garden, he hastened to join her.

"Monsieur," she ejaculated, coming to meet him, "has the ghost been slain? Do relieve my anxiety."

"Give yourself no further uneasiness. The serpent's

fangs have been extracted," replied Legrand, looking down upon her fondly, while keeping step by her side.

" But how ?" persisted she, returning his glance with equal fervor.

" I will explain at a more convenient season, sweet love. Tell me something about yourself. Our meetings are so few and restricted, that I long for the time when I can have you all to myself."

" That reminds me that it is time to dress for dinner," said Zarina, hastily dropping the rose, whose prickles caused blood to appear on the smooth surface of her white hand, which Legrand could scarcely refrain from pressing to his lips (although in plain view of the house) as it lay caressingly in his.

In drawing a handkerchief from her pocket, a tiny pink envelope fluttered down at the very feet of her companion. She could not suppress a start, or conceal a change of countenance.

Stooping down and picking it up, Legrand glanced at the address, started; re-adjusted his gold-rimmed glasses, and turned around and faced Zarina, with a thunderous countenance and a lightning-like glance of the eye.

Inwardly quaking, she leeringly glanced at the paper extended for her inspection; then feeling that her eyes were sufficiently under control, she slowly raised them to his, with a look of injured innocence.

" Why look you so, my liege ? Am I the criminal, you the judge ? In what have I ignorantly transgressed, that the thundering of Mount Sinai should be brought to bear against me ? Ah me ! would that the children of

men were not still set on miching, thereby causing justice to call loudly, as One of old in the garden, for some
hidden accusation !"

"What !" he exclaimed, ironically, "you transgress,
sweet Scythian lamb! Who proclaims it ? The sun
has its spots, the moon lends a borrowed light, the stars
cozen by their very coyness, but *you* are all innocence,
and innocence is perfection !"

"Perfection or not, it needs no *agnus castus* to repose
upon; likewise, no keen surveillance of a would-be pre-
server. Those that will not bear trusting, will not bear
watching, mark that !" raising her finger and shaking it,
while eyeing him askance. "Did all men resemble suns
in anything but blemishes, all women's faces would be
luminous, at least, with happiness. If, as some contend,
and most desire, women are mere reflectors, I, for one,
am greatly amazed at the chasteness of the reflections,
when contemplating the lights from which they were
borrowed. Be this as it may, however, you hold in your
hand, within about three inches of my eyes, (though I
have no knowledge of being troubled with either oph-
thalmy or short-sightedness) an envelope, directed in my
hand-writing, to Count LaCroix. The fact will not be
so striking as it seems, on second thought, perhaps, and
taking into consideration the circumstance that it was at
your request that I promised to dismiss the count. Now,
to one as unsophisticated as myself, a written dismissal
seemed less embarrassing than an oral one. It appears
that you are not of the same opinion, however." Affecting to be more and more enraged as she proceeded,
she snatched the letter from his extended hand and

tore it into tiny fragments, throwing them into the base
of the fountain at hand, while angrily pursuing : " There,
monsieur, are you satisfied ?   Talk about love, forsooth !
love and distrust at the same time !   You are too much
of a cat, yourself, to trust any one, monsieur.   Many
thanks one gets for trying to please you, indeed !"

" Proof conclusive ! proof conclusive !" exclaimed Legrand, enigmatically, wagging his head.

" Proof of what, Pierre the wise ?" said she, with a sar-
castic accent.

" First, that woman has a matchless facility in the use
of her tongue; second, that there are no women in
Heaven."

" I suppose you are referring to my talk ?" said she.
" But how does that prove that there are no women in
Heaven ?"

" ' There was silence in Heaven about the space of half
an hour !' " triumphantly quoted he, " and who ever knew
a woman to keep silent one-third of that time ?"

Sharp and quick came the report : " Ahem !   The
cause is quite apparent, as 'they neither marry, or are
given in marriage,' there.   If it were otherwise, and
some angel's Mary should happen to nestle at Jesus'
feet, there would be—well, the silence would be broken,
that is all."

" In which case, I should desire to be cast out, like
Lucifer," said he, with a provoking smile.

" Fah ! much good that would do you, monsieur, as
the hell of mankind is situated somewhere between the
' Gan Eden ' you told me of and earth, where, Tantalus-
ike, they hover between the choicest, fairest women

above, and the most useful, loving ones below, without
the power of reaching either !"

M. Legrand laughed, dryly, at this retort, and Zarina
soon afterwards withdrew.

Pacing up and down the cool, fragrant walks, the
suspicious schemer turned the incident of the letter over
and over in his mind.   For the twentieth time he stopped
in front of the fountain, and contemplated the floating
fragments of paper with a gloomy frown.

"Fool ! fool !" he murmured; "an angry man has
no more reason, perception or policy, than a drunken
one.   She should not have been allowed to destroy the
letter.   Perhaps I accused her wrongfully, and her anger
was genuine, not simulated, but it had been just as easy
to put the matter to proof.   Alas ! women out-general
us in deceit and intrigue !   It is a sad confession, but the
fact is indisputable.   A lovely and fascinating woman is
always master of the situation.   A man is so easily
blinded and destroyed by his love, while woman's affection is more or less fanciful and superficial.   A disappointed lover often blows out his brains; but a woman,
whose love affairs have gone contrarily, seeks 'fresh
fields and pastures new,' or consoles herself with veal
cutlets and onions.   *Parbleu!* it is a gay world !   Then,"
walking slowly towards the house, "I must appear before this company at dinner, when, in fact, it will be
more irksome than a state funeral.   Bah ! what inanities
these social civilities are !   A man that has a thought in
his head and a pain at his heart, is murdered by them!"

And he slowly sought his own apartments.

CHAPTER XXIV.

THE company was small, but select; and the dinner was pronounced a success. The last guest had departed — so one o'clock found Monsieur Legrand, Lady Clifford and mademoiselle, the only occupants of the spacious drawing-room.

" Yes; the lady's mind is unquestionably brilliant," assented Monsieur Legrand to some previous remark of Lady Clifford.

" Her mind may be bright, but her face is certainly disgusting," chimed in Zarina, glancing admiringly at the beautiful reflection of herself in the large cheval glass opposite.

" This attractive beauty of the body which is thought to be so powerful," reprovingly answered her ladyship, "is not only the snare which often leads to its own undoing, but is, also, a sore temptation to others, and mark you this, my child! that though its power may be as grateful as the cooling breath of Zephyrus to the feverish brow, its disappointments are always real and as hard to be borne as the fever burning within the veins. Beauty possesses the intoxicating power of wine. No man is wise enough, or good enough, no matter how great his intellectual qualifications may be, to allow himself the privilege of too often testing reason under the influence of either." Lady Clifford had not even glanced at Legrand, though the last sentence was evidently directed at him.

"I insist that your ladyship strengthen your own comparison by adding thereto that famous saying of the ancient sage, 'At the last it biteth like a serpent and stingeth like an adder,'" broke in that gentleman, liberally adapting the quotation, and darting a withering glance at Zarina, who still sat disporting with her mirrored charms.

"Though both fine and apt, monsieur, I see plainly that the comparison will not be complete without my contribution, also: 'They have stricken me, shalt thou say, and I was not sick; they have beaten me, and I felt it not; when shall I awake? I will seek it yet again,'" said Zarina, bestowing on Legrand a keen oblique look from her half closed eyelids, as the red lips parted in an arch smile, disclosing pearly rows of teeth which met evenly.

"There is one antique saying which Mademoiselle Echo, it would seem, has resolved to put into practice; '*Know thyself!*' that is, if studying the glass thoroughly, will impart that information," said Legrand.

"Do you mean to insinuate, monsieur, that an article should not be studied whose shadow, even, is worth contemplating?"

"Ah, mademoiselle, I only state the fact. The article is, perhaps, worthy of the attention it receives."

"Do you know, monsieur, that a woman must either be a frivolous coquette or an odious *bas bleu*. It is the result of the accepted relation of the sexes, the social situation. The field of honest competition heretofore closed, or at least partially so to women, makes duplicity and intriguing more habitual to them than open frankness or inward sincerity. All have desires which it would be better to gratify than stifle. Is not that so, mamma?" said Zarina, turning to Lady Clifford for approval.

"As to that, my child, doubtless all have some pet desires which, if fulfilled, would destroy their author — and, in truth, desire is hydra-headed. Lop off one branch and, *presto!* another takes its place. Its hunger cannot be satiated. One who was a close student of nature, the talented lady, Mary Wortley Montague, is said to have declared 'that in all her travels she had met with but two sorts of people, *men* and *women*.' Now if" —

"' *Omne simile non est idem!* ' is a simple but truthful axiom, which it would be well for us always to bear in mind, more so, perhaps, than ever, when admitting the above assertion,'' interrupted Legrand. "' A lover's angel,' for instance, 'is a rival's fiend.'" There was a pause.

"Even 'in the hereafter,'" said her ladyship, ending the broken sentence.

"It grows late, ladies," said Legrand, suddenly, as he arose, bowed and withdrew.

Then Lady Clifford and Zarina also retired, each to her separate appartments.

The next morning the sky was overcast with dull, gray clouds, from which a thick mist fell drearily. Not a ray of sunlight pierced the water laden air which crept with a sad, monotonous soughing through the burdened foliage of surrounding trees and plants, which stood swaying and drooping under their virgin cloud-bath, while each herb and shrub was a wafting censer of pleasing fragrance. The dark atmosphere prevailing without had the effect of clouding the old family mansion with duskiness within.

The soft drugget which protected the hall and staircase carpets gave forth no sound to Zarina's footsteps, as on the afternoon of the following day, she secretly entered Legrand's suite of apartments. Taking a small phial from her pocket she poured a few drops of fluid into a bottle of medicine that was on a stand by the bedside. In so doing, her cheeks did not flush, nor did a tremor shake her frame; in reality, there was a covert exultation in her heart which brightened her eyes and reddened her smiling lips.

" To-night," murmured she, " the beggar's brat — the amusing ballet dancer — the cunning lawyer's wife and ready pupil — the fair lady's charming daughter, will have reached the zenith of her highest aim — millions of money and a countess' title! Legrand gone, Lady Clifford will soon follow, and I shall reign a queen in that society which ignored or abhorred the half-starved, half-naked, though beautiful castaway, in the cloud of her poverty. A little kind attention then might have — well, no matter. A twig is easily inclined, they say, but when matured, methinks 'twould be far better to eradicate the whole than either to trim or prop its distorted growth. To prevent, is one thing; to cure, is quite another. But why dictate to that society whose highest aim is ' To seem rather than to be.' It moved and flour-

ished before my entrance, and will doubtless do quite as
well after my exit"—saying which, she left the room
as cautiously as she had entered, and regained her own
room undiscovered. Then she rang for her maid, and
after making an elegant toilet, joined Lady Clifford and
Legrand in the dining-room.

During the dinner hour, and all the evening, in fact,
Zarina seemed to be the one bit of social brightness.
The general gloom, so depressing to her companions,
seemed but to raise her spirits. She succeeded in making the dull evening bearable to Legrand, who was feeling rather ill, as he remarked to Lady Clifford.

Legrand retired to his room a few minutes after nine
o'clock, and Lady Clifford soon followed his example.

Having given her maid permission to attend a card-
party in the servants' department below stairs, Zarina
was free to keep her appointment with the count at ten.

Hastily donning a walking suit, she descended the
stairs. A semi-darkness reigned, that part of the building being closed for the night. Unfastening one of the
drawing-room windows, she stepped lightly down on
the wet grass beneath. It had ceased to rain. Through
the swift-moving clouds the moon appeared dimly at
times. Sounds innumerable mingled confusedly. Ever
and anon the glossy, green, impearled leaves sent
forth myriads of coruscations, as Luna—eternal spirit
of the night—transformed the wet drops upon the swaying branches into orient pearls. Such are human hopes;
pleasing to fancy, but dispersed, alas! by a touch of reality; gifted with the sparkle of the diamond without its
solidity.

Zarina found Count LaCroix and a priest awaiting her in the arbor.

After a whispered consultation, the marriage ceremony was duly performed—Zarina being ignorant of the legal requirements in such cases. The good father then blessed the newly wedded pair, and took his leave.

Standing in the cold, wet arbor, the count and countess planned for the future. They schemed well—ah, yes, so have others. To scheme is one thing, to succeed another.

Zarina's parting injunction was : " I have fulfilled my part of the compact, see that you now fulfill yours."

" I start for Switzerland at five o'clock in the morning. Remember that three months will be the utmost limit of my patience. At the expiration of that time, I shall return and claim my countess, cost what it may."

" Three months is all the time I ask, prince of my soul," said she, and with a fervid embrace they finally separated.

Silently as a floating mist, Zarina made her way to the suite of apartments occupied by Legrand, after first entering her own, however, and exchanging her dress and walking-boots for gown and slippers.

Upon reaching his bedside, she was somewhat startled at beholding the pallor of his face, which was certainly wetted by the dews of death.

Without expressing surprise at her presence at such an hour, he gaspingly ejaculated :

"Oh, how glad I am to see you ! I tried to ring the bell, but was too weak to rise. I am feeling very strange. Oh, Zarina ! Zarina ! I fear 'tis death ! Awaken

Lady Clifford, and send for a priest! I must confess!
I cannot go hence with such a burden! Believe me,
you will be far happier so. My snug little fortune will
be amply sufficient for you and your child—*our child.*
I will not forget that, Zarina, but will lay all the blame
where it rightly belongs—upon myself. Depend upon
it, Lady Clifford will be kind to you, and forgiving to
me, or at least to my memory, for naught prevails against
dead, insensate clay."

"You are frightened, monsieur," said Zarina, reassuringly, feeling his pulse, while kneeling at the bedside, and pressing her red lips to his cold and ashy ones.
"You foolish man, you," she continued, "to mistake the
effects of a chill for death! It is only a chill, monsieur,
I assure you."

"No, no, child; I have no time to waste! The elev-
enth hour is almost past!" cried the man, with an impatient gesture.

"Is that the limit of God's mercy, Pierre?"

"I cannot say—it is fearful to think of," he gasped.

"You are frightened, monsieur, only frightened."
She gently raised his head upon her arm.

"A priest! a priest! 'Tis verging on the hour of
twelve. I tell you, no; 'tis death! 'tis death!" shrieked
Legrand, looking wildly around the room, as she raised
him to a sitting posture. "Don't let them take me,
Zarina!" he continued, piteously; "I must confess, and
be absolved. O, that they were here! Send for them!
send now!" motioning her away.

"Do you really want to see her ladyship at this un-
seemly hour? Believe me, monsieur, you will deeply

regret this night's occurrence, when the effects of the chill have worn off," hazarded Zarina, who was bent on gaining time. "'Tis a burning shame," continued she, "that your glorious prospects, and my promising hopes, also, should be nipped in the bud, and for ever blasted before their fruition, and all for a mere whim. Only think of it, and awaken to reason and judgment, monsieur!"

Not waiting for Legrand to reply, she resumed, while seating herself in an easy chair, "It now lacks but five minutes to twelve o'clock; if you are not better by two, I shall awaken Lady Clifford and send for the priest."

"Oh *God!* GOD! GOD!" cried Legrand, beating the air with his clenched hands, "Must I die like a dog?"

"You are howling like a dog, monsieur," she replied, having a supreme contempt for the man's cowardice.

He cast upon her an awful look, then fell back, turned his face to the wall, and was silent.

When he had thus remained for some ten minutes, Zarina was surprised, upon approaching the bed, to hear him say—

"The clock struck two. Go tell her ladyship, there's not a moment to lose. Begone, I say! Do you hear me?" pointing towards the door.

"Seeing that his quietus was coming shortly she bent over him and coldly replied: "Certainly, I hear, but can you expect me to obey? You remember telling me, perhaps, that life was nothing more than a game of chess. Because you are check-mated, must I, forsooth, give up the game? Not so, my liege; for, by my soul!

the board never gave gréater promise. My aim is to win; and in the presence or absence of him who first directed, I shall not only win the game, but also, my opponent. In looking over the Book which you say that your mother prized so highly, I found this sentence: 'With what measure ye mete, it shall be measured to you again.' Now, I presume, that that is what you would call a demonstrated fact. 'Train up a child in the way he should go: and when he is old he will not depart from it,' another motto to which you have given the lie, the truth of which I intend to demonstrate also to you, who are so fond of Scriptural quotations." So saying, without another glance, she turned and quietly left the room, closing the door on her way out and once again entered her own apartments. Did she then seek her pillow — and pleasant dreams? Perhaps. Nero's fiddling was, after all, but a slight exponent of the infinite cruelty of human nature.

CHAPTER XXV

THERE are lives which know nothing but sunshine and calm, and others which are tempest-tossed from the cradle to the grave. Differences of character partly account for it, but the variable, moody winds of chance, which blow where they list, are chiefly responsible for the strange contrasts in human destinies. The gambler does well in worshipping the shadowy power he calls Luck, but he does better when he recognizes system in the operations of his deity, and best when he circumvents it altogether with loaded dice and marked cards.

Is there really a law of chance — a design in the promiscuous, hap-hazard tumbling of human dice on the board of time? Is there a sublime, though unseen sympathy, between the honey-moon tourist who has his legs cut off in a railway accident and the beggar who falls heir to a fortune? Men can never attain a god-like patience under adversity until they recognize special providences in the ordering of individual fates, or come to regard themselves impersonally as the dancing-motes in the broad sunbeams of law and love. It is doubtless true, however, that the mind of God not only regards general results, but individual cases, for the Book has said that the very hairs of our head are numbered; that not a sparrow falls unnoticed to the earth,

Through the whole doctrine of the Galilean runs the golden scheme of compensation. It is the glowing text of the Sermon on the Mount — the inspiration of those Beatitudes which hover like angels in our darkened air!

To Echo, struggling with adverse fortunes, there came, not only the consolations of a religious spirit, but she found in the very necessity of mental and physical labor a relief from the cares and sorrows that oppressed her young heart. Whatever relation labor may have borne to the ideal man in the Garden, the world, as at present constituted, owes a debt of eternal gratitude to the tree of knowledge and the daring curiosity of Eve.

"Look, Eto!" cried the voice of Wistit to our heroine, who was preparing luncheon, "the sun is runnin' 'way from the cryin' clouds. Oughten they to be ashamed of themselves?"

"Which," asked Echo, merrily, "the sun or the clouds?"

"Why, the naughty black clouds o' course," answered the child, with an emphatic nodding of her little head.

"Ah, I see. But you must understand, Wistit, that there is a vast difference between 'crying clouds' and crying little girls. Little girls spoil their faces and their frocks, and annoy their parents and friends by crying; but when the clouds cry, the earth is glad, and the grass lifts up its tiny green fingers and catches the shining tears. See," continued Echo, walking to the window and pointing to some potted plants, "how clean and sweet the flowers look after their nice bath!"

"The Chinamans might wash 'em," said Wistit, still discrediting the labors of the clouds. Then lifting up her face, illumined by an idea, she asked: "Them is clean enough for Sunday School, but 'em can't sing!"

"Indeed they can, my love. Their beauty is an ineffably sweet song in praise of the living God," said Echo, rather grandiloquently, considering her auditory.

Wistit was one of those pert children who are always bristling with unexpected questions and answers. As an instance, some itinerant divine who had been invited to address the Sunday School she attended, closed a long disquisition on the subject of Balaam and the speaking ass, by asking, "To whom, then did the beast speak?"

There was a dramatic pause of a few minutes, then the lisping voice of Wistit arose in answer —

"To the Sunday School!"

Upon calling at the home of two of her first and most influential pupils on the afternoon of the same day, Echo was met by their mother, who rather reluctantly imparted the somewhat startling, because totally unexpected, information that she thought best to dispense with her services.

"It seemed to me that your daughters were progressing finely" remarked Echo. "May I ask in what particular I have failed to meet your requirements?"

"As a teacher," replied the lady, "I must say that you have given entire satisfaction; in fact, both husband and myself were highly gratified at the progress they were making."

"If so, justice to myself forces me to demand of you, dear madam, the true cause of my dismissal," said Echo, with quiet dignity.

The lady's eyes fell beneath Echo's inquiring glance, while her face flushed slightly, as she arose and, in evident embarrassment, replied —

"You are very attractive, and my daughters young and impressible; I — in short, I have been told that your reputation is not of the best."

"The name of your informant?" rather calmly demanded Echo, though trembling slightly, and trying hard to keep the gathering tears from falling.

"I — I — in fact, it is generally so reported."

"By whom, when, and where?"

"By the members of our Church, upon whose pastor's recommendation I employed you as the instructress of my daughters. You must excuse me as I have some pressing duties which require immediate attention."

"I shall detain you but a moment," returned Echo, at the same time making an involuntary but peremptory motion with her hand, "and in the name of Him whose teaching you profess to follow, I insist that you shall be more specific and particularize some person or persons who have dared to blacken my reputation. Though only a music teacher, the good God has seen fit to temper my feelings as finely as yours, perhaps, and my good name is equally as dear, if not more so, knowing that my own food and that of others dearer than myself depends upon its vindication."

"I have said all that I intend to say upon the subject, as I do not wish my name mixed up with such affairs. I know not the truth or falsity of such reports and have had no hand in their circulation." Then, touched by sudden sympathy, she feelingly added: "Forgive me if I have wronged you, poor child, and let the love I bear my daughters be my excuse."

Echo flushed angrily as she replied, "The vilest criminal in the land is not declared guilty till the charges are proven against him, and yet you, one of my own sex, have not only refused to give the name of my traducers, but have also asserted your belief in my guilt by condemning me unheard, and you are, moreover, doing all which lies in your power to deprive me of earning an honest living by a sudden and unexpected dismissal. My plea is not for mercy, but for stern, keen-eyed justice only, in whose name I command, and, as a woman, implore you to give the names of those who have wantonly vilified a poor orphan. I would also crave a suspension of judgment till you have had time to ascertain the truth or falsity of these cruel reports."

Echo had risen, and was now standing directly opposite the woman. Her face flushed and paled by turns. Tears dimmed the luster of her soulful eyes, and brimming over, rolled unheeded down her softly rounded cheeks. Her finely curved lips, scarlet and tremulous, were expressive of deep emotion. A stray sunbeam gleaming through a crevice in the window-blind softly touched the gold-tinted crispy mass of hair which was gathered into a single plait, doubled and secured by a blue ribbon. Unconsciously her arms were slightly extended and her raised hands clasped together.

Noting her beauty, which was extremely striking to-day, Mrs. James' heart hardened as she called to mind the conversation that the Misses Richard chanced to overhear, and, moreover, there flashed into her mind the remembrance that upon a certain occasion, she had heard her eldest son express warm admiration for this same girl, and she sullenly replied—

"Your importunity forces me again to reiterate that I have nothing more to say," ending with a freezing inclination of the head.

Though secure in wealth and position and standing in the midst of her opulent surroundings, this woman fairly shrunk from the indignant blaze in Echo's eyes as she would have shrunk from the flame of a furnace, as, after a slight pause, she returned, "Pray excuse me; I mistook you at least for a benevolent lady, if not a Christian;" and, with a bow as cold as the lady's own, she made her exit with such grace and stateliness that this woman, though possessing all things which money could buy, envied the fair queen of poverty whose own shapely hands earned her daily subsistence.

CHAPTER XXVI

IN almost every community there are persons whose power of discernment is a very spear of Ithuriel in turning one's weak sides uppermost and tracing out the latent faults of character. While it may be well for each individual to recognize his peculiar frailties and study to overcome them, it will not do for them to become common property; and the sharp-beaked vultures, therefore, are known principally as nuisances in society, and some day there will be a determined movement to abate them.

Scarcely had Echo left the house on her regular round of duty, when Aunt Newbury received a call — of course it was a business call — from a coarse, ignorant, officious and pungent-flavored woman who had the scent of a blood-hound for the slightest taint in the social atmosphere. Skilled in the domestic art of making "preserves," her taste naturally ran to acids instead of sweets, and she generally managed to leave people's affairs in a pretty pickle.

As Wistit ushered in this sharp-nosed assayer of moral ore, the nurse winced inwardly and braced her nerves for an affliction.

The pleasant visitor, eyes and mouth extended and hands upraised, sank into a chair with the exclamation: "Bless my stars! if ye ai'nt a sittin' up! Heerin' you'd hed a mighty bad spell of rheumatiz, sister Newbury, and seein' its our bounden duty to visit the sick, I thought I'd just drop in a speck." During this elaborate prologue, the round, black eyes of the speaker had wandered keenly over the room and its furniture, searching for a speck or a flaw.

" Very kind of you, indeed, sister Ferret," said the nurse, dryly.

" Well, ye air a lookin' perter than I expected, for I tell ye that rheumatics has a powerful effect in tuckerin' out people. Howsumever yer spell couldn't hev been a carcumstance to a spell that tackled my Sally Ann nigh onto five years back. How that poor critter did suffer was a caution. I tell ye what, sister Newbury, it takes a 'mazen lot of grace to set up and chirp under some tribulous dispensations. Howsumever, there's no other way to carcumvent contrary carcumstances. But how might ye be feelin' bout " —

" Better, much better, thank you," hastily said the nurse.

" Wal, I reckon ye know who to thank — it aint me to besure. We had a monstrous edifying meetin' last night, sister Newbury; the parson he peppered them as needed et, an' sugared them as wouldn't be peppered, an' atween the two he did every soul uv 'em a 'mazen power o' good. 'Peared like every one had a blessed chance of enterin' the Kingdom to onst, but, awful to think uv! some uns missed et — some uns missed et! Pears as if some souls were powerful stubborn like, an' can't be driv or coaxed nigh onto the Marcy Seat. Seems like the green pastures, likewise still waters, hasn't no charms for 'em. They'd rather go grovellin' roun' on the outside whar they can allers git somethin' more sterrin' like then still waters, and some does say as how Nebuchadnezzar warnt a very enticin' example to pasturin' folks."

Aunt Newbury sighed gently, but said not a word.

"Wal, I spose I'd better be mozyin' along, only I was a goin' to ax you 'bout them cumbrous tales as has been goin' roun' bout yer little gimp of a sister."

"Tales! my sister! what in the name of Heaven can you mean?" said the nurse excitedly.

The visitor brightened visibly at the consternation she had caused, as she replied: "Wal, they do say as how she's one o' them whose feet take hold onto hell."

"What! How dare you, wretched old scandal-monger that you are, to pollute the air of this room with your second-hand lies?" The nurse was in a blaze of anger and quivered like an aspen leaf, while her fingers twitched dangerously.

"My stars! sister Newbury, don't go and git so obstropulous! Yer hadn't ought to blame me; 'twasn't me as done et. I've heern it ever since that doin's at the church, and thars them that makes no bones of tellin' et. My Sally Ann sez that brother Cason has got Helena Hoffman to go and take Echo's place in the choir. They hed a mighty-tighty time about it I can tell ye. Sister Johnson shed tears over the depravity of one that wuz so 'mazen clever. Sister Morgan got up and said she'd been a tellin' them that all along. And then sister Burress told them thet the old sarpent hisself sometimes appeared as an angel of light."

The nurse started up in a fury. "Not another word! What care I for the carrion vomit of those vultures? Off! I say? Get out of that door in an instant or I will hurl you out?"

The old wretch did get out of the door, in a hurry, too, but she halted on the step to leave this Parthian shot: "'Pears to me where there's so much smoke there must be some fire."

At the closing of the street door, the angry flush faded from the nurse's face, and the blaze in her eyes was drowned in tears, as she sank back on the chair in which she was seated, bowed her face in her hands, and wept long and passionately.

Echo returned about six o'clock, fatigued by her long walk, and very much depressed in spirit. Inward gloom overshadowed her expressive face, a circumstance which the experienced eyes of the nurse noted instantly; so, after the first kindly greeting, she said, feelingly, at the same time opening her arms —

"Come, Echo, share with me, you and I are partners you know. Then why cheat your poor old nurse by striving to withhold her share?"

As those arms closed around her, Echo's head sank on their owner's motherly bosom and wept unreservedly.

"Poor, tired darling! Do not weep so bitterly, child, but calm yourself and tell sister what has happened," said the nurse, tenderly, stroking her hair.

"I cannot tell about it just yet," sobbed Echo. Then, for the first time since her entrance, she remarked the pallor upon the nurse's face. Starting up, she exclaimed,

"You are worse.   Forgive my selfishness; you shall lie down and rest while I make you a cup of strong tea."

Before retiring for the night, Echo, sitting on a chair by the nurse's bedside, composedly related the loss of her two pupils, also, the conversation held with their mother, all of which it would be useless to repeat. "Then," added she, the three other scholars which I instructed were cross and dull.   Moreover, as I was ascending our front steps, two young men were passing, and I accidentally overheard one of them say to his companion, 'There goes the girl with whom Ainsley had an amour; he showed me the house to'— Just then Wistit sprang out of the door, and I lost the rest."

"I, too, had a visitation; it came in the person of old Mrs. Ferret," remarked the nurse as Echo paused.

"Was that all?" smilingly asked Echo.

"Was not that sufficient?" said the nurse, with a grimace of pain.

"Ah, truly."

CHAPTER XXVII.

URING the afternoon of the next day, Echo remarked to the nurse: "I forgot to tell you that I met our chorister, Mr. Cason, yesterday, and that his bow appeared stiff and his manner very cold and distant. Do you think him displeased because I have not attended lately?"

"I'm sure he must have heard of my illness, and if that was not a sufficient excuse for your absence, I do not know what would be so considered," returned the nurse, rather tartly. "Do you really enjoy singing in the choir, Echo?" asked she, moved by an afterthought.

"Yes, indeed; there is no doubt of that. Why, sister," she added, with slight enthusiasm, "I verily believe that there are those in our choir possessed of musical talent which will eventually develop into excellence of the highest order."

Aunt Newbury sighed heavily.

Echo looked up quickly: "But why that sigh and elongation of countenance, sister? There is, seemingly, more in your question than would appear on the surface."

"Has it never occurred to you, Echo, that—that the loss of your scholars dated from that public entertainment given by the Church, in which you participated?

Even before my sickness, I noticed a certain suspicious stiffening of manners and a lessening of sociality. In truth, I strongly suspect that villain, Ainsley, of maliciously putting into circulation, that very night, false reports concerning your past history."

"Oh, sister, they will not believe any great evil of me, surely," cried Echo, with emotion. "The members of the choir, especially, have known me for a year and more; will not my conduct, during that time, weigh something against the word of a man like Edmond Ainsley, even though he had made his charges openly ?"

"It seems not," answered Aunt Newbury, sorrowfully, hesitating like one who dreads to give pain.

"You have heard—you know something that you have not told me yet ?" said Echo, impetuously, with an imploring look towards the other. "Do not keep me in suspense, I pray you, sister ! Never fear, I shall find strength to bear it—as I have already borne many sorrows—with an added pain here, perhaps," putting her hand on her heart, "and a blackening and lengthening of life's shadows."

"Take courage, my poor child; these evil days will pass, and the sun will come out from behind the cloud that now obscures it ?"

"I don't know, sister; I am afraid Mr. Darwin is correct about the evolution of species, and that I, having been delayed somehow, am still of the reptilian order," said Echo, with a plaintive smile, continuing—"at any rate, it would seem so from the manner in which I am continually trodden upon and bruised."

"Tush, tush, child ! the idea is far-fetched !" responded the nurse. "You have a musical soul, which, according to Plato, once existed in the breast of a pure little nightingale. That will account for the swooping of the hawks, perhaps, which, though changing their forms somewhat, yet retain their former rapacity; also the tongue, which is said to be cloven, a mark satanic, and, by the way, accounts for their double-dealings."

"Though," said Echo, brightening a little, "I mean to live a pure life, and am also constrained to plead guilty of loving music to excess, yet my ambition soars higher than that of Plotinous, for I desire that my poor soul shall transmigrate into a life more satisfying than bird-life, however harmonious. But," here the faultless mouth drooped, the pained expression returned to the mistily luminous eyes, while a sad weariness stole into and thrilled along the chords of her magnetic voice, "why dream away the present theorizing on the past or future, when that great problem 'Now' is unsolved ? Deliver up my burden, I conjure you, sister; it is, after all, doubtless made heavier by anticipation."

"Perhaps," assented the nurse, her manner becoming constrained through sympathy. "Yesterday plague number one had scarcely disappeared, till plague number two appeared in the form of a little white envelope. It was simply addressed to Miss Newbury, and I, for the moment, forgetting that there were two bearing that title, opened it, of course." Reluctantly producing the little white missive from the depth of her pocket, and handing it to Echo, she turned her eyes, in which tears were gathering, away.

Echo accepted the missive without a word, took the paper from the envelope, and read :

CITY, Thursday evening, September 14, 187-.

MISS NEWBURY :

We, the choir of the —————— church, take this method of informing you that your services are no longer acceptable.

WM. SMITHE,
By order of the Choir.

The warm blood suffused the fair face of the reader for an instant, and as quickly receded. The paper dropped from her hand, and while giving one quick gasp as for breath, she fainted away.

CHAPTER XXVIII.

B Y the sudden and secret departure of Echo and the nurse from the gilded den of Madame Joilet, Edmond Ainsley was given the cue for the practice of a little deception towards his mother.

The good lady was easily made to believe that the governess had died of her malady.

A few months afterwards, Mrs. Ainsley returned to her old home in Quebec.

Upon the morning following her arrival, young Dr. Hoberg was sent for, and promptly came.

Lady Ainsley ended a long list of pains, aches and grievances, with the following startling question :

"Was n't it dreadful for Echo to die and leave me alone among strangers ?"

After the first violent start, her listener, who was in the act of writing a prescription, sat, pencil poised in hand, completely shocked into silence by the terrible news. Thus he sat, as if confounded, for a moment, then spoke—his words slow, short, and tottering as the steps of a child in its first effort to walk.

"Dead ! — Echo — dead ! Surely not ! Unsay that cruel word."

"No, indeed, doctor, I shall do no such a thing. She took suddenly ill, afterwards went to her room well, as it were, and in the morning was found in a raging fever."

"O, that I had known! Found, did you say? sick, and alone! Poor love! sweet love!" Then, starting up—"Made she no request? Was I entirely forgotten?"

"Request? Perhaps she did. I do not know, I'm sure; you see that the fever was infectious, and Edmond had her taken right away to—"

"Hear, O ye devils, and wonder at human heartlessness! Sacrificed, by heavens! Poor lamb! poor little lamb! Thrust out to die alone and unattended! Oh, Echo! Echo! would to God we had never parted!"

Lady Ainsley answered, peevishly:

"Dr. Hoberg, I mistook you for a man of feeling. Your manner, no less than your words, shocks one like a galvanic battery. You, of all others, ought to be more considerate of my feebleness. I did not say that she was unattended; on the contrary, Edmond, my son, had her taken to a nice hospital, which took good care of her, I presume."

Lady Ainsley's "Edmond, *my son*," was a compound of pride, ownership and reverence.

"Presume! Oh, God! presumption, in a case like that!" exclaimed Hoberg, bitterly. "You should have been positive, madam, positive. But why waste words? The care of her remains shall, at least, not be denied me. You can surely tell me the name of the hospital, which, you say, cared for her?" pursued he, producing a note-book.

"You must go to Edmond, my son, for anything

further. I have already told you all I know about it. You weary me to death. Your words fall upon my poor, sensitive nerves, like hail-stones, crushing my remnant of strength entirely;" and the lady was nearly in tears.

" Would that they could crush out your selfishness, instead," inwardly commented Hoberg, as he strode to the door, opened it, and departed without a word of leave-taking.

Hoberg's pain was now acute. He had entered the house but a short time before, with a mind full of confusion, or what the poets call " a sweet distress," a state of feeling produced by a sort of compound emotion; that is to say, the thought of meeting the object of his affection was a very pleasing thought, allied to the supposition that she was lost to him, which was in itself extremely distressing. Underlying all, perhaps, there had been a faint hope that Echo's heart would return to its old allegiance. Hoberg had prospered professionally, that is to say, financially. A wealthy patient, dying, had left him a small legacy of ten thousand dollars. Consequently, he was now sole possessor of the cottage which Echo had once so desired. Everything, even the furnishing, had been completed according to her wishes.

On leaving Mrs. Ainsley, Hoberg had walked but a short distance, when, upon turning a corner, he ran against a man who was coming up the street. His polite " Excuse me, sir," was interrupted by—" Hello ! Hoberg, as I live ! How do, old boy ? - Which way, so fast ?" It was Edmond Ainsley.

"The one, above all others, that I most desired to see,"
exclaimed Hoberg, not noticing Ainsley's extended hand,
however. "Where have you laid her?"

With uplifted brows, and a shrug of the shoulders,
Ainsley exclaimed:

"Aha! laid her! laid who? Hey, I see—been to a
wine party last night, not entirely recovered. Take my
arm, old boy; let me assist you home. 'Twon't do to
be seen by your pious friends in such a plight as this."

In truth, Ainsley was not to blame for coming to just
such a conclusion as he affected. There was a sort of
stupidity in Hoberg's manner, and his gait was unsteady,
his voice thick and guttural, his head bent forward, and
his hat pulled down over his contracted brows.

Without giving a thought to Ainsley's somewhat natural mistake, but with rather more dignity, he said, in
explanation, "'Twas but a few moments ago that I first
heard of Miss Clifford's death. Mrs. Ainsley referred
me to you for all information on the subject." Once
again taking out note-book and pencil, he added, "I wish
the address of the hospital in which you placed her, also
the name of the attending physician, and the place of
her burial. I shall have her remains disinterred and
brought home."

Here was a dilemma for which Ainsley was totally
unprepared, a Gordian Knot which plainly required a
coup d'etat. He saw at a glance that to pursuade him
from his intentions would be useless. On the other hand,
should Hoberg go to San Francisco, there was a slight
chance of his meeting Echo and thereby becoming cog-
nizant of his, (Ainsley's), villainy. To withhold the

name of the hospital would look suspicious, and be apt
to lead to an unpleasant investigation which it was
plainly his interest to avoid. It was his intention to return to the Pacific Coast and "bring down the game,"
as he styled his malicious persecution of Echo. He had
known Hoberg from boyhood, and was perfectly well
aware that he was unable to cope with him in anything
but cunning; therefore, his *modus operandi* must needs
be bold and crafty. But, aggravation! of aggravations!
a body must be produced! that was the pivot which was
most likely to turn the balance wheel of future events.
Vice has but one halting place. Its roots reach down to
hell; and those that start thereon, like boys coasting on
a steep hill-side, though intending to go but part way,
perhaps, eventually find themselves at the bottom.

"The name of the hospital," demanded Hoberg, with
testiness, "or," here a horrible suspicion flashed across
his mind, "perhaps you sent her to the city hospital?"

"Nonsense!" broke in Ainsley. "My memory is not
as good as yours. The name has escaped me for the
moment, and as it is my intention to return to 'Frisco'
in a few days, I will have the corpse disinterred and sent
to you, thereby saving you both time and money."

"Pray, what is time or money to me now?" fiercely
demanded Hoberg. "I shall leave my patients in
charge of a brother practitioner, and to-morrow morning will find me on the way to San Francisco."

Ainsley was disconcerted, but he said, with apparent
unconcern, "If you are determined to start on your
quixotic journey to-morrow morning, I shall accompany
you and render you all the assistance in my power—

though my advice would be to let the dead rest in peace."

"I am much obliged, Ainsley, for your offer," responded Hoberg, "but all I ask of you is to furnish the address of the hospital and the place of her burial. I am perfectly competent to attend to everything. Besides, Mrs. Ainsley requires your attention at home."

I've already told you that I intended returning to 'Frisco;' a day or two sooner or later makes no difference to me. You will find me ready and waiting for you at the depot in the morning. The matter is settled, so there is no possible use of further dilly-dallying. As your time for preparation is limited, allow me to say good-bye for the present," saying which, he turned and walked rapidly away.

Shortly afterwards Ainsley entered a telegraph office and sent the following dispatch:

QUEBEC, CANADA, October 17th, 18—.

DAN VINTON, 310 —— St.,

San Francisco, California:

I start for 'Frisco' to-morrow. Rent a nicely furnished house in a respectable neighborhood and hold till I come. Answer.

AINSLEY.

In the course of a few hours he received a telegram announcing that a suitable house had been secured,

OBERG and Ainsley arrived safely at their place of destination. Their long and hurried journey was fatiguing and monotonous, unrelieved by the slightest episode of interest. During all the time, Hoberg had spoken only when it was absolutely necessary. Ainsley's levity must have grated harshly upon his state of feeling, but after that first outbreak, he had shielded himself in impenetrable reserve. Though inly grieving, he was outwardly serene.

The dual quality of human existence is too evident to admit of dispute. Mankind lead a twofold life, and are always better or worse than they seem, and therefore the inner capabilities and slumbering probabilities, like the gold in the mine, are sometimes brought to the surface by laborious effort or by sudden upheaval. Daily some struggling one, just on the verge of the under-world, perhaps, awakens to the possibilities within, and discovers his true self, much to the surprise of old acquaintances.

"Oh, pshaw? that can't be our Tom? Impossible? Why, I've known him quite intimately ever since he was born, and never discovered anything remarkable about him!"

And, may be, should "Tom," himself, speak the truth

upon his first great achievement, his sentiments would differ nowise from those of his friend. Though it may be well, on the one hand, to freely turn the tap of our being and let the inner stream of sweetness and brightness flow, yet on the other, to those who are inly evil and whose safety lies in suppression, the experiment is dangerous in the extreme. Nurtured in the lap of luxury, Ainsley had heretofore restrained himself from turning the tap fully, so the slow droppings from his "inner consciousness," when noticed, had been kindly characterized as "youthful indiscretions," whose proper corrector was Time. It is also noticeable that though the "youthful indiscretions" of the rich are left to the gentle ameliorations of Father Time, reformative schools, prisons and penitentiaries are the usual correctors of those who have not the cunning to evade or money to pervert the law.

"Half past nine o'clock," remarked Ainsley to Hoberg, when crossing the bay of San Francisco. "It is too late to attend to the matter in hand this evening. We will stop at the 'Grand,' retire early and be ready for business in the morning."

Securing rooms at the Grand Hotel, Hoberg immediately retired to rest. Ainsley left the house soon afterward, and hailed a passing hack, which, under direction, bore him to No. —, Broadway street. Leaving the carriage, Ainsley entered a brilliantly lighted saloon. Upon exchanging certain cabalastic signs and pass-words with one of the attendants, he was ushered into an elegantly furnished back room. Writing his name upon a card he handed it to the polite waiter, saying, "Give this to Vinton and say that I await him here."

Some twenty minutes elapsed before Mr. Vinton entered the apartment.

"How do, Ainsley?" was his salutation, while advancing with extended hand which Ainsley shook heartily. "Glad to see you, boy!"

"Same fix myself, Dan, extremely glad. I'm completely badgered, by Jove! Forced to walk obliquely, as it were, pushed aside from my straight and narrow course. In fact, I've a friend who must be *hocus-pocused.* Hobson's choice you know — no possible alternative! You received that telegram?"

"Of course; and did as you requested. Its all right, so far, old boy," said Vinton, jovially, clapping him upon the shoulder."

"Well, not to elongate, there was a young girl who accompanied Mrs. Ainsley to this coast as a companion, leaving behind a betrothed lover in Canada. Now this girl and I took to each other as ducks take to water," winking at Vinton, who nodded understandingly, and both laughed noisily. "There are hearts which bill and coo without priestly sanction," continued Ainsley. "Of course the affair must needs be kept from Mrs. Ainsley, so, when the girl was smitten with a fever, I had her removed to a hospital and taken care of; but my mother returned home while laboring under the impression that the girl was dead, and so informed the fiery young lover, who called immediately. Well, what did this Don Quixote of a lover do but demand the name and address of her attending physician, saying that he should re-

10

move the body to Canada! By Jove! Dan, its a fix!"

"The lover, in question, is a doctor by profession, the son of a minister, who is an old acquaintance of my mother. As money is no object," pursued he, after a moment's hesitation, "I thought I would get you to manage the affair. You can easily arrange about the hospital business. Give him the name of some doctor who has left the city, or 'fix' one for his benefit. The procuring of a proper body is the straw which seems most likely to break the camel's back."

Ainsley paused. With keen, half-shut eyes concentrated on the main chance, as it were, Vinton sat before him expectantly, his head thrown well back. At the mention of money, both hands opened involuntarily.

"Risky business, Ainsley; for which you say that money is no object — an indefinite expression. Give us an offer."

"A thousand?" said Ainsley, twisting his mustache, nervously.

Vinton shook his head.

"Two thousand?"

Vinton brushed the ashes from his cigar with a dexterous movement of his little finger, and shook his head again.

"Name your price, then," said Ainsley.

Vinton leisurely blew a wreath of smoke into the air, and began to muse, with a look of pious concern. "It's a tough business, perhaps a dangerous business, seeing that I must take your word for the real status of the intrigue," he said, slowly, "and the man that mixes in it must be well paid. The judgment of the court is, therefore, Ainsley, that five thousand dollars from a man in your circumstances will about cover the time, trouble and risk of the undertaking."

Ainsley helped himself to a glass of brandy from the decanter that stood on the table between them, and then replied —

"Five thousand! by Jove, Dan, you would have done credit to yourself in the Claude Duval business! Isn't five thousand rather cool, rather steep?"

"Just a trifle frigid and declivitous, old man, but business is business, the world over, and I am deucedly hard up these days. You wouldn't come to me with a *bagatelle*—of that I am assured. Come, shall it be five thousand and a clean job?"

"I have no other recourse, you Richelieu of finance!"

Then the two friends held a long consultation on the ways and means of their projected villainy, and the streets were almost deserted when Ainsley finally separated from the other and sought his hotel.

CHAPTER XXX.

EFORE the events last narrated had occurred, additional misfortunes had befallen our heroine. Why is it that some of our great modern thinkers do not explain the gregarious character of calamities? A full knowledge of the law would undoubtedly be of inestimable service to mankind. How many old sayings turn upon this pivot of the world's faith! The poets are full of beautiful references to it, as the following from "Hiawatha:"

"Never stoops the soaring vulture
On his quarry on the desert,
On the sick or wounded bison,
But another vulture, watching
From his high aerial look-out,
Sees the downward plunge and follows;
And a third pursues the second,
Coming from the invisible ether,
First a speck, and then a vulture,
Till the air is dark with pinions.
So disasters come not singly;
But as if they watched and waited,
Scanning one another's motions.
When the first descends, the others
Follow, follow, gathering flockwise
Round their victim, sick and wounded,
First a shadow, then a sorrow,
Till the air is dark with anguish."

Aunt Newbury had suffered a relapse, and little Wistit had been stricken with a fatal disease.

It was a glorious night for the passage of the pure, young spirit. The rays from the brilliant luminaries swimming in the vault of space kindled the clear, California atmosphere almost as resplendently as the beams of the noonday sun — and yet it was a strange, sweet light — as still, shadowless and mysterious as the patient smile of God upon the populous immensity of His Kingdom.

Sunshine and shadow chase each other around the arena of life, and the heavy footsteps of sorrow trample upon the golden skirts of fleeting pleasures. The joy-bells hung within the chambers of the heart scarce ring their welcome to some new-found love, till a sob of bereavement rises in their music, and the shadow of the grave falls across the still threshold of the soul.

The noise and bustle of the busy world without had ceased to mar the solemn stillness. The softened splendor of the star-light had crept through the apartment and given to the modest interior a dreamy peacefulness, as lovely as the sacred reveries it inspired.

Wistit was still sleeping. One tiny hand, so soft and white now that a snowflake might have marred its delicate purity, lay grasping the counterpane. The tender eyes were closed. There was a faint smile seated upon the gentle mouth which told that sleep had brought freedom from pain.

Echo, gazing fondly upon her perishing waif, parted the damp curls from her waxen brow and kissed it softly, while tears of anguish coursed their way down her pale cheeks. Then, going to the window, she stretched out her arms towards heaven as if, groping in the darkness of uncertainty, she longed to grasp "the substance of things hoped for, the evidence of things not seen;" and gazing upward, as if her love could pierce the misty curtain of ethereal blue and compel an answer, from the depths of her stricken soul arose a silent prayer, more eloquent than words can frame. It was the burning call of the subject spirit to the Sovereign for help when the sea of shadows rises to clasp the poor feet faltering upon the rocks of despair.

The silvery tones of the little time-piece chimed out the hour of twelve, and still Echo kept her watch beside the couch of her dear one, whilst the nervous clasping and unclasping of her hands, and the flames of anguish illumining her dark eyes, betrayed something of her soul's struggle.

The damp of death slowly gathered upon the brow of the sleeper, as morning dew upon a withering lily, plucked by some careless hand and left to perish. Would the white-winged soul depart silently thus, and make no sign? Would those dear treasures — the last word, the last glance, the last kiss of the dying — not be vouchsafed to the darkened household?

The child's pulse was growing fainter. The dreadful paroxysms of pain were gone forever. The hectic flush was fading from her cheeks. The fever which had raged in her veins for many days was cooling rapidly under the icy breath of the slayer of humanity.

There was poignant, though suppressed, grief in that chamber — a sorrow more deep and true than that which

gives way to tears, groans and cries. Noisy sorrow is
more or less selfish and ephemeral; they suffer most
and longest whose hearts bleed in silence.

While Echo stood there, watching with silent dread
the parting of the spirit from its statue of painted clay,
the eyes of the sleeper suddenly opened wide with a
scared look, as turning them in the direction where her
protector had last been seen, she asked in a frightened
voice,

"Where is you, Eto?"

"Close beside you, darling," Echo replied as she knelt
beside the bed.

"I hear, but can't see, Eto. I'm afraid of the dark,
and it's very cold."

The groping hands felt fondly over Echo's face and
rested upon her neck as the shivering, pallid lips murmured faintly, "Hold me close, Eto; I'm so cold and the
big black cloud is coming nearer."

Then she was silent for a while. Suddenly, a beautiful smile broke over the pale, childish features, as, pointing outward and upward, she exclaimed in a voice of
rapture —

"Oh, Eto! look there! look there!"

"What is it, my sweet darling?" said Echo, stifling a
great sob; "I can see nothing."

"Look! Oh, how sweet and pretty! It is the beautiful country that mamma said I should come to by-and-
by—I can see it behind the cloud ! There are no clouds
there ! The gates are open, and they shine like the
moon when the sky is blue. I can hear the music and
see the happy children—and look ! you must surely see

her—there is mamma ! Oh, good-bye, Eto ! mamma is holding out her arms to me, and she is so pretty now ! Good-bye ! Wistit will wait for you at the gate !"

It was all over then ! The prison-gates of life were unlocked by the silent warden, Death, and the happy soul went forth, to feel the pain of death no more. The invisible spirit retired unspotted from the misty vales of time, and passed into the opening cloud of mystery for-ever.

Thank God, for these glimpses of the eternal world that shine before the feet of the dread messenger ! Thank God, for the beautiful " superstition " that wreathes these glowing visions on the brows of our dying children !

We will not unveil the sorrows of that sacred chamber any further. Years afterward, in a happier time, Echo twined this poetic garland for the little grave at Lone Mountain :

Softly the winds are sighing,
    On the mountain by the sea,
Where my Waif is lonely lying,
    Far away from love and me.

No costly marble, shining,
    Marks the sacred little spot,
Only a rose-bush twining
    'Mid the blue forget-me-not.

The dewy morning, weeping,
    Drops for me a trembling tear
Upon the rose-bush, keeping
    Its watch throughout the year.

The fairy moonbeams sparkle,
  And the pearly mists roll on;
The eddying rainbows darkle,
  And, like gleaming hopes, are gone.

But my heart still mourns her truly,
  And her angel wing, I know,
Fragrant from flowery Beulah,
  Beareth away my woe.

CHAPTER XXXI.

A WEEK had passed since the death of her little protege, and Echo was still in the depths of gloom. Aunt Newbury was slowly recovering, but still not a ray of hope lighted the music teacher's future. Oh, how short her praying breath was in those days—how stricken and dead her faith! Providence can crush the strongest of us so easily. The atmosphere that rings with the music and laughter of the happy, is heavy with the groans of broken spirits. The juggernaut of fate grinds some of us utterly in the dust, but the world goes on as merrily as ever without us. If we be Christians, our daily and nightly prayer must be for strength to bear the burdens that are cast upon us; if we be not Christians, we can only clench our teeth and die as the dumb brutes die. Some Minneapolis flouring mills were blown to atoms the other day, occasioning great loss of life, and the scientific people say that it resulted from the explosive quality of the impalpable powder of flour suspended in the air—that is to say, that an atmosphere impregnated with the best elements of life is suddenly aroused to hurl the terrific bolts of death. We are, everywhere and always, at the mercy of the mighty forces of nature. And yet we must not falter, even in the routine duties of life, but must find our relief from heart-sorrows in the labor that wins our bread.

But Echo's world had conspired to deprive her even of labor. The number of her pupils had fallen off to a very few, and the necessities of sickness had exhausted the money she had laid by for a rainy day. Surely the blackness of despair had fallen upon her now—that darkest hour, which is said to precede the day.

She had changed much of late. A strange pallor had succeeded the fresh glow of her complexion, and a deep shadow seemed to hover about her drooping eyes.

She sat at the window with a book in her lap, but she had no intention of reading. The book was simply that sort of silent company she would have preferred in her best friend. There are dark times when there is no solace in book or friend.

While thus sitting, her cheek resting upon her slender white hand, and gazing dreamily into the street, she was suddenly startled, so far away had been her thoughts, by the appearance of Mr. Farrish at the front steps. He lifted his hat, with a grave smile, at her sudden movement of surprise, and she arose to give him admittance. He took her hand in gentle greeting at the door, and held it for an instant as he looked into her face, and remarked its exceedingly sorrowful expression. He was completely overcome by his sympathies, and could not say a word as he took the chair she proffered him. At last, with a quiver of pathos in his rich voice, he said :

"I am afraid that you have been very unhappy, and very, very much in need of friendly offices. I have been out of the city for many days, and have just returned and learned of your loss."

The tears coursed silently down her faded cheeks as she answered :

"Yes, my friend, the Lord has seen fit to afflict me very sorely."

The strong man could restrain himself no longer at this, and bowed his head in his hands and wept. Both were in tears, and it was several minutes before another word was spoken.

Raising his head, finally, when he had sufficiently conquered his emotion, he said :

"Ah, my dear lady, you are so utterly alone, and your fortunes are so untoward ! Do let me have your confidence, and be your friend."

She could no longer hesitate, having seen the tenderness and truth of his nature, and thus responded :

"My sorrows have broken me sadly, but I know that I can trust you, and I will, therefore, confide to you the story of my life."

And so, while the mystic twilight was gathering in the apartment, she began at the beginning and told him all she knew concerning the events that had affected her life.

As the narrative progressed, it was apparent that Mr. Farrish was laboring under the strongest excitement, and when she had finished he rushed across the room and seized her hand, exclaiming :

"Let me salute you, then, by a stronger title than that of friend—I am the cousin of your father, and therefore a relative of yours ! Why, I was named after Cleave Clifford, and we attended the same school ! Bless my soul, what a happy discovery !

Echo was no less joyfully agitated than her new-found kinsman. A mysterious orphan, having never known any relative but her grandmother, there had always been in her heart a hungry yearning for the deep and indefinable sympathy of kindred blood. It is strangely true, as the old adage has it, that blood is thicker than water. The crimson currents of the heart flow intuitively in gulf-streams of eternal affection.

Therefore a bright flush mantled Echo's wasted cheeks, as she cried, enthusiastically :

"Oh, my friend, my kinsman, it is indeed a happy discovery ! It is more to me than the discovery of a continent. An oasis has appeared in the desert of my life, at last ! A golden anchor of hope has dropped to me from Heaven, and I shall be tempest-tossed no more !"

She wept again, for joy this time, and he tenderly kissed her forehead, and thanked God for the new blessing that had arisen in his prosperous life.

"Do you know, Echo, dear," he said, "that glowing vistas of joy open up before you now ? We will clear away the mystery that has shrouded your life—we will find your parents !"

She placed her hand on her heart, to still its wild throbbing.

"Oh, if we do, the crown of Elysium will be mine on earth ! And why may it not be ? We do not know that they are dead; and while some great calamity must have befallen them, it is possible that grandmother may have been deceived as to its true character, and that no dishonor really clouds their names."

"Yes, dear, you are right. Your grandmother, advanced in years and living alone, was a strong, self-contained woman—one, above all others, whose family skeleton would be kept from the sight and hearing of the world. That you, the child of her wayward and unfortunate son, were living with her, was a fact that she never, doubtless, revealed to her nearest living kindred. She kept you secluded, as you say, and in her later years seems to have repented that she had done so. In the pride and reserve of her nature, the family trouble, whatever it may have been, must have assumed unnatural proportions, and it is just possible that she was thus led to commit a great wrong in withholding from you the secret of your parent's misfortunes."

"I believe that you are correct in the estimate you have given of her character," said Echo, as her thoughts turned reverently to the memory of her dead relative, "but she was none the less the truest and noblest woman that ever lived. She was guided by a high sense of duty in all things, great and small, and her judgment was so clear that she could not have often erred; and yet, in any matter affecting her family name, she might have fallen into a mistaken line of conduct."

"By the way, since you know so little of the family history, may there not be others, former friends and neighbors of your grandmother, who have some information in regard to the matter?"

"Ah, indeed, that is a happy suggestion! At the death of my grandmother, I resided for some time in the family of the Rev. Mr. Hoberg, our parish pastor. He was grandmother's dearest and most intimate friend, and has in his possession some sort of mysterious souvenir—

a legacy from the dear old lady—which was to be delivered to me only on my marriage day. Dear me, I had nearly forgotten that !" said Echo, for the first time seeming to realize the strategic importance of that legacy in unraveling the dark tangle of the parental history.

" Why, that legacy will put the clew of the whole mystery in our hands !" said Farrish, rising in his excitement and pacing the floor. " But hold ! your marriage day ?"

Echo colored at this suggestion, as she thought of her disappointed love, but she replied :

" That is another difficulty, perhaps an insurmountable one, but then the pastor doubtless knows enough about the affair to put some frail thread of discovery in our way."

" Do you know," said Farrish, gazing quizzically at the ceiling, after the manner of a man in pursuit of an idea, " that it is my candid opinion that your affianced never really turned away from you ?"

" The evidence seems indisputable," said Echo, with an instantaneous return of her former melancholy; " I have the letters of his sister and himself in regard to his change of feeling."

" That may be; but letters can be counterfeited where there is a long purse to sustain the experiment. I suspect that rich young villain, Ainsley, of having been at the bottom of the trouble."

" I should like to hope so," said Echo, with a sad smile; " but a true lover would have followed me and found out the truth, personally."

" Undoubtedly, cousin, under ordinary circumstances; but perhaps he is also relying on the testimony of false letters, and was, as I hope it may prove that you were, entangled in a subtly woven plot. But that matter shall be looked after, too," concluded Farrish, with an energetic shake of his head.

"Oh, dear," said Echo, rising suddenly, " I have completely forgotten Aunt Newbury in the startling interest of our conversation. Let us repair to her room at once, and acquaint her with the new aspect of affairs."

The tender-hearted invalid was inexpressibly delighted at the information they conveyed, and declared that she needed no other elixir to insure her immediate recovery.

When the whole story had been told, Farrish observed that they must make up a programme.

"It is necessarily a simple one, too," he continued, "and may be briefly stated. In the first place, you have no particular reason to desire to return to Canada, just now, so that you and our dear Aunt Newbury may take up your residence at a delightful little summer home of mine at San Rafael—where both of you will find release from present anxieties, and the most healthful atmosphere in the world. As for the party of the second part, I shall immediately visit Canada and leave not a stone unturned to discover what we seek. Come, cousin," lifting his finger, playfully, towards Echo, "not a word of opposition! I claim my prerogatives as a relative, and am not a man to be thwarted, I can tell you."

This arrangement was agreed to, and Farrish soon

after took his leave, amid mutual expressions of esteem and affection.

Once again, that night, in the pure maiden's heart, welled up the eternal fountains of faith, love, trust, and hope—and she was a living, beautiful soul.

WHEN Mr. Edmond Ainsley, on the night of his business interview with Vinton, retired to his luxurious apartments at the Grand, he did not immediately court his pillow, although the hour was late.

He lit another cigar and sat for a long while in partial undress, and the profoundest meditation. No qualms of conscience beset him. He was not subject to internecine struggles of that kind. He was anxious, principally on his mother's account, to maintain his social standing at home; what, then, if his stupendous scheme, with all the ugly incidents yet to ensue in connection therewith, should finally leak into the public ear at Quebec? That was not all; there was another danger more material than the probability of social ostracism—the avenging wrath of Dr. Hoberg!

But how could he avert the vengeance of Hoberg now—in case he should choose to let the matter drop? The thing was impossible—that cruel scalpel, "red with insufferable wrath," menaced his path, turn which way he would—with the greater chances of safety in favor of a forward movement.

While at home, he had satisfied himself that Echo no -longer corresponded with any of her former friends. With her present silence assured, he believed that he could trust himself with the management of her future. He was a rake and high-flyer of the wildest pretension, and he conceived that the accomplishment of his black designs with reference to the unfortunate young lady could not possibly be long deferred. Having once achieved the destruction of her honor, he would be safe —no pale face would ever reappear among former scenes to vex the slumber of the fraudulent remains.

Echo was the loveliest girl he had ever pursued, and she had repelled him so disdainfully that he meant to have revenge, the sweetest and best the case afforded. He had hunted down so many women successfully, that the word failure was no longer in the vocabulary of his wicked amours.

Does it occur to this easy-going world that a frightful number of its millionaires, wine-heated, thick-blooded men, are the slaves of their brutal lusts, and that much of their money goes towards conquering fresh territories of female virtue? It is a sickening thought—one that may well constrain us to despise men and to blush for the frailty of women.

"I must gain time for Vinton's machinations by giving out that I have a frightful headache, when that tragic doctor calls, as I am sure he will at an early hour," murmured Ainsley, as he finally threw away the stub of his cigar, and got into bed.

Doctor Hoberg was in a fever of unrest all night, and arose at six o'clock. For two hours he wandered aimlessly about the streets, had a cup of coffee, and then returned to the hotel. Ainsley was not yet visible, and a waiter was sent to inquire after him, and inform him that Doctor Hoberg would be glad to see him as soon as possible.

The servant brought word that Mr. Ainsley was much indisposed, and had not yet arisen.

The doctor hurried up to his room and found him just putting a fresh application of wet towels to his head, while an ominous glass of claret and ice ornamented the stand at his bedside.

"Good morning, doctor," he drawled. "By Jove! I'm horribly bruised! Never had such a villainous, racking headache in my life. 'Pon my word, it's killing."

Hoberg felt very much like kicking him into immediate convalescence, so great was his vexation, but he said, quietly:

"Will you not be able to be out soon?"

"Not until the afternoon, I fear; but there will then be time enough to attend to the matters contemplated."

"At what hour shall I call, then?"

"Say about two o'clock, doctor; I shall struggle upon my feet by that time, and be able to accompany you."

"Very well; I am suffering great anxiety, and shall be here promptly at the hour."

"I was born for a prime minister, by Jove!" exclaimed Ainsley, as soon as the doctor had gone; and he threw off the wet bandages, and took a glass of wine.

Doctor Hoberg had an age before him, seemingly, until the hour appointed; but the wheels of time, roll they never so heavily, yet constantly roll, and two o'clock was finally at hand.

He found Ainsley, elegantly attired and looking clean
and cool, waiting for him in the hotel parlor.

As they passed out again together, Ainsley remarked :

"The physician we desire to see has an office on
Kearney street, and we had better take him along."

Hoberg nodded his head in acquiescence, and the office
of Doctor Turner was soon reached. He was a large,
fine-looking man, and his manner had the charm of dignified affability. There was a trifle too much gloss of
broadcloth and glitter of jewelry in his outward adornment, perhaps, but dress is no criterion of the quality of
the man.

"I was very much interested in the case of that young
lady, Doctor Hoberg," said he, after the usual introduction had passed, and their business had been made
known. "I struggled hard to save her, but the disease
took one of those sudden turns which so often baffle the
truest skill, and all was over soon."

"Was she conscious at the last ?" said Hoberg, with a
stifled moan. "Did she leave no parting word for her
friends ?"

"She was conscious, my dear doctor, but too weak
for utterance. Her breath passed as gently as the sigh
of a summer wind, so gently that I was scarcely aware
that the catastrophe had occurred. Before that she had
raved continually, calling often upon some one named
'Arthur.'"

A great sigh shook the bosom of that Arthur upon
whom the dying girl had called.

After that they walked along, conversing on indifferent topics, until they appeared before the establishment of Madame Joilet, Stockton street, where Echo had so nearly passed to her "long account."

Houses of this kind, like the great gambling hells, are always shrouded in an atmosphere of quiet. Respectability sits throned above their carved portals, the deadly sins are stealthy. The assassin creeps and whispers—never talks or walks.

When the gentlemen had been ushered into a spacious and richly appointed waiting-room, Madame Joilet, dressed in subdued taste to suit the occasion, appeared. She had become in appearance a complete epitome of all matronly virtues.

She greeted the city doctor with a meek smile of recognition, and extended the same favor to Ainsley, expressing the hope that they found themselves well. Doctor Hoberg was then introduced, and the business nature of the call stated.

Madame Joilet, although a native of France, spoke English with a perfect accent, her language being illustrated with a limited number of Gallic shrugs and gestures.

"Ah, indeed!" said she, glancing at Hoberg, with a look of mournful interest; "you are, then, the relative or friend of that beautiful and unfortunate creature?"

The doctor bowed.

"I have thought of her so often—so often," resumed the kind matron. "It will give me the greatest pleasure to aid your affectionate undertaking."

She then handed him the certificate to the proper authorities, which she had just written at his request, and the gentleman withdrew.

Madame Joilet had nearly warbled the gay " ta-ta !" of frivolous people, at parting with the sombre trio, but caught herself in the act and gravely bowed her adieus.

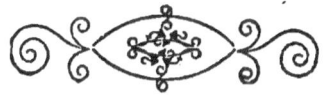

CHAPTER XXXIII

ONE Mountain, the grand and solemn cemetery of San Francisco, was dedicated in the years agone by the matchless eloquence of Baker. The sea never rolls its anthem from the cliffs, and the wind never sighs among the funeral trees, but the mournful echoes of that immortal voice return again, still singing a requiem for the dead. There lies Broderick in the gory mantle of his historic quarrel; there lies Baker, himself, "stricken and pale from the field of sacrifice."

The cemetery extends over a series of sand-hills and depressions, which affectionate art has made green with shrubbery and bright with flowers. The fashionable Cliff House drive skirts its silent walls, and the gay metropolitans may be said to whisper their loves and intrigues in the shadow of its sacred gates.

In an obscure quarter of this cemetery, on the day following the interview with Madame Joilet, were several people, gathered about a low, sand-swept grave. The little mound might have been heaped but yesterday, or six months, or six years before. The sands measure time — they do not bear the impress of its power. They are always the same — dry, blank, hoary!

Not a shrub or a flower marked the spot — only plain

white boards at the head and the foot — the former of which bore in black letters the name —

ECHO CLIFFORD.

Under the direction of an unctuous man in black, two laborers began to dig in this grave, while several gentlemen — apparently much interested in the work that was going forward — stood apart. The vigorous laborers threw the light soil up with startling rapidity, and their spades soon struck an obstruction below.

One of the men got into the opening and threw up some loose boards. Ropes were then handed him, when the other gentlemen stepped forward, and some of them assisted the laborers in raising a long, rough, wooden box, which, to all appearances, must contain the remains of a human being. The lid of the wooden box was then pried up, and a respectable coffin, draped in black velvet, was disclosed within.

It was then noticed that a terrible odor crept into the air, and there was a general movement backward.

"Putrefaction must be far advanced," said Doctor Turner to Arthur Hoberg, who stood beside him with a face appalling in its expression of grief and horror; do you desire " —

"No, no!" murmured the other, bursting into sobs, "It is too terrible not to be true!"

The undertaker who had paused, hammer in hand, hurriedly replaced the lid, and the remains were conveyed to a hearse in attendance at the gate. The party of gentlemen entered a cab, and were just turning into the road in the rear of the hearse, when a lady and gentleman drove up in an open carriage, their faces expressing the utmost surprise at the spectacle of a funeral cortege going citywards. The gentleman was Cleaveland Farrish, and the lady Echo Cliftord!

Before leaving for San Rafael, Echo had desired to pay a last visit to the resting place of the child she had learned to love so well, and this was the occasion of their visit to Lone Mountain.

Had Arthur Hoberg only looked out of the window as the others drove up, ah, heavens! what a scene there had been! But his head was buried in his hands and his eyes were blinded with tears.

Ainsley began to breathe more freely, but the cloud of anxiety had not entirely cleared from his brow. It was a desperate business, he felt, and he was almost sorry that he had undertaken it. "By Jove!" he murmured, "it is playing with death!"

But the job was done, and he must face the consequences. Vinton had acted superbly. "You are an ideal mechanic, Dan," said Ainsley to him when the funeral party had disbanded at the undertaker's on Market street, and he had had an opportunity of finding him at the old rookery on Broadway. "How did you manage it?"

Dan poured himself out a glass of liquor, saying, "I'm an ideal orator, too, and I never attempt a speech without due preparation." Having finished his libation to the shades of Demosthenes and Cicero, the orator began:

"Well, in the first place, I 'fixed' the Kearny street doctor and Madame Joilet — that was a bagatelle. The cemetery job was the real sticking point, and I strug-

gled with it a long time unavailingly. In the heat of
the combat I happened to think of an anecdote told upon
John Morrissey. John had a row with a man in a saloon,
and his opponent assaulted him just as he was in the act
of taking off his coat. Hampered by the half-drawn
garment, he was knocked down, when his opponent fell
upon him and began raining in his blows with awful energy. A thought occurred to John; instead of trying
to pull the coat off, he would put it on. He did so, with
a single movement of his herculean shoulders, and the
other man was carried off to a doctor ten minutes afterward.

"The recollection of that anecdote saved me. Instead
of trying to get possession of an established grave, I
made one. Of course, I had to take our undertaker into
my confidence, and through his professional assistance,
the whole thing was exquisitely managed.

"The grave was prepared yesterday afternoon, and it
was, essentially, tenantless."

"There was a horrible odor," said Ainsley with a
grimace.

"Drugs," said Vinton, sententiously.

CHAPTER XXXIV.

SUNSET on the Mediterranean. The sea lay clasping its lovely isles, like a maiden dreaming of her gems. The sun's rays, fused in a soft, glowing mass of matchless color, flowed over the whole western arch, until it lifted and shone like the gateway of that Heaven we cannot see. Peaks, ridges, hills, vales, cities, and villas, put on the glory of the pageant, and were lovelier than any dream of Enchanted Lands or Happy Isles. Upon the mighty picture rested, too, the lights and shadows of ancient, classic and mediæval time — the solemn and tender nimbus of the history of man; for in those shades and gleams War shook his crimson spear, Love displayed her hyacinthine locks, and Art lifted her immortal face..

Near a city on the shore, a solitary traveler was ascending a mountain which, environed with white-walled villas at its base, reared its rocky cone high in the purple bloom and golden mist of the evening.

Reaching the summit, the traveler sat down on the crumbling fragment of an ancient ruin, and surveyed the scene. He was, apparently, somewhat past middle life, tall, well-proportioned, and muscular. His dark hair and whiskers were tinged with gray. His bronzed face was regular, yet massive in outline, his eyebrows boldly marked, and his eyes dark, luminous, splendid.

He did not belong to the race inhabiting the city below him. He was of the stock of those conquering islanders in whose veins flows the mingled strength of Saxon, Norman and Danish blood. For long years he had been exiled from home and friends, and had been a wanderer in many lands.

He had gone forth in the hot blood of youth and was yet in the meridian of his vigor, but his wild passions were subdued, and his thoughts and purposes flowed in a deep and tranquil current.

The truest, sweetest, most enchanting period of human life is not found in childhood or in youth, but in its tender autumn time, when the first frosts have fallen, and dim, ineffable regrets weave a misty veil over the glowing landscapes of the heart. It is the turn of the leaf — the dirge-haunted Indian summer of our years. It is then that the soul takes on its richest, fullest coloring. The sunshine is sadder, but dearer to us, then, because it slants across the fallen castles of our hopes and the grass-grown mounds that cover our dead. Perhaps it is then that the exiled spirit thinks, for the first time, of some far, forgotten home, and thus lies lapped in reveries stranger and more delightful than were ever wafted from the flowering lotus.

The gad-fly of remorse had driven this solitary man into the unknown regions of the earth, and as he sat there musing in the mellow radiance of the evening, his old life at home seemed to be connected with an existence in some other world. A great yearning to return began to grow upon him. The scenes and incidents of the old time began to revolve before him in living distinctness, and he wondered how he could have remained away so long. Faces of loved ones came to him as never before, and his anguish was almost insupportable. Why should he not return? His life was worse than wasted in this idle journeying from land to land, and he might find among those who were near and dear to him a life-purpose and a hope. All other considerations perished and passed away before this one flaming idea and desire, and he resolved to act. So must the Prodigal Son have felt, when he said, " I will arise and go to my father's house."

There was a grand light in the brown face of our traveler as he arose, and with one parting glance at the fading splendors of the sunset, hastened down the mountain. His preparations were soon made, and the next day he was pacing the deck of a steamer bound for Marseilles. His journey terminated in Paris. Having secured respectable lodgings in a quiet neighborhood, he employed an intelligent and active young man as messenger and sent him immediately with a sealed note to an old Captain of the Guards named Ducrot, whom he had formerly known, and of whose present residence he had taken care to inform himself directly on his arrival.

During the absence of the messenger, the traveler paced the floor continually, muttering to himself and contracting his brows as if in serious and disturbing thought.

After the lapse of an hour or so, a carriage drove up in front of his temporary quarters, and there alighted therefrom a stalwart man of about fifty-five — habited in the undress of a retired officer. His hair was nearly white, but strong and abundant, and his leonine visage was not subdued in ferocity by the heavy sabre-cut that extended across the right cheek obliquely, from the point of the flowing gray mustache nearly to the temple.

This man of warlike presence mounted the steps with a firm step, and was admitted by the traveler himself, who closed the door and faced his visitor with folded arms.

The two men regarded each other for a moment in perfect silence, and then the Frenchman opened his arms with a stentorian shout,

"*Io triumphe!* It is Clifford, my friend and brother, come back from the dead!"

"It is indeed I, Captain, and it does my soul good to see the lion-hearted Ducrot erect and vigorous with unabated youth." And these two men embraced like brothers.

"In the name of God, Clifford," said the Captain, when the first transports of surprise were over, and both were seated, "to what ends of the earth have you been gone so many years?"

"I have sojourned in many climes, Captain, and toiled in many since last I saw you, but I assure you that I have never ceased to remember you with affection and gratitude," said the traveler, still clasping the hand of his friend.

"But why did you not return? Did you never hear the truth?"

"I supposed that I knew the truth," said the other mournfully. "I have had no new light since going away."

"*Ma foi!* then, my friend," said the Captain, ener-
getically slapping his knee, "I will strike you with a
thunder-clap of revelation.

Clifford shook his head as though he were hopeless of
any new phase of facts in the case.

"In the first place, then, my Sinbad the Sailor, what
have you to say if I tell you that the man did not die?"

"Not die?" said Clifford, starting angrily, "that is
bad news, indeed."

"But I tell you that is good news."

"You seem to have changed your opinion, Captain,"
with a lowering of the heavy brows.

"Shall I tell you why it is good news, Monsieur Sinbad?" persisted the man of war.

"I am most anxious to know why my friend, Captain
Ducrot, the soul of honor, calls the intelligence of so
great a misfortune, good news?"

"Simply because the man did not deserve to die; he
was innocent."

"Are you trifling with me, my noble friend?" said
Clifford, huskily.

"I swear by the grave of my father, that the man
was innocent!" said the Captain, solemnly.

"Innocent! my God! that would imply that my —
that " —

"That your wife was innocent too, my poor brother,"
said the Captain yet more solemnly and tenderly.

"After all these years!" groaned Clifford, as he laid
his head upon the table, convulsed by the power of his
emotions.

A plaintive silence of several minutes ensued, and

then the Captain laid his strong hand softly on the other's shoulder, and, in a low voice, began:

"The whole truth came out immediately, my friend, and your wife was utterly exonerated from all blame."

Clifford neither looked up nor spoke, and the Captain continued,

"The man you struck-had been clandestinely meeting a young lady, a friend of your wife, to whom he was engaged to be married, in your house — and thus the whole mistake and catastrophe occurred."

"Oh God! how I have wronged her!" cried Clifford, agonizingly.

"And how you must have suffered!" interposed the Captain. "Come, my friend," he resumed, encouragingly. "Your action was justified by the facts as they seemed to you. If you made a mistake; if you did wrong, in fact, in not having been more deliberate, let all these years of miserable exile atone for that, and look you only to the present and the future."

Clifford regained his composure and again sat erect.

"Lady Clifford is in Paris?" he finally asked.

"Yes, having recovered her daughter, she has re-entered society."

"Recovered her daughter?" said Clifford, starting up excitedly.

"That and nothing less, monsieur," said the Captain, rather enjoying the dramatic *esprit* of the situation.

"When, and how was she recovered?"

"An agent sent out by Lady Clifford discovered mademoiselle in America, whither it is claimed you had taken her at the time of your flight, and brought her to Paris but a few months ago, I believe."

"You will see them, of course?" continued the Captain.

"Yes; I can do no less. The yearning of a husband and father finally overcame my pride, my fears, and every conventional scruple, and I have returned. God only knows what reception is in store for me, but my purpose is clear and true, and I shall not abandon it. The revelation you have made gives me much cause to hope that the golden bow of promise may yet span my darkened sky. Whatever the mother may do, the child will surely not desert me."

"Bravo, Sinbad, your life shall yet blossom with returning joys. Your wife may have been incensed at you for having so readily believed evil of her, but she has borne herself discreetly in her worse than widowhood, and must be one of the noblest of women. I am confident that she will forgive all in memory of your terrible sufferings, and that your hearts will flow together again in peace, trust, and love."

"God grant it!" exclaimed Clifford, devoutly.

The two friends then adjourned to a neighboring café, where they lingered long over their wine, brightening the links of their ancient friendship.

CHAPTER XXXV

THE footsteps of Zarina, passing to the privacy of her own chamber, and the innocent companionship of her individual thoughts, had scarcely died away along the carpeted hall, when an unaccountable spasm, deadly in its violence, seized the person of M. Legrand. He threw himself over on his spine, and, doubling his knees back almost to his chin, suddenly shot his legs forward with the velocity of a thunderbolt, hurling the entire drapery of the bed to the other side of the room. Then he kicked and clawed the air, and spat into it, with a fury that was fearful to behold.

Finally, when he had exhausted himself by a series of the wildest and most grotesque movements imaginable, he quietly arose and secured his door against all possible intrusion. His sallow face was illumined by a strange white light, and his eyes glowed with the smothered flame of some mighty purpose. Going to his dressing-case, he opened a drawer and took therefrom a glittering, pearl-handled knife, of the kind gentlemen usually carry in their pockets. What was he going to do? His fell purpose was soon apparent.

He sat down on the side of the bed, and coolly began to pare his finger-nails, some of which had been torn in the muscular carnival through which he had just passed.

"*Pardieu*, madame!" he said, in a malevolent whisper; "it is a long road that has no turning. You were like this," and he held up the bright blade, "keen, cold, cruel, beautiful, but I was warned in time, and I come back from the borders of the grave to overthrow and destroy you."

Yes, he had been warned in time, and you could see in every ghastly feature of the man as he sat there attending to a trivial necessity, that he had been into the shadows of the sombre land.

Jealousy, the green-eyed, the Argus-eyed, had saved him. He had tracked Zarina and the count to their trysting bower, and had been a hidden witness of the anomalous marriage.

Restraining the tigerish impulse to spring upon and destroy them both, he had ceased to use the medicaments left for him by his physician, rightly suspecting that his rapidly failing health had not been without a definite and criminal cause.

He had affected the mortal agony of that night in order to further entangle and confuse his paramour, and lead her to the hideous unmasking of her satanic design.

"Ha, ha!" he chuckled, softly, as he smoothed his hungry-looking talons; "the man that loves is a fool, and doubly a fool is he that loves his wife."

Having shuffled off his infatuation for his covert spouse, Legrand gave back his allegiance to the sordid interests that had ruled his life before he entered the lists of love.

His course was chosen with the inspired promptitude of a Napoleon. Rehabilitating his disordered couch, and binding a damp towel about his temples, he went to bed, and slept soundly until a seasonable hour in the morning.

Arising briskly, he began an elaborate toilet, suspending his labors occasionally to take a glass of wine. When he had finished he was a marvel of artistic grooming, and the wine had lent a slight flush to his pale cheek and an animated sparkle to his eye.

As he sauntered gracefully into the breakfast parlor, it might have been thought that he was the owner of the mansion—young, rich, happy, and honored—instead of the villainous adventurer that he was, treading close to the gulf of an awful ruin.

"The compliments of the morning, ladies," he exclaimed, with gay suavity. "May I venture to express the hope that both of you are well ?"

Lady Clifford acknowledged his salutation quietly, and moved towards her place at the table.

Zarina, who had been scanning the columns of the morning paper and teasing a white lap-dog at her feet, looked up suddenly, turned livid, gasped, and only saved herself from falling by clutching the arm of her chair with despairing energy.

Luckily Lady Clifford did not notice her supreme agitation, and Legrand had a motive for not calling attention to it.

Zarina was a woman of masculine nerve, however, and

she soon gained control of her feelings, whatever they may have been, and addressed some commonplace remark to Legrand, which he answered in kind.

As the meal progressed, Legrand's conversational qualities shone out as never before. He was more profound than Johnson, more brilliant and poetical than Coleridge, and more witty and piquant than Madame de Stael. He was absolutely oppressive in the glare, flash, roar, and ripple of his talk, which soon assumed the character of a towering and despotic monologue, the ladies having been altogether silenced in its desolating course.

The repast concluded, Legrand turned to Lady Clifford :

"May I have the honor of a private interview with your ladyship this morning, on a matter of the highest moment ?"

His tones were clear and distinct, so much so that Zarina recoiled from their peculiar emphasis as if it bore a poignard thrust of intimation to her very heart.

"Certainly, monsieur," said Lady Clifford, rising and leading the way. "Let us adjourn to the library."

Fully an hour passed, and still Zarina sat in the dining-room waiting the event of the interview, for she felt sure that a crisis of some kind was at hand.

At last Legrand came out of the sitting-room and went up stairs, no movement being observed in the apartment he had left. Half an hour passed, and then he came down again, arrayed in his traveling-dress, and carrying a small portmanteau.

Entering the dining-room, he went straight to Zarina and held out his gloved hand.

"Zarina," he said, in almost tender tones, as she mechanically put her hand in his, "do you remember the cry of the Old Guard, when, for the first time in history, they recoiled at Waterloo?"

Her lips were white, and she moved them once or twice vainly before she could articulate:

"I do not know, monsieur."

"*Sauve qui peut !*" he said, in a low tone, bending and kissing the hand he held, then turned, passed through the door without once looking back, and was gone—forever!

A traitor to every principle of truth, he had sold his own villainy. He had been gone but a moment when the door-bell rang, and a visitor was announced. Going into the hall, Zarina heard Lady Clifford, in strange, broken voice, tell the servant to show the gentleman in.

She advanced so as to command a view of the room, and saw a tall, bronzed man halt for a moment on the threshold and look towards Lady Clifford, who rose with difficulty from the sofa upon which she had been sitting, and returned his gaze.

Not a word was spoken, but in an instant the flash of a divine lustre, the reflection of an awakened love, swept their faces, and they rushed into each other's arms with simultaneous cries:

"Husband !"

"Wife !"

And then Zarina remembered the forlorn cry of the
Old Guard at Waterloo—

" *Sauve qui peut !*"

CHAPTER XXXVI.

ORNING on the Summit of the Sierras! The eastward bound train of the Central Pacific railroad was just rounding one of those appalling curves which, in that sublime and gorgeous region skirt the brink of immeasureable abysses, when, suddenly, its motion was observed to diminish—then, cease altogether.

The train had stopped.

After a brief delay the door of the express car was seen to open, and a plank was pushed out until its extremity rested on the outer edge of the grade.

Then a large body, glittering like an immense silver brick in the sunlight, was placed upon the plank. It appeared, on closer scrutiny, to be an oblong, irregular hexagon—that figure which, from association, has become so terrible to the human race. The incline was steep, and when all was ready, a brakesman stepped forward, and with a single impulse of his hand, shot this mysterious body like a meteor into the abyss.

The train moved on.

To understand this curious proceeding, we will have to retrace our steps a little way into the events that preceded it.

Reconsidering her first decision, Echo concluded to revisit her old home, in company with her cousin. Aunt

Newbury was provided with a comfortable home, mean-while, where she was to await Echo's return from Canada —when both were to proceed to San Rafael, according to the original intention.

Doctor Arthur Hoberg, having had the supposed re-mains of his affianced enclosed in an additional metallic casket, took passage in the same train with our friends, as the Fates would have it, and there was, every moment, therefore, imminent danger of a collision.

By the greatest good fortune, Echo, in glancing out of the car window at Sacramento, was the first to realize the situation, having seen Arthur plainly, as he stood facing her and conversing with some gentleman for a moment before he got on the train.

She was astounded, of course, and gave a little scream, which she could only explain to her cousin by attribu-ting it to the true cause. This she did, in an agitated whisper, pointing out Arthur to her cousin. Farrish was no less surprised.

"Why, he must have been searching for you," he said.

"I hope so," said Echo naively, blushing painfully, however, the moment she realized the masculine audac-ity of the remark.

"Noble looking fellow, too," said Farrish, musingly; then, with a sudden transition to activity —

"Do you know what I propose to do?"

"Certainly not, cousin; nothing rash, I hope."

"Well, our Adonis there is smoking, as you see, and will probably go into the smoking-car. When the train gets in motion, therefore, I shall call upon him and find out the true history of the whole affair. It's providential that he is a passenger on the same train, for I intend to throw him over the precipices of the Sierras unless he shall show the true color."

"Oh, but — cousin" —?" faltered Echo, whose womanly sensibilities began to be aroused as she thought of the letters she had received.

"Never mind, my dear; I shall act considerately, and your situation shall not be compromised in the least. I know that there is villainy at the bottom of your estrangement, and the sooner an understanding is had, the better for all concerned."

When the heavy train, with many a groan and splutter, had finally begun to move, Farrish was as good as his word, and bidding Echo, who by this time was distressingly agitated, to be of good cheer, departed in quest of Arthur.

As he had expected, the Doctor was in the smoking car, and he approached him directly —

"Haven't I the pleasure of addressing Doctor Arthur Hoberg, of Quebec?" he politely asked.

Arthur started at the sound of his own name, and rose as he answered,

"The same, sir, and I" —

"Mr. Farrish"—taking a seat at his side.

"Learning, accidentally, who you were," continued Farrish, "I made bold to approach you. I am a relative of an old neighbor of yours, now deceased, Mrs. Clifford, and now on my way to Canada to look up some matters of family history."

"I am inexpressibly glad to meet you," said Arthur, brightening electrically at the name of "Clifford." Then he thought of his mournful charge in the express car, and the sunshine fell away from his face like the white mask of Khorrassan, leaving his features dark with unutterable gloom.

"If your mission to Canada pertains to the affairs of that unfortunate family," said Arthur, chokingly, "I have most sorrowful intelligence for you. I suppose that you are acquainted with the various branches of the family?"

Farrish inclined his head, adding, "I am the namesake of Cleaveland Clifford, the deceased widow's only son."

"Indeed! Then you doubtless have heard that he left an only daughter, who was reared by her grandmother?"

Farrish nodded his assent.

"Well," said Arthur, drawing a long breath and trembling visibly, "Echo Clifford was the loveliest and purest of her sex. After the death of her grandmother she came to live in my father's family for a time, and we became greatly attached to each other, Echo and I, and were engaged to be married." The young man almost broke down at this juncture, but made a desperate effort at self-command, and continued:

"Echo at length engaged herself as companion to a wealthy lady named Ainsley, a resident of Quebec. Having passed the medical schools I also established myself in Quebec and auspiciously began the practice of my profession. We were frequently in each other's society in those golden days, and the time of our nuptials was near at hand, when an event occurred which postponed that happy day forever."

Arthur passed his hand across his brow and had again to struggle for self-control."

"The event to which I allude," he began again, "was the burning of the Ainsley mansion, in which Echo and Mrs. Ainsley very nearly lost their lives. Mrs. Ainsley's health was prostrated by the nervous shock she received, and her physicians advised travel and change of scene. Echo had become indispensable to her comfort and happiness by this time, and she refused to travel without her. This was a cruel whim, so far as its bearing upon our fortunes was concerned, for Echo could not find it in her heart to desert the pampered invalid, and it was arranged that she should go. California was chosen as the place of their temporary sojourn, and Echo and I, at first, maintained a constant and affectionate correspondence; but a cloud soon came between us, and I saw plainly that her love had grown cold. To be brief, she finally, in a constrained, unnatural way, wrote asking a release from the engagement, and I could do nothing less than consent. Then we heard nothing more of them until Mrs. Ainsley's return, a short time ago, with the terrible intelligence of Echo's death, by fever, in San Francisco."

Arthur bowed his head for a moment and did not see the wonderful expression that passed over the face of his auditor.

"The blow almost deprived me of reason, but I suspected them of having neglected the poor girl, and I almost forced Edmond Ainsley to accompany me to San Francisco, where I intended to have her remains exhumed and brought home for burial. That sad duty I have performed, and I am now returning with all that is left of my lost, lost love!" Arthur's head fell forward again, and a heart-rending moan issued from his lips.

Farrish was in a blaze and quiver of excitement.

"Young man — Doctor Hoberg!" he said, laying his hand firmly on Arthur's shoulder,

"Look at me, look me in the eye!"

Arthur lifted his pale face and looked at him in stupid wonderment.

"Now tell me," said Farrish, in a measured, solemn voice,

"Are you in your right mind?"

"I have no reason to doubt it, Mr. Farrish," said Arthur, suspecting the other, in his turn of mental aberration.

"Well, then," cried Farrish, bringing his clenched hand down on the back of the seat with a force that almost tore it from its fastenings,

"You are the victim of the most stupendous fraud that has been perpetrated in this century!"

Arthur could only gaze at him in stupid astonishment.

"Brace your nerves," resumed Farrish, "for a marvelous revulsion of feeling." "Can you not guess what it is?"

"No, I cannot, unless it be that —"

"Echo is alive!" said Farrish, finishing the sentence, and catching Arthur's head upon his arm, as he fell forward in a swoon,

*   *   *   *   *   *   *

Autumn had come. The northern forests were aflame
with the inverted torch of the passing year. The railroad journey had been joyously concluded, and a long
ocean voyage had, soon after, closed with marvelous
revelations and the celestial harmonies of happy souls.

The night was crisp and clear, and the old parsonage
was aglow with festival lights. Lady Clifford was there,
leaning on the arm of the bronzed traveler. Arthur
Hoberg was there, happy as a prince, and Echo, blushing
at the consciousness of her own loveliness. Aunt Newbury was there, too, and Farrish, and Mary, and others
that we need not name.

The venerable pastor had at last been allowed to be-
stow the mysterious casket upon her for whom it was
intended, and every cloud that had obscured the earlier
fortunes of our heroine had passed away.

Let the mantle of oblivion rest upon the fates of those
who bore a sinister part in the story. Be assured that
their shadows never again fell across the pathways of
our nobler characters.

Reader, let us part kindly. We have invited you
upon a rugged and, perhaps, an unprofitable way, but
the end is here. It is a rude tale, inaptly told, but under
its tattered gabardine beats the warm heart of a Christian purpose. And so, closing, as all good stories must
close, with the music of marriage bells, let us borrow
the toast of Tiny Tim, and say:

"God bless us every one."

WAIFS AND ESTRAYS.

WRECKED.

I'T is a fearful thing to contemplate a shipwreck; to see the masts dismantled, the helm useless, the rudder gone, the noble vessel at the mercy of every fierce billow, to be dashed to pieces on the rocks and the ruins stranded upon the shore.

But how much more fearful to contemplate a life wreck ! What are the iron-bound masts and machinery of ten thousand vessels, were they built of gold, ribbed with rubies and freighted with diamonds, compared with the mind which conceived them ! A few dollars will rebuild the useful vessel. But where is the cunning skill that can again restore the strength of body, the peace of mind, the squandered opportunities of the wrecked human life? Where is there a more pitiful object than a poor, silly creature, clothed in the habiliments of a man or woman, who has never learned to say *no* with emphasis — one who is tossed about on life's tempestuous sea as the leaves of the forest in the autumn gale?

Can we not emulate the beautiful example of those self-denying Sisters of Charity, as they go scattering seeds of benevolence more precious to the heart of the life-wreck than a drink of ice water to the parched throat of a dying soldier! It is all very well for those

who are living in opulence, well fed and richly clad, to
go to the hungry and cold, talk of reform, and remind
them of their sinful state. Words are many, but do they
feed the hungry? Prayer is a blessed privilege, but
does it clothe the naked? The gift of a Bible is a precious gift, but will it shelter the homeless? The sound
of music is delightful, but what would avail the most
ravishing strains that ever flowed from the famous harp
of Orpheus, to one when gaunt, meager want was
fiercely gnawing at his vitals. Prayer without work
is like a farmer who has sown seed but neglected the
harvest.

When a vessel is wrecked there is a great "hue and
cry," but when a precious human soul and a beautiful
human body is wrecked, physically, mentally and mor-
ally, perhaps a few will say, "Poor wretch! Such a
wreck! Why I knew him when he was a promising
young man!" and then dismiss the subject.

One cannot go anywhere without meeting these un-
timely wrecks; in the cars, in the street cars, on board a
ship, walking upon the streets, you behold these wrecks.
Wrecked in health, wealth, strength and manhood—
purity, veracity and integrity, all gone, only a misspent
life remaining. Oh, how we pity the wives, mothers and
daughters of those wrecks of manhood who, with smiles
upon their faces are outwardly, patiently and silently submitting to the inexorable! But a glimpse at the ineffable
misery of the inner life would startle and terrify the beholder. We all live two lives: our external life is cold,
plain, practical and selfish; our internal life is full of

high aspirations and great expectations, which are rarely realized.

And it is when our anticipations are blasted, our hopes deferred, our motives and actions misunderstood, our body tired and our minds weary with labor, the tempter entices us, alluring us on and on, and we lack the physical and ethical capacity to successfully cope with so skillful an adversary. Then it is we need Christian succor, divine judgment, and the divine aid. Then it is when we are decoyed, life-wrecked. Oh! Christian man and woman, that you should come forward and not stand far off with pretended sanctimoniousness, "thanking your stars" that you are so much better than the rest of humanity! What do you know of the past life or of the terrible temptations of the one under present public condemnation.

Ah, my friends, suppose the mask could be lifted from all our hearts and our most secret thoughts exposed to the public gaze; would we not all make swiftly to some dark closet. Suppose the mask would drop from every professed Christian in any assembly, and all their sins of omission and of commission would be written upon their forehead, just imagine the scattering! There would be none left; no, not one. You should go to the poor despondent and despairing sinful ones of earth, for they, in their debasement, are afraid and ashamed to come to you.

Yes, go to them. *You* are not dead yet, neither are your children. The Omnipotent only knows the future, and that life-wrecked man and woman was once as innocent as that pure little rosebud which you so lovingly rock to sleep upon your bosom.

Why need it wither! Why must the virulent canker of disease and sin, of mistrust and selfishness, enter into the inner portals of the exquisite bud, destroying its fragrance and beauty, even before it is matured into full bloom!

A good gardener is exceedingly careful of a choice rose-bush, shields it from the fiery rays of the summer sun, waters, prunes and guards it from the rough hands of the ignorant and the rude attack of the destructive insect. How patiently he waits for the first tiny leaves! How he rejoices alike at the fragrance of the chased bud, and the exquisitely rare beauty of the full blown rose.

How many of us tend our precious human rose-bushes as carefully as the hired gardener does the natural!

Do we mothers do our duty, our whole duty, to the frail, tender, impressible little plants which are entrusted to our keeping? Do we make our bosoms the port for all their little joys or sorrows, and our strong mother-love the trestle work upon which the tender plants can, and do, climb upward? Do we attend as carefully to the ethical needs of our children as the physical? Do we kindly and patiently prune the faults from our own daily lives and conversation so as to shield the little blossoms from the taint and mildew of selfishness and scandal? Do we shelter the frail plants from the storm of untruthful, windy words, and guard it from rude, vicious companionship? Do we watch the coming bloom of our precious plants with jealous care, making home the real "Utopian Isle" of perfect felicity ?

If we have not done all this, and more, we are not worthy the excellent diadem of motherhood, and we fear the gate-keeper at the "golden gates" of the Eternal city, will turn away with a sigh as he refuses us admittance.

We sincerely hope that futurity will clearly see the fallaciousness of the judgment which upholds the human law in guarding and protecting the rose-bush in one's yard, making it a fine or imprisonment to the "maliciously disposed person or persons who would or should impair or destroy the said bush," and permit the same person or persons, if so disposed, to enter the "Sanctum Sanctorum" of home and destroy our most promising human flowers.

Fie, fie! upon *the law* which permits the desolation and desecration of a home, be it the rich man's palace or the lowly hovel of those sorely tried people, the miserably poor.

We are told by an eminent historian, that "Cicero vindicated the truth and inculcated the value of the precept that 'nothing is truly useful which is not strictly honest.'"

Can a man be strictly honest and wantonly injure another ? Webster gives the definition of the word honesty, to be "upright, just, fair in dealing with others; having the disposition to act at all times according to justice or correct moral principles."

Now in God's name, in the name of truth and justice are *you* and *you* acting fairly, justly and honestly to others when you uphold and elect men to office who will not, or do not, pass laws for the good of their constituents ?

'Tis a fearful thing to contemplate a shipwreck in imagination; you can feel the shivering of the ship as she dashes and plunges along.   Will she outride the storm ?   The captain is an old sea-king, wise and sober, the man at the helm is strong and brave, not a rotten plank, not a weak place, her ropes and sails are new and good, her masts are iron bound, her sides ribbed with steel, her keel strongly bolted.   Surely she will outride the storm, and arrive safely in port.   Hark ! what is that ? Look again.   Her sails are torn into shreds, her masts shivered into splinters, her helm useless, her rudder gone.   Her gallant captain stands firmly at his post of duty, and gives orders in a sonorous voice which trembles a little in spite of himself, for on board that vessel is a much-loved and only daughter upon her bridal tour. The boats are lowered, but what boat could live in such a violent gale ?   Hear the booming of the signal gun. See the cowering forms, and white, pitiable faces.   Listen to the prayers uttered by shaking voices and trembling lips, as visions of the safe home-harbor come galloping swiftly through the frenzied brain.   The monarch of the deep and the king of the wind have united their forces, and the roaring of the waves increases in fierceness. The booming of the gun grows fainter and fainter. Hark to the dreadful shrieks, feel the violence of the shock, the fury of the wind as the ship breaks into pieces; see the horror-stricken faces as they are tossed upon the maddening billows; hear the wild exultations of the ferocious monarch of the deep as he shouts his orders to his vassals, the demons of the gale.

In the morning the waters of the lake are placid, with here and there a white-robed swan gracefully rocking upon her swelling bosom. There is nothing left to tell of the fierce storm of yesternight but the ruins of a vessel stranded upon the shore and a corpse or two, "Somebody's darling," with the good-bye kiss almost warm upon their lips.

Who can portray a life wreck?

Have you never seen a young girl, pure as a snow-flake, and as fair as pure, whose presence filled the room with sunny gladness, whose voice was sweeter than the song of many birds, and whose laugh was more musical than an Æolian harp? Have you never known such a one to be wrecked upon the rocks of pride and fashion?

God pity her, whosoever she may be, and throw around her His broad mantle of charity, for she has irrevocably lost what a life-time of the most remorseful agony cannot restore.

'Tis exceedingly dreadful to contemplate the vast army of life-wrecks, and hear their sturdy tramp down, even to the portals of the loathesome tomb. There they go, young and old; you have known some of them in their better days. How pleasant were their expectations as they went to battle manfully with the common occurrences of life. Truth was their rudder, honesty their helm, integrity their captain. They were iron-bound by a mother's love, and steel-ribbed by the tender memories of home.

Their vessel will outride the most furious tempest, and

be wafted into port by fragrant winds and ambrosial dews. But they, too, were allured by the deceitful sirens and were tossed on sin's tempestuous sea, till truth, honesty and integrity were all swept away in a storm of inebriety. The iron bands of a mother's love and the steel-ribbed principles were first burst asunder by the furious hurricane, and the hand of the recording angel grew stiff with horror as it penned the words "Life Wreck."

Oh, the ineffable misery of the life wreck, when the cold fingers of the icy monster, Death, are clutching at their heart-strings, and they are standing on the precipice of despair, with the eternal chasm of desolation yawning beneath their feet!

Let us not quiescently repose at home, vainly sighing for the return of the golden age, but earnestly work to raise such a holy rebellion that Ate and her legions will be overwhelmed, and the reign of Astrea, the goddess of justice, re-established.

Is the exquisite workmanship of the Infallible?— the amazing mechanism of the extremely wonderful human body, even beyond the giant intellect of man himself, to be life-wrecked, while God lives, and reason sits upon her throne, and the warm human heart beats within the breast of men and women that walk these streets? Shall we not vigorously inculcate and vindicate the divine attribute, benevolence, and obliterate the superstructure of all human depravity, selfishness?

JOHN MARVIN.

—

NOW had fallen to an unusual depth; the cold was intense, and rendered more intolerable by the fierce wind which pierced the thinly clad pedestrians to their hearts, and chilled the warm blood in their veins, as a blast from the north pole chills a bank of summer violets.

By ten o'clock the streets were almost deserted. About eleven the door of a fashionable saloon slowly opened and there entered a gaunt and hungry looking man, with bare toes, red and shining, peering through an old pair of boots, and tattered clothes, which gave evidence of a life of dissipation. The man's clothing seemed to be endowed with the traits of humanity, for there was a gulf between the vest and trousers; the vest, being not quite so ragged and of finer cloth than the trousers, objected to a social union, however strongly the piercing winds of winter hinted at the comfort of such an arrangement.

The man was five feet, ten inches in height, broad-shouldered, full-chested, and a form emaciated and slightly bent; head and beard unshorn, very dark, and thickly sprinkled with gray. His forehead, deeply seamed, was white and almost massive, and his head of faultless mould. His eye was dark gray, sunken, and of peculiar and fascinating power. There was nothing rough in his manner; on the contrary, there was an easy grace, almost elegance, which betokened a day of education and refinement. He stood by the door awhile, as if blinded by the brilliantly-lighted interior, then, staggering up to the polished bar, he spoke in a trembling voice to the bar-keeper:

"Once I was the possessor of thousands; to-night I am dying of starvation and cold. For three days I have not tasted food; for God's sake give me something to drink!"

The answer came cold and cutting.

"That's played out, old chap—worn thread-bare long ago; only gentlemen are allowed on these premises; git!"

\-   *   *   *   *   *   *   *   *

"Has it come to this? Can this be death? Ground under the heel of poverty, shivering with cold, hunger gnawing at my heart-strings, what matters it? One by one the leaden grains are disappearing; the hour-glass is almost empty. Where are the butterflies which circled round the golden shrine of summer? King John they used to call me. King of what? a few grains of yellow dust. Born in a palace, starving in a garret. Who can unweave the tangled web of destiny? What have I gathered from the past, but ashes of bitterness? My purposes have been broken reeds, and at last I stand at the gates of death, groping in the shadow. To die and be forgotten! Oh, dreadful thought! To be extinguished as a breath of air exterminates yon flickering candle; rot like a dull weed, disappear like a meteor,

the soul incarcerated within the mouldy walls of the
grave forever. ·Impossible! the inextinguishable fires
of hell would be far more preferable. Oh, Jesus, thou
son of David, have mercy on me!"

The reverberation of the voice of Him who said,
"All that come unto me I will in no wise cast out,"
came from the tomb of the past and rekindled the embers of the ruins of former consciousness, partly con-
sumed by idleness and dissipation, but still glowing
upon the altar of the noble and impassioned soul, estab-
lishing the immovable certitude of divine law which
truly sways the lever, whose fulcrum is justice, whose
extent is rectitude, whose weight is the universe, and
whose sweep is endless duration. So, on the very verge
of eternity, his weary soul drank in the incarnate rapture
of divine mercy, and from the billows of remorse arose
an ardent heart-prayer which sprang from inner depths
of the soul's life, and condensed the repentance of a life-
time. On the marsh of despond the crystalline dews of
hope fell, transfiguring the rank weeds into lilies of holi-
ness, whose perfume was wafted by the soft winds of
perfect peace into the purple chamber of the soul for-
evermore.

The night was bitter cold, but he knew it not. The
moon shone gloriously through the attic window. Physical suffering for him was past. The gnawing of
hunger, the piercing of cold, was gone. In the solemn
pauses of the wind storm he saw a visioned summer,
heard the birds sing, and smelt the perfume of the
violets which grew in the old garden at home. A delicious drowsiness stole over him. He was a child again,

From the dim glades of the past, soft and low as angels' footsteps, down the purple tide of weary day came the sweet voice of his mother singing to him his cradle song. So, repeating to himself the childish prayer which always followed after the song, he fell asleep.

Three days after, the lifeless body of the once fashionable John M—— was found by a little newsboy, his only earthly friend, and buried by the city. His funeral procession consisted of two drunken Irishmen, who buried him, and a little ragged boy, who wept great tears, which fell upon the rude pine coffin in the form of a wreath; tears which were frozen as they fell, and, when tinted by the golden sunbeams, resembled a crown of orient pearls which were in fact a priceless diadem of beauty gathered from the mine of human sympathy.

Poor John never having been taught the dignity of labor, his unfledged wings were useless; he was like a tropical bird caught in a northern blast. He lacked the necessary experience which the stern teaching of poverty imparts to her favored children, rendering them almost invincible. Prosperity is but a shadow upon the dial-plate of time; the winds arise, the clouds gather, and it is gone. All pay reverence to the giant oak upon a summer's day; but few prop up its trembling branches during a winter storm.

We all understand the brevity of human life, but few, very few, extract the sweets from the golden flowers of the present. The beauties of the morning sunrise pass unnoticed. Like a vast multitude of moths, we are longing to singe our wings in the fierce blaze of noonday, which we spend in vain regrets, delusive hopes, and foolish fears. Amid the glories of an evening sunset we stand in the marsh of despond, whilst adown ethereal space a gleaming flood of gold gilds the landscape with marvelous beauty.

John M—— was but one victim in a thousand of the false teaching that honest labor is dishonorable. Slave to society, which demands of its votaries nothing but senseless extravagance, which enwraps the sons and daughters of America with the strength of a boa-constrictor, till their souls are shriveled as the body of an Egyptian mummy; truth, trust and honesty are blown away like fallen leaves in an autumn gale, while the accursed inbreathing of dishonesty, flowing from the golden sluices of political aristocracy, invades the air like miasma from an African swamp.

Every series of human events repeats its own history; every human act inscribes itself on the globe of memory, and can never be entirely obliterated from the scroll of time when written by the sunbeams of truth.

When the flame is gone, the smoke and ashes remain. As the clouds gather vapor, so life gathers atoms. As the clouds would be useless without the wind, so would human life without the immortal spirit. At one time the sheeny, purpling clouds glide majestically through a smiling summer sky, at another, driven violently along, accompanied by vivid flashes of lightning and rolling thunder, they are at last torn and scattered by their death winds. This, too, is an emblem of life, and though the rain storm was of short duration, it left its sepulcher in the smiling fields and wrote its modest epitaph upon the lofty trees, bladed grass and blooming flowers.

The sun prints a map of its presence on the face of nature more or less lasting — writing with his gold pen his past course upon the plant and the pebble, the rock and·the leaf, the snow upon the mountain, the soil in the valley. His power is in the sky, his mercy in the air. The universe is a memorandum of his signature, which speaks to the intelligent.

COMPARISON BETWEEN VOLTAIRE AND ST. PAUL.

HOM have we here? Voltaire. Endowed with genius, intellectually great, dignified, graceful, and fascinating in a remarkable degree; not only courted by those who wielded the scepter of government, but also by those who wielded the scepter of knowledge; crowned with celebrity, admired of men, and worshipped by women, surely he was greatly blessed. His opportunities for doing good were ever ample. Did he improve them? Lives there to-day, one person upon the face of the globe, who can truly say that the gifted Voltaire was a real benefit to mankind? Was ever any one better or happier for having gained his friendship? Do parents, as a general thing, place his writings in the hands of their children? Possessing wealth, love, fame, friendship, wit, genius — everything that the world could give, yet was he happy? was he satisfied? Let him speak for himself — hear what he says: " The world abounds with wonders, and also with victims. In man is more wretchedness than in all other animals put together." By what did he judge mankind? by himself. He furthermore says: " Man loves life, yet he knows he must die; spends his existence in diffusing the miseries he has suffered, cutting the throat of his fellow creatures for pay—cheating and being cheated; the bulk of mankind are nothing more than a crowd of wretches equally unfortunate. I wish I had never been born." You perceive that Voltaire was weary of life; but were his anticipations joyful, when he could not avoid going out upon the unknown current of eternity? Forsaken by friends, he stretched forth his hands, but their clutch was weak, few tears fell, no loving arms clasped him Human skill was vain, and he went drifting, drifting, past the arches, and the columns, alone and helpless, down the long arcade into the infinite, lost, lost, lost !

Here is St. Paul. He, too, was educated in manners, law and science—beloved and extolled by the Jews; for he was an enthusiastic admirer of the traditions of the Pharisaic school and a zealous persecutor of the Christians. But when his eyes were opened, how nobly he retrieved the past. What an honor to his country and a blessing to humanity. Though generation after generation has faded from sight, like the glory of the sunset from the evening sky, the memory of St. Paul is very pleasant, and his writings are in every home. While the beautiful gems which dropped from his lips in the long ago fall upon the ears of the invalid of to-day like the softest strains from the golden wires of an Eolian harp; when desponding and world-weary, how it lightens our burdens to think of Paul, and as the North Star guides the mariner safe to harbor, so the heroic example of faithful Paul shines before us and guides us on and on, over the thorns and up the rugged way, nearer the throne. From a persecutor, Paul became persecuted.

He was arrested and arraigned before King Agrippa. Behold him as he stood up manfully while surrounded by enemies and eloquently pleaded the cause of the "Lord of Lords, and King of Kings." His life was in danger; he was scourged, stoned, driven here and there, imprisoned, and persecuted in every manner. Despised and forgotten by former friends, he wandered along the way-side of life, scattering seeds which were to spring up and yield such a bountiful harvest in the future. Was Paul happy? Through the past, for the good of posterity, comes the echo of those immortal words : "I have fought a good fight, I have finished my course; I have kept the faith. Henceforth there is laid up for me a crown of righteousness, which the Lord, the righteous judge, will give me at that day." Paul was happy. And though he suffered decapitation in the reign of Nero, he died a glorious death. "Angels hovered around" the dying scene, and "the spirit of the living God" brought such mental joy that his physical suffering was unfelt.

ERNEST TREMAIN.

AINTER and fainter became the rolling thunder as the dark clouds parted slowly and sailed majestically away. The rain ceased. The sun peered through the racking clouds. A rainbow arched the heavens, then disappeared as the sun shone forth warm and bright. The passing breeze like the kindly hand of a friend tenderly shook the over-burdened trees, lightened them of their load, and softly brushed the tears from the hearts· of the flowers, while the sun changed those which remained into shining pearls, just as the Holy Spirit turns the drops of penitent agony in the human heart into a casket of sparkling jewels which in God's own good time shall blaze forth in the glorious halls of eternity.

The grand loveliness of the landscape mingled with the genial air and the perfumed breath of flowers seemed to invite Ernest Tremain to solitude. He left the city and ascended the mountain. The beautiful storehouse of Nature opened her richest treasures at his feet and seemed to reproach him for his past vileness, as he sat musing alone on the trunk of an ancient pine tree, fit symbol of fallen greatness. A host of phantoms with their mighty voices came creeping from the past, kindling strangely bitter fires, causing them to burn and torture his fiercely throbbing heart anew. Hopes, dreams, and memories that he thought had fled upon the receding waves of time forever, came mournfully surging back through the rusty bars of forgetfulness into the brightened corridors of memory, mastering pride, and driving the currents of anguish against the "windows of his soul" and there breaking and falling into a silent spray of pain.

The bright summer days of his youth had gone forever. The fond dreams of his fancy had been dimmed somewhat, whilst wandering through the green-woods of life. Autumn came and the grand loveliness of the waning summer fell around him dark and cold, then the winds arose and the ominous rain of unbelief fell in copious showers from the lowering clouds of sorrow, and overflowed the deep founts of his heart and turned them all to bitterness.

For the first time in life Tremain prayed, wrongly prayed, for death, for oblivion, for annihilation, anything but his present remorse. Darkness gathered around, darkness which could be felt as the wailing wind sobbed through the moaning pines. He saw himself just as he was, in all his baseness, and hated himself accordingly. His faithful dog made several attempts to caress him but he drove him away with curses. A storm arose. The rain descended, the lightning flashed, the thunder rolled, but he heeded them not, for the storm without was peaceful to the terrific storm which raged within.

Morning dawned at last, bright and beautiful. The powerful sire of day arose in majestic splendor and smiled beneficently on the universe, whilst the great Sire

of sires looked down with infinite mercy upon a poor,
fallen soul lying prostrate with anguish, on the lonely
mountain.   So, by and by, the tempestuous storm abated,
and the transient sunbeams of hope shone through the
brightened clouds, and down the dim, dry glades of
memory came faintly, so very faintly, the soft sweet
strain of forgotten music from the lips of Faith, sweep-
ing away the dark webs of scoffing and selfishness, awak-
ening the viewless spirit of the mind to nobler action,
and soothing the secret longing of the soul by softly
whispering " Love, labor and wait."

Why does it take years of sorrow, months of suffering,
weeks of pain, and days and nights of sharpest agony,
to teach us the simple little lesson of loving, laboring
and waiting aright?   Why have we the courage to let
the blighting air from the desert of sin sweep the golden
fringe of purity from the purple chamber of our souls,
and not the fortitude to cease mourning its departure?

Ernest Tremain fell upon his knees and prayed aright,
as he had never prayed since childhood, and God blessed
him, and the vail of darkness was rent from the eyes of his
understanding, the demon of misery fled and the white-
robed angel of tranquility smiled peace into his soul, as
he arose and threw away the powder which he had been
treasuring in the magazine of appetite, plucked hate
from his heart and scattered the ashes of the past to the
winds of oblivion, as one by one a vast procession of
shades passed before him, then faded into the past
forever.

He stooped and patted his patient dog on the head
and spoke kindly to him, the dog whom he had cursed

the night before. His voice was changed, his step was firm, his eye was earnest, and his head erect, for he had resolved to regain his squandered birthright, to take up the world unto himself, and surmount the mountain of difficulty which lay in his pathway, and no longer cumber the ground a dead and fruitless tree.

Life resembles a high mountain. In the spring-time of youth the trees bud and blossom, the birds sing sweetly, the primrose and violet bloom along our pathway; we are happy and hopeful, and eagerly grasp at the surrounding beauties. We begin at the base with joyous laughter, but spring wears on apace. The mountain becomes more rough and rugged, and summer finds us but half way up, the blossoms begin to fall from the trees, as innocence from our young hearts, our way becomes more rocky and uneven, the sun beats down fiercely upon us, and we murmur, lose faith, and are easily discouraged; some wander off here from the true path and enter a green land. The lane is pleasant at first, but ends in a gulf, the gulf in infinite despair. Others have gone from the trees, only the fruit remains, but some of the fruit is sour, worthless, bitter; on one hand trees are shorn of leaves, fruit and blossoms, the words of unbelief have at last gained admittance into their hearts and they stand dead and sapless, whilst on the other they are laden with fruit grateful to the eye, pleasant to the touch, luscious to the taste and strengthening to the inner man, but will it all keep pure and spotless through the winter? I'm afraid not.

'Tis winter, we can go no farther; we must descend; like a band of pilgrims we fain would stop and rest, but remorseless Time pushes us down, down! Happy are the trees which cling closely to the rock of life, as the storms of winter close around them, and retain their life-giving sap to blossom again in the resurrection morn, in the garden of the Eternal.

RELIGION.

—

TRUE religion is a leveler — it causes the head of the haughty to bow, and raises the eyes of the humble. The exclusive aristocrat and the liberal democrat should meet as equals around the altar. The ponderous doors of the Divine ark are not opened by routine or method, but by active faith and earnest prayer. The steps which lead into the ark are rough, high, and hard to climb. The first is repentance, followed by amendment; the second is firm reliance on the veracity of God; the third is charity, or liberality in judging the words or actions of others; the fourth is unselfishness, which is only another name for active goodness. The path of rectitude, though sometimes rugged, always leads to peace and pleasure. The indulgence of one wrong and unselfish act can only be rectified in thought of regret. No self-denial or atonement can recall the past. By the divine gift of memory we are warned by the past and cautioned to pay more strict attention to duty in the present, and also taught to do right and rely on the wisdom of our Father to provide for the future.

A great many of the wise and learned of every age seem to have been laboring under the impression that "the Christian religion is a religion of sorrow." We

13

presume that this idea arose from the fact that horrible
atrocities have been perpetrated in the vain hope of crushing out this great human leveler, and bitter enmities im-
planted which the recent massacre of Acapulco teaches
us centuries have not availed entirely to eradicate. We
are proud to admit that many of the brightest gems of
manhood and womanhood have suffered persecution, in-
carceration, crucifixion, decapitation and martyrdom at
the stake for the upholding of the royal standard of
King Jesus. Yes; we glory in a religion which permit-
ted that grand old man, Bishop Latimer, at whose feet
the fire was already lighted, to give utterance to these
prophetic words: " Be of good comfort, master Ridley,
and play the man; we shall this day light such a candle,
by God's grace, in England, as I trust shall never be put
out." And though the fagots were already burning
around this God-like Bishop, he did not seem to be very
sorrowful. Ah! Bishop, the fire with which thine enemies sought to destroy thee, served but to perpetuate thy
memory, and caused others to vindicate thy principles
and emulate thy virtues. Although the miseries of
those who have lost life and property for vindicating
and inculcating truth and justice, are great, yet the candid are forced to admit they are small in comparison with
the enormous amount of wretchedness originating from
unbelief and sin. Christianity ennobles and elevates;
sin debases and demoralizes. Science tells us that the
moon of itself is dark and covered with barren rocks.
Blot out the king of day, and you immediately blot out
the majesty of the queen of night. Mankind, like the
moon, is naturally dark and barren of goodness; but the

majestic light emanating from the King of Righteousness enlightens, beautifies and dignifies humanity, until,
in our amazement, we are apt to forget the source from
whence it comes.

It cannot be agreeable to suffer in any sense of the
word. It is emphatically a disagreeable evil, though it
may be our duty to bear it, and the knowledge of having
saved others from its endurance is of course a grand and
noble satisfaction. If it were a pleasant thing in itself,
we should wish others to suffer, but the gratification lies
not at all in the sorrow or suffering, but in the thought
of having averted it from those we love. It is surely a
proof of overruling beneficence that humanity can thus
obtain a pleasure from the fires of agony.

But why should we mislead ourselves and others by
attempting to conceal the fact that misery in every form,
whether physical or mental, is but an evidence of our
own imperfections which we should deplore and seek to
mend. Why was Christ a man of sorrow? Because
he suffered for the sins of others. Every one of the
sorrows of Christ originated from the disobedience of
humanity. Take away sin in every form, and sorrow
and suffering will cease. How can the Christian religion be a religion of sorrow, when the Participator and
Alleviator of all sorrow hath said, "Your sorrow shall
be turned into joy?" The human heart is the most wonderful piece of mechanism which God ever created. It
is pained by disappointment, excited by passion, moved
by pity, and ruled by love. We are amazed at our own
actions; we mark out for ourselves a path from which
we do not intend to deviate; but passion ensnares us,

and we are astray. We form resolutions which we firmly intend to adhere to, even at the loss of life; pity weeps a tear, and they are shaken; love takes possession, and the high purposes, grand aspirations and pure principles of a life-time yield to inclination as straws yield to a whirlwind. Our present life is an incomprehensible mystery, but the Christian religion is not "a religion of sorrow" by any means. Only those who possess it are capable of enjoying true happiness. We pity the contumacy of the nature that will persist in dwelling in the shrouded Cimmerian darkness when, by a single effort, it could push out into the cheerful sunshine and boundless riches of a Father's love.

UNCHANGEABLE LOVE.

NVIABLE is the lot of those that are never forgotten; equally happy are those who receive from their fellows sincere trust and perennial friendship. What is true friendship, but Platonic love? What do we love with? With our souls, of course. We are told that the soul is immortal; if that be true, the love of the soul may be as much immortal as God himself, and Heaven would not be, without those we love. Where God is, there is Heaven. Be it deep down into the bowels of the earth, or far up, above the blue pavilion, beyond the glittering constellations to the infinitude of space, it matters not, so God is there.

The fundamental principle of Heaven is love. The superstructure of the infernal region is built on selfishness, envy and hate. If it had not been for the most inflexible friendship and the divinest love, where would we be to-day? Upon what a fearful precipice would we be standing! How dark would have been the present! what infernal gloom; what utter darkness would have enshrouded the future as we went gliding down the precipice of time!

When we are smitten with disease, and hemmed in by the darkness of desolation, and weep with bitterness of

heart, and lament with the wailings of the lost; when
human trust and love fail, and we sit in the lowermost
pit of dismay and sin; when we stretch forth our hands
in supplication, and raise our woeful eyes in pleading for
human compassion and succor—pleading with those
whom we have loved and trusted; those who in former
days had loved and trusted us—to see such turn away,
and with words of ice pass by on the other side, it is
then, and then only, that the mind of man can clearly
grasp the wonderful truism contained in those precious
words, "God is love." Love is Heaven; hate is hell;
wealth is a deceiver; worldly fame and honor continue
not; the head that bows, and the voice that extols in
prosperity, shall condemn and not hold you innocent in
the trial of adversity.

That being does not exist in any land, no matter
how exalted—were he peer of kings, and did he
possess the strength of Hercules, the wealth and wisdom
of Solomon, the beauty of Narcissus and the unselfishness of Moses—but must lie down and sleep at last; and
the sun will shine, the dew fall, the rain descend, and
the withered flowers hold up their heads and smile as
happily as if the city of decay had not received another
occupant.

As the water impresses the stones, so love impresses
the immortal soul; and love shall live again, glorified,
sanctified through all eternity.

Save and hoard, you men of wealth; cramp and grind
the honest poor; have ye forgotten that deeds of charity
are as acceptable to the Divine heart as drops of dew to
a land of drouth?

To dress and be fashionable seems to be the highest aim of a democratic American lady now-a-days. One ring from that soft, white hand, would make some poor family not only happy, but also comfortable all winter. All the gew-gaws that wealth can buy are but trash to one clasped in the arms of the angel of death.

Your days are numbered. Your opportunities for doing good are vanished. Death prevails; hope flies away. The worms feed as greedily upon the rich man's dainty darlings, who are lovingly laid to rest with funeral pomp and pride, as they do upon the weary one who sleeps in a rude coffin in an unknown grave, with none to mourn and but two to break the sod.

What is life but a shadow ? We look back upon the past and are astonished. We think of the wickedness and snares that obtain in the present, and are well nigh overwhelmed. We meditate on the future and the wondrous claims of love with the very essence of happiness, and hope binds us with her golden fetters to earth, and follows our loved ones to the empyrean regions of felicity.

EMINENT ENERGIES.

LOVE and perseverance are the most valuable traits of character which can be cultivated. Without their possession happiness is impossible. Nothing affords us more gratification than friendly intercourse with those we love. It seems to be natural that all pure social feeling should be attended with pleasure. Benevolence, sympathy, sensibility, love and affability, necessarily produce agreeable sensations in the minds of the participants.

Let all social intercouse founded on true love and constancy, depart from the world, and the golden grain would rot in the fruitful field; the waters of the commercial oceans would stagnate, and the loud whirling of machinery and noisy manipulation of labor would cease. Men would prey upon one another, and life and property would be insecure. Witness the state of things in southern localities, where the beautiful angel of love has fled weeping from the dark demoniac spirit of hate. Behold Mexico, where bloodshed and riot obtain in place of tranquility and happiness, where the progeny of that Old Python not only desecrated the holy of holies with their presence, but stung to death the pious devotees of the Living God at the very foot of the altar.

Without the sweet solace of love, the prolific plain of

the human heart would soon become a barren desert.
It is the mainspring of all human action. It strengthens
the arm of the laborer, sharpens the wit of the lawyer,
and gives endurance to the widow, perseverance to the
missionary, and calms the mind of the sailor as he climbs
the mast in the furious hurricane, with visions of a safe
home-nest where dwell his household gods in peace and
safety. It is the love of civil liberty which animates the
soldier as he stands firm and never falters, while one by
one his companions fall around him. He sees not their
pale, upturned faces, nor heeds their dying moan. It is
enough for him to know that the glorious constellation
of liberty is in danger of obscuration; and the mournful
cry of the wounded eagle closes his eyes and shuts his
ears to other sights and sounds.

When you were hungering for sympathy, and stretched
forth your hand for the soft, warm bread of appreciation,
and received instead the hard, cold stone of distrust and
dislike, does that prove that all bread is stone ? surely
not. Because your friend has misunderstood you, is that
any reason that you should begin sowing the thistle seed
of hate ? Have you done for your friend what Christ
did for you ? Do you wipe the bloody sweat of agony
from his brow by accepting the stupendous sacrifice
which he made for the healing of sin ? Do you never
distrust his mercy and love for yourself ?

The divine attributes of perseverance and love bring
their own reward; they are the frost-work of pure gold
to the purple chamber of the soul. We cannot very
well help being pleased with ourselves, not only for the
purity of our motives, but for the unselfishness of our

purposes, therefore be not dismayed if you have cast the rarest jewels of your heart before one who looked upon them as paste. Were these not more valuable than ever when they came from the grinding mill of the lapidary of sorrow ?

That great rock—Christianity remains unshaken, while the white-capped waves of infidelity roll back broken by the persevering love of the finite, who faithfully bore the cross that all might gain the crown of immortality.

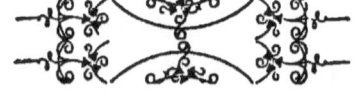

THE LEGEND OF LIFE.

All the sweet stars sang and glittered,
  In the radiant olden time,
Till the cup of Life, embittered,
  Flashed along their feast sublime;
When the chorus fell, and ever
  Though they smiled through falling tears,
Like a far, resplendent river,
  Ran the music of the spheres.

And the moon uprose serenely
  In that plaintive time of old,
And her mantle, lustrous, queenly,
  Like a silver mist unrolled;
But her brow was pale, and stilly
  All her beauty clasped the air,
And she wore the mystic lily
  In the glory of her hair.

Then the crimson lips of morning
  Kissed the world to life and light,
And the blue seas caught the warning
  With a revel of delight;
And the bold peaks towered grandly
  To the arches of the sky,

While the perfumed zephyrs blandly
  Waked the meadows with a sigh.

Birds in hues of floral splendor
  Flamed and sang in tropic woods,
Tinted vapors, dim and tender,
  Wreathed the sky in lovely moods;
And the winding rivers, dreamy
  With the shadows that they bore,
Trailed their crystal robes and beamy
  To the ocean's misted shore.

Gemmy lakelets lay enchanted
  In the glamour of the East,
And the trees immortals planted,
  Dropped a gold and purple feast;
And the yellow lion, sleeping
  In the hyacinthe shades,
Saw the fearless lambkins leaping
  Down the clover-scented glades.

White-limbed mortals, idly roving
  In Elysian ecstacy,
Knew no duller task than loving,
  And were God-like, fair and free;
For their lives were but the summing
  Of the sweets the angels sip—
Drowsy as the brown bee's humming
  At the woodbine's fragrant lip.

'Twas the happy age, the golden,
  Which the elder poets sang

When their measures, rare and olden,
  Up to heaven rose and rang;
But a north-wind blew, the flowers
  Curled and withered in its breath,
And above the trysting bowers
  Ran the whisper : "Labor—death !"

And the palm-tree lisped no longer
  Tales of love and peace benign,
For a music, braver, stronger,
  Shook the plumage of the pine;
And the surges, shoreward bending,
  Rolled the thunder of a prayer
That was half a pæan, blending
  Battle, vict'ry, and despair.

Still the fair moon wandered nightly
  In enameled fields of blue,
And the springing dawn still brightly
  Showered rubies on the dew;
Phœbus still passed on and over,
  Crowning earth with regal charms,
And caressed her, like a lover,
  In the rose-wreath of his arms.

But the bugle-call of duty
  Echoed down life's rocky stair,
And the world's receding beauty
  Told of tempests in the air;
For the slow and strange uncoiling
  Of the wondrous fate of man,

In the dust and din of toiling,
  And the rush of strife began.

On the clear, unspotted pages
  Of the pearly book of mind,
Through the weary lapse of ages,
  Shades of truth were dimly lined;
Words were blotted, phrases tangled,
  But a transcript grew apace
Of the features, O how mangled !
  Of Jehovah's hidden face.

Genius spread her purple pinions
  For a flight beyond the stars,
Valor called his fiery minions
  To the wreck of savage wars;
And the sheen of cities, founded
  By the rivers and the seas,
Marked the periods grandly rounded
  On the roll of destinies.

Many gods, with wild grimaces,
  Led the faith of men astray—
Temples rose in sacred places,
  And the priests bore kingly sway;
But the keen sword, never sleeping,
  In the twilight flashed and rang,
Where the stormy hosts, at reaping,
  To a moon of scarlet sang.

Like a sail that glints in turning
  On the ocean's cloudy rim,

Hints of truth, a moment burning,
  Touched the spirit's border dim—
Touched and passed, and left the tremor
  Of a flitting sense of light,
On the soul of sage or dreamer,
  Watching, listening through the night.

Sweet as vesper bells, recalling
  Weariness to prayer and rest,
Were the words of wisdom, falling
  From the lips the gods caressed;
For the minds of some, uplifted
  O'er the tumult of the years,
Through the veil of shadows, rifted,
  Caught the sunlight's leveled spears.

On prophetic temples, visions
  Of redemption blossomed then,
And, beyond the sword's decisions,
  Shone the star of peace again;
But the pall of superstition
  Hovered still o'er courts and camps,
And the seers, in pale contrition,
  Stumbled on by misty lamps.

I.

'Tis a gala night with immortals above,
And sweet, as the sigh of the woman you love,
  Is the loitering breath of the breeze;
And the tresses of moonlight are drifted and blown,

On the lips of the sea-waves, subduing their moan,
And tangled in odorous trees.

II.

And the stars, from their beautiful vases of gold,
Besprinkle the earth with ambrosia untold,
And the scintillant laughter of light;
But the vale of Judea is waiting the crown
Of a kinglier splendor than stars shower down,
Or wreathe on the brow of the night.

III.

The waters of Jordan salute as they pass
The flowers that lean to the whispering grass,
With a crystalline tinkle of song;
And the olives kiss hands to the mystical palm,
The queen and the priestess of luster and calm,
As the moments of Jubilee throng.

IV.

O, fair as the bosoms of maidens, the hills
Heave soft in the ocean of rapture that fills
The domain of the prophets and kings;
And the shepherds, reclined on the blossomy swells,
Talk low as they listen to murmurous bells,
Or the bird that awakens and sings.

V.

Is it dawn that the stars are so suddenly pale?
Is the daylight aflame in the shimmering veil
Of the pensive and lingering moon?
Ah, morn never rose and the day never shone

With a glory like this, which doth seem to be thrown
From the disk of some marvelous noon !

VI.

For the gates that the poets and psalmists have sung,
At the nod of the Father have suddenly swung,
    And the planets their splendor enfurl;
As a flash of the Throne, an ineffable beam
Is an instant astray, and has left us a dream
    Of sapphire and diamond and pearl.

VII.

There's a step on the stair that the angels have trod,
And the Prince of the Manger, our brother and God,
    Is the guest and the grace of us all;—
Our captain in battle, the rose and the wreath
Of our life and our love, and our triumph when death
    Shall trumpet the welcome recall.

VIII.

Oh, Jesus of Nazareth, comfort us still,
For the pathway is dim and the tempest is chill,
    And our sorrows thou only canst tell;
And the spheres never roam in the clear amethyst,
But they beckon and say thou wilt come to the tryst,
    And we know that the rest will be well.

Lo ! the torch of Heaven, streaming
    O'er the devious ways of earth,
Left full many a beacon gleaming
    On the altar and the hearth;

In the desert sparkled fountains
   That were never known before,
And the cold and craggy mountains
   A serener aspect wore.

Then the heavy tome of Science
   Slowly loosed its mighty maze,
And no longer bade defiance
   To the paly student's gaze;
On the canvass blushed the beauty
   Which the soul of art doth keep,
And the sculptor's priestly duty
   Woke the marble's snowy sleep.

Woe befell, and nations wandered
   In the slimy sloughs and fens,
And a wealth of hope was squandered
   In Cimmerian glooms and glens;
But the goal of all endeavor,
   Like a soaring shaft of flame,
Tossed its plumy crest forever,
   Till the peoples onward came.

There was heard the moan of bondage
   And the lingering shriek of pain,
And Olea's glossy frondage
   Dripped with battle's costly rain;
For the years, with flying shuttle,
   Wove a sombre web of doom—
Brightened only by the subtle
   Thread of Hope's refulgent loom.

Yet the ocean swung the censer
  Of its worship evermore,
Though the days were darker, denser
  Than the Pagan nights of yore;
And the graceful rivers, straying
  In their shining scarfs of mist,
Sang of summer, and, delaying,
  Meads and musky gardens kissed.

*   *   *   *   *   *

O, the woven lights and shadows
  Of the rolling tide of time—
Purple tents to-day, and meadows—
  On the morrow cliffs to climb !
But the broad sun stands forever,
  As the planets wheel and wheel,
And our fears depress us never
  When the days at parting kneel.

Leaf by leaf, the stony record
  Of the strata rises still,
And the life of man, so chequered,
  Owns the same eternal will;
In the dust and blood and ashes
  Of a thousand wild defeats,
Vict'ry springs, the spirit flashes,
  And the pulse of courage beats.

Lo ! the human mind advances
  In the nimbus of her pride,
And within her starry glances
  No delusion shall abide !

In the trackless depths of ether,
  Roving worlds display her sign,
And to prisoned Truth, beneath her,
  Patiently her ears incline.

Yet, beside the tranquil river
  Flowing brightly by our doors,
Hearts with old emotions quiver
  As the spirit sinks or soars;
Love is still the sweetest warble
  Lips of ruby ever know—
Death is still a sphinx-like marble,
  Still a white and speechless woe.

Isis and Osiris, listening
  To the voices of the Nile,
Saw such tears of mortals glistening,
  Knew the sunlight of our smile !
Lo ! while thought has grown and builded
  Temples brighter than the sun,
Joy alone our lives has gilded
  Since the reign of Christ begun !

Up, and on, O mind of mortal,
  To the far, imperial heights !—
Up, and touch the jasper portal
  That delays thy daring flights !—
Touch and turn, the way is weary,
  And the stars no warmth impart,
Thou shalt lay thy treasures dreary
  On the threshold of the heart !

S. L. S.

THE SOUL AND THE FLOWER.

Springing, like man, from the dust of the ground,
Diffusing the sweetest of fragrance around,
Opening its bosom to the sun's bright ray,
A beautiful little white floweret lay.

Like the soul of a saint in calm repose,
The heart of the flower its leaves enclose;
Receiving with rapture the dew and the sun,
Breathing more sweet as its brief race is run.

As purple pansies on the spotless snow,
The lives of Christians should with virtue glow,
Attracting all eyes by their modest worth,
The fairest pledges of a fruitful birth.

Not like the Dahlia, vaunting and vain,
Proudly flaunting the poor with cold disdain,
But like the Daisy, as becometh its name,
Blooming in alley and highway the same.

The sun, as adversity sternly distills
Bitter blight in the heart of the flower,
With healing dew-drops and with pleasure refills,
Like dews from the Word every hour.

The heart of the Christian beneath the rod,
Blossoms the sweeter in the garden of God;
'Twould be well for us all in the last sad hour,
If our souls did resemble this pure little flower,

MOTHER'S GRIEF.

Fold the little white hands at rest
Upon the little guileless breast;
The death-damp will never again
Rise on the forehead freed from pain.

Softly sever a silken tress,
Gently smooth the spotless dress,
Gather rare lilies waxen white;
How can a mother say good-night?

Drive me not hence, I love to stay
By the little fair form of clay;
Respect my grief, nor heed my moan,
But leave me with my dead alone.

Tender is the trace which lingers,
Made by little baby fingers;
Only a mother knows the worth—
My child was all I had on earth.

WHOSE CHURCH IS THIS?

It is told of a man poorly dressed, that he went to a church seeking an opportunity to worship. The usher did not notice him, but seated several well-dressed persons who presented themselves, when finally the man addressed the usher, saying: "Can you tell me whose church this is?" "Yes, this is Christ's Church." "Is he in?" was the next question, after which a seat was not so hard to find.—*Christian Union*, November 25, 1874.

" Whose costly church is this ?" the poor man cried;
" Was it not to save all that King Jesus died ?
Or was it for those who wear silks and laces,
And who attend church with scornful faces ?
Is it, then, such an awful and grievous sin,
For the very poor man to seek shelter within ?
I'm old and feeble with many a care,
I had found a few roses here and there,
Like scattered sunbeams or words of prayer,
But they, too, faded in life's frosty air.
My loved ones have gone where we all must go."
Memory whispers of the past, and lo !
A pleasant scene upon the stage appears,
Surrounded by friends, as in former years,
The sexton smiles and bows, without a fear
Of soiling the pew with poverty's tear,
Duly attends and opens wide the door.
The dream, it has past; in a moment more

Again I stand at the church door and wait,
The rich, esteemed for their fair estate,
Are seated, and, with haughty pride elate,
Would bar the portals of heaven's golden gate.
Beneath many a vest, ragged and old,
There beats a manly heart of worth untold.